Rock, Paper, Scissors

B Baskerville

Hyem Books

*Apart from the woman with the Welsh terrier. That's me.

- Chapter 1 -

THE CITY DIDN'T LOOK right to Macey Gallagher as she stumbled out of the club. The lights of the traffic left red and white snakes across her vision as if her brain was set on long exposure. Her eyes couldn't keep up with the world, and her body couldn't keep up with her brain. Every movement required meticulous concentration. Right foot. Left foot. Right foot.

A neon pink sign blinked at Macey, but she couldn't read it; the letters looked jumbled, and they didn't make sense. All around her, Newcastle's party people were enjoying their Saturday night. They hugged, kissed and danced, oblivious to the nineteen-year-old's worsening state. Pearl would be around here somewhere. She must be. Macey just had to find her.

"Watch it." A woman with an angry face and impossibly black eyebrows shoved Macey out of the way and into a brick wall. "Look where you're going."

The bricks grazed Macey's arm, and tiny globules of blood popped to the surface, turning her skin into a Lichtenstein artwork.

Where was Pearl? She didn't like feeling like this. She'd only had a couple of drinks. Hadn't she? Two glasses of wine with dinner before switching to Diet Coke in the club. It wasn't that much, but her head pounded and she desperately needed to pee.

It was April in Newcastle upon Tyne and bright, clear days gave way to chilling, teeth-chattering nights. In these parts, the locals declined to wear coats despite the nighttime temperature barely reaching five degrees.

"Coats are for southerners," Alison had told her on her first day at Newcastle University. "If you want to fit in, leave your coat at home. Besides, who wants to cover up an outfit as cute as yours?"

An ambulance raced past with its lights flashing and siren blaring. Macey covered her ears and closed her eyes. Everything was louder and brighter than it should be. She could hear people laughing, and paranoia told her they were laughing at her. Across the road, two squat men got into a fight. Their heavy fists flew at each other's heads in great arcs until a ginormous man in black with an earring in one ear separated them. One stormed towards the taxi rank; the other marched towards Macey.

Macey backed herself as far into the wall as possible, hoping to make herself invisible.

"Alreet, pretty lass?" His scowl turned to a smile as he edged closer. Macey tried to focus. He was old, not granddad-old, but probably mid-forties at least, maybe fifty. Lines carved across his forehead, and whilst his head was bald, his beard was mid-brown with patches of white. "Now, where've you been all my life?"

Macey clutched her bag to her chest. Her mouth was drier than the Sahara, but she managed, "For most of it, I wasn't born."

It was a mistake. The man's scowl returned. "Bitch," he spat, edging closer still.

It wasn't the first time Macey's mouth had got her into trouble. She was quick-witted, like many of her Dubliner compatriots, and while some thought of her craic as endearing, the insecure could react badly.

A slender woman with brown spiral curls walked by.

"Pearl?" Macey called. *Thank God.* She ducked under the man's arm and made a run for it, though it could hardly be called a run; a stagger would be more accurate. "Pearl?"

The woman turned and looked Macey up and down. She wasn't Pearl. "You all right, love?"

Macey rested her back against the wall and nodded. The gesture satisfied the woman, but Macey was far from all right. She wasn't well, the bald man was still staring at her, and her flatmate was nowhere to be seen. They'd promised to travel back home together, to share a taxi and order a dirty great pizza to finish off the evening. Pearl would be mad that Macey had gone home without her, but the doorman wasn't going to let her back into the club, and she couldn't stay out in the cold all night. She took two steps towards the taxi rank and teetered over in her heels. What a total waste of money. The shoes looked amazing, but they were nearly impossible to walk in, and God knows why anyone would design something so uncomfortable to wear. She tried again. Right foot. Left foot. Her ankle buckled once more, and Macey fell straight into the arms of the woman who wasn't Pearl.

"Oops. I've got you." She had a kind face and wore a fluorescent vest, the sort of one a workman would wear. "You don't look like you're doing so good. Do you need help?" The good Samaritan propped Macey back upright and supported her around her tiny waist. "What's your name, love?"

"Macey." The word didn't come easy to her. Her brain was becoming foggier by the minute, and her jaw wasn't responding as expected.

"Great accent. Where in Ireland are you from?"

"Dublin."

"Oh, fantastic." The stranger helped push Macey's blonde, wavy hair behind her ear. "I've been there for the odd boozy weekend. Great place. You here for uni?"

Macey nodded. She felt nauseous and bewildered and didn't want to be sick, not on the street.

"I'm with the Tyne Pastors," the woman said, pointing to a logo on her yellow vest. Did you have too much to drink, Macey?"

She shook her head. "No," she managed. "No, I—I don't think so."

"We work with the police. We help people who could do with a sit-down and a glass of water, or people who are lost, that sort of thing. We have a van across the road." She pointed to a dark van with sliding doors. "If you want to shelter from the cold, we have blankets and can make you a nice cup of tea while we try and get a hold of your friends. Sound good?"

The thought of a warm drink drew Macey over the street as if she were being pulled by a magnet. She was steered away from a kebab that had been dropped in the road and supported as she stepped up the kerb.

"Careful of your footing here." The stranger waved to an amicable-looking man holding a pile of fleece blankets. "This is Macey. I think she'd like some tea and to rest her feet.

"Hi, Macey," he said as he handed her a blanket.

Macey wrapped it over her shoulders and pulled the ends tight to her chest. Instantly, she felt comforted.

"Take a seat." The woman smiled and indicated a bench that ran the length of the van. A slim woman with mascara running down her face was sitting on the bench and sobbing into her mobile. She hiccoughed and continued crying. Between her feet, some strong-smelling coffee steamed into the cold air.

"Thank you." Macey smiled at her curly-haired new friend. She was blurry but gentle, and she had a familiarity about her. It was like talking to an aunt or a cousin.

"Where do you live? We usually stay out until four. If we can't reunite you with your friends by then we can give you a lift."

"H— Heaton," she stammered. Heaton was a popular suburb that sat to the east of the city centre and was only a short drive away. "Rothbury Terrace. Near... Near the mosque." Macey sat on the bench and tried to make herself comfortable. The bench was hard, but the fleece cushioned her bottom and she was already feeling warmer. She slumped back and closed her eyes for a moment, then looked at the screen on her phone and tried to make out the logos that no longer made sense. Pearl and Alison were probably dancing. Had they even noticed she'd gone?

"Here you go." The man handed her a mug of tea. He screwed the lid back on the flask and returned to the driver's seat. This would all be over soon, she told herself. Either Pearl would come and find her, or she could wait an hour and the pastors would drive her back home. She craved to be back in her bed. A trip to the medicine cabinet and a pint of water and she'd be right as rain.

Curls returned to the van. "Any luck with your boyfriend?" she asked the crying girl. The girl shook her head and tucked her phone into a pocket. "How about we stop this awful draught?" She reached behind her and slid the van door until it clicked closed.

The driver looked over his shoulder, and Curls nodded to him. The engine started and the van pulled away.

"Are you taking me home?" Macey asked.

The driver didn't answer. Nothing sobered a person up quite like the sickening knowledge that something awful was about to happen to them. For as Macey Gallagher's hands were bound with a cable tie, she realised all too late that these were not the Tyne Pastors and the good Samaritan was not so good.

- Chapter 2 -

DCI Erica Cooper stepped out of the Crown Court onto Newcastle's Quayside. It was a drizzly morning; the grey sky muddled with the grey Tyne, casting a usually vibrant part of the city into dullness. Around her, paparazzi gathered with their cameras trained on the revolving doors of the courts. They hoped to catch the families of The Tarot Card Killer's victims in their most vulnerable moment. *Vultures*, thought Cooper.

The only reason the scavengers were ignoring Cooper as she strode past them was because she'd brought a change of clothing. She'd learnt this tactic during the month-long trial of notorious gangster Eddie Blackburn. Unless Cooper needed to address the press, she preferred to escape unnoticed. Her coat of choice featured an oversized hood that covered not only the top of her head but also her forehead and eyes too.

Once a safe distance away, Cooper dropped her hood and tilted her head to the sky. Droplets of rain splashed against her number two buzzcut and helped cool the rage that had been building inside her. Brian Hutchins's defence team had been arguing a case of diminished responsibility. Cooper's self-control had been tested as she listened to their sob stories. Hutchins had taken the lives of four teenagers and had been minutes, possibly seconds, away from killing Cooper's daughter when her team had apprehended him. Tina had suffered from nightmares ever since, and although Cooper hadn't told anyone, so had she.

A little further along the quay, a stooped woman sold flowers from a cart. She wore her hair in curlers and tied a plastic bag around her head to protect it from the rain. "The usual, pet?" she asked Cooper in a friendly, northern voice.

"Please."

Cooper took the single yellow rose and followed the quay to the spot where she'd seen her best friend murdered. Thirteen years ago, some drunken lowlife had pushed eighteen-year-old Cindy Howes into the river, and she'd drowned before anyone could get to her. No one was ever charged.

"I still miss you," said Cooper in a whisper. She brought the flower to her nose and inhaled. "And I'm still sorry we never caught him." Cooper kissed the petals before tossing the flower into the river.

Cooper had parked in a multi-story near the courts, and by the time she got back to her car, the April showers had soaked her to the skin. She decided to nip home to change before returning to Northumbria Police Headquarters. Once in a dry suit and with a fresh layer of make-up, Cooper picked up an extra-large chicken supreme pizza from the retail park next to HQ. She knew from experience that her team worked best on a full stomach, and anything was better than the staff canteen or the vending machine.

"You're not listening to me." A young woman with a Yorkshire accent slapped her hand on the front desk.

"Miss, take a step back and calm down." The desk sergeant got to his feet. "We do not tolerate the abuse of our staff."

"Abuse? Abuse?" The woman shook her head in disbelief. She was slim, dressed in sporty lycra and had a head of dark chestnut spiral curls. "She'll die if we don't find her soon."

"Miss, please lower your voice. We'll have someone take your statement as soon as we can, but we're very busy today. There'll be a bit of wait." He pointed to some plastic chairs.

Tears began to roll down the woman's pretty face. "Something's happened to her. I know it."

Cooper didn't know what was going on, but she felt for the woman; she was clearly distressed. She approached the desk and placed the pizza on it. "It's okay, Davis. I'm free. I can take her statement. Can you send this up to CID? Tell them to save me a slice."

Davis looked longingly at the box before nodding.

Cooper turned to the woman. "I'm DCI Erica Cooper," she said by way of an introduction. "What's your name?"

"Pearl," she sniffed. She couldn't have been more than nineteen or twenty. "Pearl Baxter."

"Follow me, Pearl. We'll get you a glass of water, and you can tell me what's going on."

It took a few moments for Cooper to calm Pearl Baxter down. From what she could gather, Pearl's flatmate had gone missing after a night out.

"But you said she's been texting you?"

Pearl shook her head. "No. Someone's been texting me. But it's not Macey. She said she was going to stay at the flat that night, but when she wasn't there the next morning, I thought she must have hooked up with her boyfriend. They're at that totally loved up, can't keep their hands off each other stage in their relationship, so I wasn't worried when I didn't see her on Sunday morning. When I hadn't heard from her by Sunday afternoon, I texted her to ask if she was at Aaron's."

"Aaron is Macey's boyfriend?"

Pearl paused while a couple of officers raced past. "Yes, Aaron Quinn. I asked her if she needed anything from the shop, and she replied with *no thanks*. That's not like Macey at all. She'd ask for something ridiculous like a tamed baby walrus or a glow-in-the-dark dildo."

Cooper tried not to smirk.

"And she always signs her texts XOXO. Always. Look."

Pearl handed Cooper her phone and scrolled through the girls' messages. "I see what you mean," said Cooper as she scanned hundreds of messages, all ending with XOXO. "And you don't think she's really at Aaron's because..."

"Because Aaron showed up at the flat yesterday looking for Macey. He hadn't seen her since Saturday morning."

"Ah."

"All the time I thought she was at his, he thought she was with me."

Cooper's hand moved quickly across the page as she noted down Pearl's statement.

"She'd messaged Aaron too," continued Pearl. "Well, whoever has her phone did. It didn't sound like Macey. Aaron actually thought she was in a mood with him because of the one-word replies."

"Have you tried calling her?"

"Of course I have. Dozens of times. It just goes to voicemail."

"Has Macey ever done this before? Could she have met a new man? Be avoiding Aaron for that reason?"

"No," snapped Pearl. "That's not her style. Like I said, she was loved up. I know it's only been a couple of days, but none of our friends have seen or heard from her. I checked her wardrobe, and I don't think anything's missing. Her toiletries too. They're all still there. And her medicine."

"Medicine?"

"Insulin. She has a kit that she takes on nights out because alcohol sends her hypo, or hyper. I forget which. But she only took one night's worth with her. The rest is in the flat."

A chill ran down Cooper's spine, and she knew why Pearl feared the worst. If Macey hadn't taken her diabetes medication with her, she was high risk. Wherever she was, Cooper needed to find her. And fast. Cooper placed her hand on Pearl's arm. "I can see why you're concerned. This is more worrying. Have you spoken to Macey's parents?"

Pearl shook her head. "I don't have their details. Aaron might. I'm not sure. Our landlord should have them, though. We had to name guarantors when we signed the lease."

"Pearl, I'm going to take some more details and open an investigation into Macey's disappearance. Then I want you to go home, make yourself a nice cup of tea and call this number." She handed Pearl a pamphlet for Missing People, a charity that provides support and advice for the families and friends of missing persons in the UK. "They offer round-the-clock emotional support. You're understandably distressed. These people can listen. I'll pop over to see you later today, okay?"

Pearl's lip trembled again. She was on the verge of falling apart. "Thank you," she said, taking the pamphlet. "I just hope we're not too late."

- Chapter 3 -

CID smelled of pizza. Sadly, as Cooper stared into the empty box, she realised her request that the other detectives leave her a slice had gone unanswered.

"You seen Tennessee?" she asked Detective Neil Fuller.

Fuller, a squirrelly man whom Cooper was once romantically involved with, looked up from his computer. "I still can't get used to you with that buzzcut. Suits you, though. Makes you look more, you know, confident."

Cooper ran her hand over her head. She liked the feel of the super-short hairs against her palms. Last year, she'd lost her hair to chemotherapy and had worn a wig to cover the evidence, but thanks to her daughter's enthusiasm and insistence that she looked like a total badass, Cooper had begun to embrace the look. She ditched the wig and bought herself a pair of clippers. Fuller was right; it did suit her.

"He's over there," nodded Fuller, and Cooper followed his eyes to a desk at the far end of the department.

DS Jack Daniel, who had been known as Tennessee since he was a bairn, was taking a bite out of the last slice of pizza. Strings of cheese stretched from his mouth to his hand like strands of yellowy spiderweb. Cooper approached with stealth, grabbed what remained of the slice and shoved as much into her mouth as she could manage before handing the crust back to Tennessee.

"Urgh," he grimaced.

"Now, now," teased Cooper. "Eat your crusts, or your hair won't go curly."

Tennessee pulled a face and turned his eyes upward towards his mop of blond curls. "What you got?" he asked, pointing to the file in Cooper's hand.

"Missing girl. Nineteen-year-old student named Macey Gallagher, originally from Dublin. Reported missing by her flatmate Pearl Baxter. Hasn't been seen since a boozy night out on the eighth and doesn't have her insulin with her."

Tennessee sat up. "Since Saturday? How'd the flatmate not realise until now?"

Cooper shrugged. "She assumed she was staying at her boyfriend's, and her boyfriend assumed she was with the flatmate."

"Is that likely?"

"I'm not sure, but the flatmate's been receiving texts supposedly from Macey, only she's convinced the messages aren't really from her." Cooper stole a chair from a neighbouring desk and sat down.

"And that's why you haven't handed it over to Mispers?" Tennessee asked, referring to the common abbreviation for missing persons. "You smell a rat?"

Cooper drew her lower lip in between her teeth and slowly released it. "I smell a rat," she confirmed, "but I hope I'm wrong. Listen, there's not much of the day left, but I'm going to make a start by contacting the girl's landlord and getting her parents' contact details. Can you put a request in for the missing girl's phone records? And get a trace while you're at it. Hopefully, it's still switched on."

"Consider it done," he replied with a yawn.

Cooper frowned at the DS. "Another restless night?"

Tennessee took the name and phone number of the missing girl from the file and got to his feet. "Little Alfie woke up about twelve times last night. I mean, I want to be a hands-on dad, I don't believe in leaving all the baby stuff to his mother, but Hayley didn't even stir. I swear that woman could sleep through a bomb blast. Anyway—" he waved the phone number. "I'll be back in a bit."

Cooper watched him walk away while she dialled the number Pearl Baxter had given her for their landlord. The first five months of fatherhood had ravaged Tennessee's fashion-model looks. The man was drained. His skin was dry and colourless, apart from the skin under his eyes, which had been stained a sickly shade of purple.

"Hello?"

Cooper could hear chewing noises. "Mr Walker? This is DCI Erica Cooper from Northumbria Police. I'm calling about a tenant of yours. Macey Gallagher?"

There was more chewing. "Gallagher? Gallagher? Oh, yeah. Blonde girl, Rothbury Terrace. Let me guess, noise complaint? Always is with the student lets."

Quieter than the chewing noise but still audible was the sound of excitable sports commentary. "No, Mr Walker, it's nothing like that. I'm afraid Macey's been reported missing. I need the contact details for her parents; I believe you have them listed as guarantors?"

"Missing?" The television was turned down but not muted. "Er, yes, I have their details somewhere. Can I call you tomorrow? I have a lot of properties. It'll take me a while to dig them out."

"Sorry, but I'm going to need them now. Your horse race will have to wait."

Several seconds of silence was followed by a sigh and, "Fine. Hang on. I'll just pop you on hold."

Cooper drummed her fingers on the table for a moment and checked her mobile for messages. She had two. Tina had messaged to say that her father was taking her and her boyfriend, Josh, to the cinema and asked if she wanted to join them. Cooper declined. She and Tina's father, Kenny, had split up the moment they found out she was pregnant. They'd barely spoken for the best part of twelve years, but recently, they'd been making an effort with each other. *Maybe next time, T. Have fun, and don't eat too much popcorn.*

The second message was from Justin Atkinson, a highly skilled scene of crime officer, silver-haired environmentalist, and Cooper's new beau. *Berlin is beautiful. Great conference. The Germans are making huge strides in forensic podiatry. Fascinating stuff. Miss you. J.*

Cooper smiled to herself. Not many people would consider forensic podiatry fascinating, but that was what made Atkinson so brilliant at what he did. As a teen, she'd always been attracted to alpha males. Strong, silent types with biceps bigger than their brains. After falling pregnant at seventeen, joining the police at eighteen and dedicating herself to a career that could provide for her daughter, Cooper's romantic confidence took a tumble, and she ended up in a string of on-again, off-again relationships with men like Detective Neil Fuller. Thankfully, her thirties had awoken Cooper's dormant sapiosexuality, and she couldn't get enough of Atkinson's extensive vocabulary. His tall, lean body was a felicitous bonus.

"You still there?" Matt Walker was back on the line and had interrupted her thoughts about something else that was extensive. "I have the names and address you wanted."

Cooper shook herself back to the present and grabbed a pen. "Yes, okay, go."

"Iris and Sean Gallagher. Six Kildonan Avenue, Perrystown. You want their phone numbers?"

"Please."

Cooper noted the landline and mobile numbers for Macey's parents and thanked Matt Walker for his help. She was just about to dial the Gallaghers when Tennessee returned.

"Here," he said, handing her a coffee. "Phone records will be with us tomorrow or Thursday at the latest."

"Cheers. I was just about to inform the family. Want to do the honours?"

Tennessee's mouth twitched. "Ah, Coop, you know I hate that."

"And you know everyone hates it. You're a capable DS. If you can handle the domestic we saw the other night, you can handle this."

The younger man rubbed his jaw and went to take a sip of coffee before realising it was far too hot. "Fine. Give me the phone. What are their names?"

"Iris and Sean Gallagher."

Cooper picked up a second line to listen in and take notes.

"Hello? This is DS Jack Daniel from Northumbria CID. I'd like to speak to Mr Sean or Mrs Iris Gallagher, please."

There was sniggering on the other end of the phone. "Aye," came a deep, male voice, "and this is Mr Jim Beam hoping to speak to Captain Morgan. Good one. Who is this? Mikey?"

"Sir, this isn't a joke. This is Detective Sergeant Jack Daniel from—" There was more giggling, and Tennessee turned to look at Cooper.

"Fine," she mouthed. "Sir? Sir? DCI Cooper here, DS Daniel's colleague. We're calling about Macey."

The giggling came to an abrupt end, and his voice hardened. "Macey? Should I be sitting down?"

"Macey was reported missing by her flatmate today. She and her friends haven't seen Macey since the evening of the eighth. When was the last time you spoke to your daughter, Mr Gallagher?"

"Missing?" Strangely, Cooper thought she heard him laugh again. "I thought you were going to tell me she'd been shot or something. Well, thank God."

Cooper and Tennessee frowned at each other. Sean Gallagher didn't sound too concerned for his daughter's safety.

"The last time you spoke to Macey, sir?"

"Oh, it's been a while. A month at least. I'll check with her mother, but this is classic Macey."

"How do you mean?"

"Well, she's always running off, isn't she? Did it when she was ten. Jumped on the train to Galway to see her aunt without telling anyone. Sparked a massive search. It made the news and everything. At fifteen, she stole her sister's ID – double of each other they are – and she went off to Amsterdam with a boy from her school. Got high on pot brownies and stole a pedal boat. And at eighteen, after telling us she was going to Trinity College, she runs off to Newcastle. She's a wanderer. Always has been, and always will be. I'll ask around, see if anyone's heard from her, but if history's anything to go by, she'll show up when she's hungry or runs out of money."

"Mr Gallagher," interrupted Cooper. "Macey's flatmate doesn't think she took any of her belongings with her. She also left her insulin at the flat they share."

"Hmm," he was quiet for a moment. "Well, that's more unusual. She'll pick up an emergency prescription, though. She was always very good at remembering to do her injections. I'll speak to Iris and Kate."

"Kate?"

"Her sister. It's Katherine, but we call her Kate."

"When you spoke to Macey last month, how was she?"

"Besotted with some boy."

Cooper consulted her notes. "Would that be Aaron Quinn?"

"Yeah, that's him. She said he'd never been abroad before and she couldn't wait for the summer break to come around so she could show him Bangkok. She's probably with him. They'll be holed up doing what young lovers do."

Cooper took a deep breath. She wasn't sure if Mr Gallagher was indifferent to the danger his daughter could be in, whether she genuinely was the type to disappear and not tell a soul, or if he was hiding something. "She's not with Aaron," Cooper said. "He's just as worried as Macey's flatmate. I'll be speaking with him first thing in the morning. Thank you, Mr Gallagher. I'll be in touch regularly to update you on the investigation. In the meantime, could you call me immediately if you hear anything?"

"Of course."

Cooper recited her number and hung up. She sipped her coffee as she mulled over the conversation. She and Kenny would be beside themselves if Tina disappeared again, and Tennessee would be the same way with his infant son. Sam Sutherland, a DI, had been so concerned about his daughter, Caroline, during the Tarot Card Killer case that he'd pulled her out of school. Sean Gallagher did not appear to be cut from the same parenting cloth.

"What now?" asked Tennessee.

"Put in a request for her bank records and meet me downstairs in fifteen. We should visit Macey's flat before we finish for the day."

Tennessee saluted and grabbed his coat. "What did you think of Sean Gallagher?"

She ground her teeth before speaking. "I think Papa Bear's a little too laid back about his baby girl going missing."

- Chapter 4 -

Tennessee opened an umbrella and held it over his and Cooper's heads as they strolled through Heaton Park. The young detective was as physically protective of Cooper as Cooper was emotionally protective of him. He reminded Cooper of a younger brother who always looked out for his much smaller *big* sister. She was worried about him; he'd checked his phone eight times on the short drive over here.

Heaton Park was a beautiful oasis of greenery in a diverse and fashionable area of Newcastle. The suburb of Heaton was close to the city, with good schools, independent cafés and restaurants, as well as the usual chains. The rain pitter-pattered off the umbrella as Cooper and Tennessee strolled towards the park's exit. The trees lining either side of the pathway were blushed pink with blossom petals while blooms of yellow daffodils erupted in patches over grassy verges. Even on a miserable spring day like today, the park was alive with colour.

On Cooper's right, the ancient ruins of The House of Adam of Jesmond stood proud against the downpour. A knight and loyal ally of King Henry III, Adam de Gesmuth rose to Sheriff of Newcastle only to become hated by his community for extortion and embezzlement. Fearful for his safety, the king allowed Adam to fortify his home. After Adam's death during the crusades, the house fell into disrepair, but two walls remained defiant to seven hundred years of wind and rain.

"What's that smell?" asked Tennessee.

Cooper sniffed the air. "Wild garlic."

"Can you eat it?"

"You can. Some fancier restaurants forage down here and use it in their menus. Please don't ask me how. You know I can't cook for toffee."

Tennessee kicked a pebble with his boot. "Did I hear Sutherland was called to an armed robbery?" he asked, referring to detective Sam Sutherland.

"Yeah, some jokers turned over a pawnbroker's in the city. He's got Keaton and Martin with him. Bit of a hostage situation going on. I'm sure they'll fill us in once it's all over."

The pair left the park, passed the Islamic Centre and turned up Rothbury Terrace. On one side of the street, substantial Victorian terraces housed well-to-do families. On the other, smaller terraced houses had been converted into flats for the city's ever-expanding student population.

Cooper double-checked the door number of one flat before ringing the bell. A red-eyed Pearl Baxter opened the door and hurried the pair in. “Come in. It’s pissing down.”

“How are you holding up, Pearl? Did you call the number I gave you?”

Pearl nodded at Cooper. “Spoke to some lady. She said I can call back whenever I want to talk.”

Cooper placed a hand on the young woman’s shoulder. “That’s good. Pearl, this is DS Daniel. Could you show us Macey’s room, please?”

“This way.”

Pearl led the pair to the back of the house. “Macey had the back bedroom. She wanted the smaller room as the rent was cheaper.” She pushed open the door. “I’ve left everything as I found it,” she added.

Macey Gallagher’s room was a shrine to Ikea. Cooper recognised the Malm range of furniture from her daughter’s bedroom as well as a free-standing mirror she’d admired on her last visit to the Swedish labyrinth of flat-packs and temper tantrums.

Tennessee picked up a hairbrush from Macey’s dresser and slipped it into a paper evidence bag.

“What are you doing?” asked Pearl. The corners of her mouth turned down accusingly as if Tennessee were stealing from her flatmate.

He sealed the bag before answering. “The hair on her brush includes the root. We can take a DNA sample from it.”

“In case she turns up dead?”

Tennessee’s face tensed, and he nodded. It was enough for Pearl to leave the room.

“Poor kid,” he said to Cooper.

"Can't be easy." Cooper slid a MacBook out from under Macey's bed and opened it. "Her laptop's here; password-protected, though. We'll take it to the techies."

Tennessee continued to scan the room. "I have to agree with the flatmate. It doesn't look like anything's missing. Nothing obvious anyway." He opened a drawer and closed it again.

Cooper opened a second drawer. "Here's her passport." She flicked to the photo page and took in the image of Macey Gallagher, a pale blonde with rosy cheeks and blue eyes that seemed too big for her face.

"So she hasn't left the country."

"Her father said she'd travelled on her sister's passport before. We should check with the sister. Make sure she still has her passport."

"Any sign of a diary?" Tennessee said, continuing his search.

"No. There's plenty of notepads here, though." Cooper flicked through the pages of a beige exercise book. "Uni notes by the looks of it. Personal notes in the margins. *Dentist two o'clock, buy bread,* that sort of thing."

"Worth taking them?"

Cooper nodded and slipped the books into a bag. "Martin can comb through them when he's finished at the pawnbrokers. See if anything stands out."

"He'll love that," Tennessee said with sarcasm.

"He doesn't have to love it. He just has to do it. Right, I think we're done here for now."

Cooper found Pearl on her living room sofa, gripping a bottle of Czech lager with both hands. When she saw the DCI, she lifted the bottle, toasted the air and took a long swig. "It's been a shitty, long day."

In front of the sofa, a coffee table was littered with photocopied posters of Macey's face under the words *Have you seen me?* Tennessee picked one up. "Did you make these?"

Pearl shook her head and took another swig. "Aaron did. He feels a bit helpless. Wants to stay busy. He's been up and down Heaton Road handing copies to all the cafés and shops. He's going along Chillingham Road tomorrow morning and then Osborne Road in Jesmond."

"Can you tell me what Macey was wearing on Saturday night?" Cooper pulled a pen and pad out of her coat pocket.

"I can show you." Pearl opened her phone and scrolled through images until she found a suitable one. "This is Macey," she pointed to a short, slender girl in the middle of a group shot. "She had on these new Kate Spade heels. Apparently, they hurt like hell. That's a French Connection wrap dress, and I don't know what brand her handbag was, but it was a black clutch with silver trim. She kept an insulin pen in there, make-up too, and the silver bracelet..." Pearl zoomed in on Macey's right wrist. "It's a medical alert bracelet. Says she has type one diabetes."

"That's great, Pearl. Can you send that photo to this number?" Cooper handed Pearl her card. "And these girls are the ones you mentioned to me at the station? Imogen and Alison?"

"That's right."

"Who's this?" asked Cooper, pointing to a man who stood close to the group whose eyes were trained on Macey.

"A friend of Imogen's. Nick, I think. It was loud in the bar. Might have been Rick."

"And did you see Nick or Rick after you noticed Macey wasn't with you anymore?"

Pearl's shoulders lifted for a moment. "I don't know. I was pretty out of it. Too many shots. Sorry, I know I'm useless."

A tear rolled down her cheek, and she tipped the remaining beer into her mouth.

"You're not useless," Cooper told her. "You're doing well. Don't be too hard on yourself. Now, is there anything else you can think of? Anyone Macey was scared of? Or a reason she might want to disappear?"

Pearl wiped the tear away and left a smudge of mascara on the back of her hand. "No. She was happy. She was enjoying her course, and Aaron doted on her."

Cooper closed her notepad and gave Pearl a sympathetic look. "Thanks, Pearl. Call us if you think of anything else. We'll see ourselves out."

LIKE PUPPIES ABANDONED BY their mother, the girls huddled together for warmth. They whimpered and whined. Annoying little bitches. He was sick of them. Especially the Irish one. She was nineteen, according to her ID. Older than his boss would have liked, but luckily, she looked younger. Her eyes were big for her head, giving a baby-like appearance that would fetch some big bucks. The driver had done well picking her out of the crowd, and the lure knew what she was doing, knew how to get them to trust her. It was a shame the Irish girl was so noisy. Where she was going, they didn't like noise and backchat.

"Please," she begged, her voice loud but quivering. "Please." Her wrists were secured in front of her with cable ties, and she held her palms together as if praying. "Please, I need my medicine."

"I told you to pipe down," he replied, pushing her away so she fell into the others. She needed to be quiet. Their location wasn't as isolated as he would prefer, but his bosses had picked it out, and he had to make do. If she kept making this racket, she could blow the whole operation.

"Please," she tried again, louder this time. Snot streamed from her nose, and tears ran under the blindfold and into her mouth. "I need insulin. If I don't get it—"

He cut her off with a swift kick to her ribs. "Quiet."

She curled up in the foetal position and squeezed her upper arms to her sides, trying to protect herself from further blows. He stood watching her for a second and relaxed in the blissful silence that followed. His violence has worked. He'd have preferred to punch her in her pretty little mouth; it would have given him more satisfaction, but it would have split her lip or knocked a tooth out. His boss would be furious. He liked them young, beautiful and unmarked.

He crouched down and could smell sweetness on her breath, brought on by high blood glucose levels. "Listen," he whispered, "I'll get you some fucking insulin, all right? But you need to keep your gob shut. Understand?"

She cowered further into the other girls. As if those skinny bitches could protect her. They were bound and blindfolded just as she was.

"Understand?" he asked again. Growling this time because he didn't like to repeat himself.

She nodded and wiped her tears.

"Good." He placed a bottle in her shaking hands. "Drink some water. It'll help. I'll be back with food and insulin later. But I swear, if the guard tells me you've made so much as a peep, I'll flush the insulin down the bog, and you'll be tossed in the fucking sea."

- Chapter 5 -

"How did you manage to burn porridge?" Tina Cooper furrowed her dark brows as she stared into the pot on the hob. What should have been creamy porridge oats was now a brown, dried-out mess.

"Sorry, T," said Cooper with an apologetic smile. "I got distracted reading the news. I'll make some toast instead. So, what are your plans for today? And what in God's name are the seagulls so worked up about?"

There was an almighty racket coming from the roof of Cooper's home. Seagull squawks were part and parcel of living near the coast, but the family of herring gulls that had made Cooper's chimney stack their home seemed especially agitated today.

"They've been like that since dawn," yawned Tina. "And yeah, I've got a metric tonne of homework to do. The Easter holidays are hardly going to be a holiday at all. I'm going to hang out at Dad's this morning while I finish up a biology assignment and an English essay, and then I'm going to Josh's this afternoon. We'll do maths together, then take a walk down Longsands."

"Nice," said Cooper. "The beach bit, anyway, not the homework." Truth be told, Cooper knew Tina was just playing a part, saying the words she thought she ought to say. If she knew her daughter, and she believed she did, Tina would be far more excited about ploughing into a maths paper than getting sand between her toes.

The toast popped out of the toaster, and Tina slathered a healthy amount of chocolate spread on two slices and began to devour them. "Here," she said, handing Cooper two slices and a jar of ginger jam.

"Don't worry about me. You have them. I'll eat at the station."

Tina rolled her eyes and gave her mother the *no, you won't* stare. She was probably right. When Cooper was worried about a case, her appetite seemed to disappear, and she was extremely worried about Macey Gallagher. The longer it took to find her, the more danger she would be in.

The doorbell chimed at ten past eight, and Tina opened the door for Kenny. He greeted Tina with a kiss on the top of her head and Cooper with a clumsy hug. "Got you a present," he smiled.

Cooper was sure he meant Tina, so she busied herself by making a flask of tea to take with her, but when Kenny dragged an A1-sized framed poster from a Metallica gig through the door, with a grin worthy of the Cheshire Cat on his face and proudly declared "Ta-dah," she knew the gift was for her.

"Recognise it?" he asked.

Cooper grabbed the frame and held it up at eye height. "Is this what I think it is?" Memories flooded back to Cooper. Her mind conjured images of cheap lager in plastic cups, bodies bouncing off one another, and music so loud your ears hummed for days. "Our first date."

Technically, it wasn't a first date. Cooper had met Kenny at the concert when she'd crowd-surfed over a tide of head-banging moshers and had landed in his big, strong arms.

"Where did you find this?" asked Cooper. She could smell Kenny's aftershave from that night and could still feel her best friend, Cindy, squeezing her arm in excitement as they waited for James Hetfield to take to the stage.

"On an eBay auction," replied Kenny. "I thought you'd like it. Got the frame at a charity shop. Thought it was quirky."

"It is." The frame was made up of pin badges and buttons of all shapes and sizes. The classic yellow smiley face badge - synonymous with the nineties rave scene - stood out the most.

"I brought my tool kit. Thought I'd hang it for you before I whisk young Tina away for a morning of studying."

Tina was still nibbling on her crusts. She grunted, "Fun times," as crumbs fell from her mouth to the kitchen floor.

Kenny didn't wait for approval; he lifted the poster from Cooper's hands, heaved it upstairs and looked around Cooper's room. It felt odd, having him in her room. It took her back to being a teenager and enjoying stolen kisses and naughty moments under the sheets when her parents were at work and she was supposed to be at school. She hoped this wouldn't take too long. She didn't want the smell of Kenny's aftershave to linger until Atkinson returned from Germany. Not that she'd done anything to feel guilty about.

"Above the fireplace?" asked Kenny. He extracted the correct drill bit from his tool bag and held it between his teeth while he found a corresponding wall plug. Cooper nodded; the poster would look great there.

Kenny was finished in less than a minute. Impressive work. It would have taken her three hours of measuring, double-checking and working out how to use the damn drill to achieve the same result, and it would still be wonky.

Kenny's hands rested on his hips as he admired his handiwork, and then his eyes flickered to the dresser where Atkinson's spare glasses were resting on a Yuval Noah Harari book.

"Does the Science Man like Metallica?"

Over the last few months, Kenny had stopped referring to Atkinson as Justin and had instead started calling him the Science Man. It didn't bother Cooper; the name was pretty apt.

"He doesn't dislike them."

Kenny shrugged his large shoulders and left the room. Cooper followed him downstairs, where she found Tina balancing a pile of textbooks in her arms.

"Ready to go, sweetheart?"

Tina nodded and gave her mother the briefest of goodbye hugs. Cooper grabbed a leather jacket and her keys and followed Tina and Kenny out the front door, only for her ears to be assaulted by a chorus of caws. Whatever was bugging the winged rats, Cooper hoped they'd get it out of their system by the time she got home. Before her backside could reach the driver's seat, her phone buzzed. Cooper glanced at the screen and saw that it was Detective Chief Superintendent Howard Nixon.

Oh, bloody hell. What had she done now? "Sir?"

"Cooper, I have the results of the phone trace for your missing-presumed-dead girl."

Relieved that she hadn't done anything to warrant one of Nixon's notorious bollockings, Cooper braved correcting her superior. "She's not presumed dead, sir."

"Diabetic lass, out drinking alcohol till the wee hours, wearing next to nothing, and no one's seen hide nor hair from her since? If she turns up alive, I'll eat my hat."

"How about, if I find her alive, you give me a raise?"

Nixon chortled. "That's a big if, but like my ma used to say: Shy bairns get nowt. Right, note this down. The phone's been switched off since Monday lunchtime, but its last triangulation point was fifty-four degrees, fifty-eight point four minutes north, one degree, twenty-seven point three minutes west."

Cooper keyed the coordinates into her sat-nav and found they led to Bede Industrial Estate in an area called Jarrow. "Thanks, sir. I'll be in touch."

Cooper hung up and collected Tennessee from the corner of Front Street and Percy Park Road in Tynemouth.

"Get in," she yelled over the noise of car horns from the traffic building up behind her. "And I hope your tetanus is up to date. We're headed for darkest Jarrow."

"Christ. What did we do to deserve that?"

Jarrow, on the south bank of the Tync, had been a powerhouse of the shipbuilding industry. When the local shipyard closed in the 1930s, over eighty per cent of the working-age men found themselves unemployed. Without investment in the area, the local population continued to suffer more than their fair share of crime and unemployment.

"It's the last known location for Macey Gallagher's phone. Thought we should check it out. You sleep better last night?"

The detective sergeant picked some sleep from the corner of his eye and flicked it out the Mazda's window. "Got a whopping three and a half hours."

Cooper turned her Mazda onto the A19 and headed for the Tyne Tunnel. It didn't take long for them to reach their destination. Tennessee emerged from the car and scanned the road back and forth. "There's nowt here."

"There's a bus stop," said Cooper. She approached the stop and studied the timetable. "Only one route stops here. The number twenty-seven. Goes to South Shields."

"You think she got a bus from here?"

Cooper pulled a face. "I'm not sure she was even here, but her phone definitely was. Phones hold secrets. Photos, emails, private messages."

Tennessee shuffled along the road's edge, checking under shrubs and kicking his feet into long blades of grass.

"Here." Cooper pulled a pair of gloves from her field kit and handed them to Tennessee. "Make yourself useful," she said, pointing to a rubbish bin next to the bus shelter.

Tennessee's face wrinkled as he approached the bin and stared down into it. "Seriously?"

"Seriously."

The DS didn't argue. Piece by piece, he pulled litter from the bin and laid it on the ground.

"Anything interesting?" asked Cooper.

"Crisp packets, cans of Monster energy drink and something that resembles a dead mouse. Oh, shit, it *is* a dead mouse. Gross."

Tennessee held the creature by the tail, at arm's length, before dropping it next to a soggy copy of The Sun.

"But no phone?"

"No phone."

Cooper sighed. She wanted the phone. CID would have Macey's call and text history soon enough, but there were other things that her records wouldn't show, and those were the items Cooper was most interested in. Besides, any prints could be run through the system. If they matched with someone with a record, they could pay them a visit. She pulled her own mobile out and called the operator.

"Hello? Yes, put me through to South Tyneside council, please. Environmental services." She watched Tennessee place each item of rubbish back in the bin, peel off his gloves and chuck them in the bin as well. "Hi, this is DCI Erica Cooper from Northumbria CID. There's a bus stop on Jarrow Road. I need to know when its bin was emptied."

A woman with a high-pitched Geordie accent conducted a quick check on her system. "It would have been collected on Tuesday. Could have been anytime between six a.m. and five p.m. I can contact the team and try to narrow it down for you."

"No, that won't be necessary. Where did they take it? Great. Thank you."

Cooper hung up and winked at Tennessee before dialling DC Oliver Martin, the youngest and most image-conscious member of her team. She put him on speakerphone.

"Oliver, it's Cooper." She spoke quickly, not giving him a chance to protest. "I need you to get a team together, don a fetching white coverall and get yourself down to the tip at Boldon. Ask the site manager where the refuse collections from Jarrow Road were dumped on Tuesday and sift through the landfill until you find me Macey Gallagher's mobile. A Huawei Y7 in a red case. Cheers."

She pictured the young man's face as she pocketed her phone.

"You know he's losing his shit right now?" said Tennessee, suppressing a grin.

"Well, he keeps saying he wants us to let him get his hands dirty. It's not my fault if I interpret that literally."

- Chapter 6 -

It took fifteen minutes to drive to Heaton, during which time Tennessee told Cooper about the gurgles baby Alfie had been making at two in the morning and how he was convinced he was trying to sing along to Tennessee's rendition of Fog on the Tyne.

Aaron Quinn, Macey Gallagher's boyfriend, lived in a student let above a betting shop. Tennessee knocked on the door and was greeted by a young man with bloodshot eyes, a stubble-covered jaw and joggers worn so low on his hips that at least three inches of his boxer shorts were visible. Cooper had to restrain herself from going into Mum-mode and yanking his trousers back up to his waist where they belonged.

"Aaron Quinn? I'm DCI Cooper. We spoke on the phone. This is DS Daniel."

Aaron led the pair up the stairs and into his living room. Cooper did a quick scan of the room;

it hadn't seen a duster or a vacuum cleaner in at least two months. Empty beer bottles and energy drink cans littered the dining and coffee tables, Playstation controllers lay on the sofa, a game of FIFA had been paused, and an ashtray overflowed with cigarette ends. On the arm of the sofa was a bundle of the same posters they had seen in Macey and Pearl's flat.

Aaron hastily cleared some space for the detectives and invited them to sit.

"Erm, you want a coffee or something?"

Cooper couldn't see the kitchen from where she sat, but judging by the living room's standards of hygiene, she decided to decline his offer.

"No, thank you. Aaron, can you tell me when you last saw Macey?"

"That was the morning of the eighth," he answered. "She'd spent the night on the seventh, and we had breakfast together. Then I drove her to her flat. It's not far but it was raining."

"And how would you describe her mood that day?"

His nose wrinkled as he considered the question. "Just normal I suppose. She was looking forward to going out that night."

"Aaron, I'm sorry to ask you this. I know it's difficult for you right now, but did Macey ever give you reason to think she may harm herself?"

Aaron's eyes widened as his gaze met Cooper's. "God, no. I appreciate you have to check, but Jeez, no, not Macey. She wasn't depressed or suicidal, if that's what you mean."

Cooper watched Aaron pace back and forth while she asked her next question. "Did you hear from Macey again once you dropped her off at her flat?"

He shook his head. "No. I told her to text me if she wanted to meet up later on or if she wanted to crash here."

"But she didn't text you?" asked Tennessee.

"No. Not until the next morning, but I don't think that was really her. Did Pearl tell you we don't think the messages are from her?" He stopped pacing and checked his mobile.

"She did," Cooper assured him. "What did you do for the rest of the day, Aaron, after you dropped Macey at her place?"

"Erm, God, let's see. I played some footy in the park, then came home and did some uni work."

"You said it was raining." Tennessee looked up from his notepad.

"It was. The rain doesn't bother us. Getting covered in mud's half the fun."

"And what did you do in the evening?"

Aaron stared at Tennessee for a moment. "Why do you want to know so much about what I was doing that night? Seems like a waste of time. Shouldn't you be finding out what Macey was doing?"

Cooper gave him a supportive smile. "We are, Aaron. This is all part of the process. We want to establish what everyone in Macey's circle did that day so we can piece together exactly where Macey was and when."

"Ah, okay then. Well..." He started to pace again and played with something in his pocket as he spoke. "Me and Mikey, he's my flatmate, we went to the Blue Bell on the other side of the park with the lads in the flat next door and played some pool and had a few beers. Then we walked back, stopped in The Chillingham for a few more and got an Indian on the way home. I played some FIFA, but when I hadn't heard from Macey by two, I decided to go to bed."

"Thank you, Aaron," said Cooper. The man seemed nervous and agitated. Not surprising, given his girlfriend had disappeared. "This is helpful. You're doing a good job. Can you tell me when you first became worried about Macey?"

Aaron seemed to relax a little. He sat down at his dining table and rubbed his jaw. "I wasn't worried at first because she was texting me. But she seemed pissed off, like I was bothering her or being a pest or something. Her answers were just one word. I thought she was being short with me. I was more worried that she was upset with me for some reason, or—" his voice cracked with emotion. "Well, I can be a bit insecure when it comes to Macey. She's so gorgeous, and I'm just a daft scruff. I was worried she'd met someone else. I got a bit panicky. I've never met anyone like Macey before. She's amazing." Aaron's eyes turned glassy. No doubt his mind was frantic; going over everything he'd said or done and hoping to God he wasn't the reason she'd disappeared.

"She said she wanted to take me to Bangkok this summer. We've been saving up for the flights.

Anyway, I was freaking out that she'd met someone or was sick of me because I'm not interesting or exciting enough. I was proper paranoid. So I thought I'd pick up a little gift and go over and see her. I got pastries and a Frappuccino, but when Pearl answered the door and I said I was there to see Macey, her face sort of fell. She pulled me inside and started going on about how she thought Macey was with me, and I told her I thought she was there. Pearl tried to call her, but it went straight to voicemail. I tried as well but the same thing happened. That's when we properly started to fret. Pearl was hyperventilating. We rang everyone we knew but no one had seen her."

Cooper crossed her legs and tapped the end of her pen against her notepad. The way Aaron Quinn was pacing and constantly fidgeting had caught Cooper's attention. It would be perfectly natural for him to be anxious about his girlfriend's disappearance, but he was coming across as more nervous than worried. The traits were similar, but in all her years of police work, Cooper had learnt the difference.

"Aaron, do you mind if DS Daniel takes a quick look around while I finish up my questions?"

His eyes darted to the door leading to the hallway and bedrooms. "Why?" he asked. "Don't you need a warrant?"

Cooper kept her face neutral. "The hair sample we took from Macey's brush yesterday didn't have enough root to provide us with a DNA sample; I was hoping we could find something with Macey's DNA here." It wasn't a lie, but it wasn't the truth either. The hair sample was with the lab and she hadn't heard yet if the quality was good enough to extract DNA from. "And, we only need a warrant if you won't let us look around. Is there a reason you wouldn't want to cooperate?"

Back and forth, Aaron's eyes flickered between Cooper and Tennessee. "Okay, go ahead. Sorry about the mess though. Three lads under twenty. We're not the tidiest." He took a seat and immediately stood up again as Tennessee excused himself.

Cooper gave a little cough to bring his attention back to her. "Does Macey have any friends in Gateshead or South Tyneside?"

"Gateshead?" His expression turned to one of a man racking his brains. "South Tyneside? Don't think so. I mean some of her uni friends might be from there but not that she's mentioned."

"No relatives in that area?"

"No." He shook his head. "Her whole family's in Ireland. Why?"

"We heard from her network provider that her phone was in Jarrow on Monday." Cooper saw Aaron's pupils dilate. "That doesn't mean she was there, of course. Her phone could have been stolen, and I appreciate that you think Macey was in a good place, mentally, and that you don't think she would have harmed herself, but there's also the possibility that she left and doesn't want to be found."

Aaron's exterior toughened. "That's not her style," he said gruffly.

"Mr Gallagher, Macey's father, seemed to think Macey had a habit of running away or going AWOL."

A look of hurt passed over Aaron's face as he contemplated the idea. "She had no reason to run away. She loves me, and she loves Pearl. She's doing well at uni. She's happy. I promise you she's happy. You can't give up on her, we have to find her."

Cooper stood as Tennessee re-entered the room. "It's okay, Aaron. I'm not giving up on Macey. I promise. I don't think she would leave without her insulin and I'm going to do my very best to find her."

Aaron wrapped his arms around himself and let his chin fall to his chest.

"Call us if you can think of anything else, and be careful with those posters, Aaron. There's a lot of sick people out there and you'll no doubt get hoax calls, time-wasters and cranks."

His jaw slackened for a moment. He hadn't considered that.

Out in the cool breeze of Heaton Road, Cooper turned to the DS. "Find anything interesting?"

"Some alt-right literature and about fifty Adderall pills, but no sign of foul play if that's what you mean."

Cooper started walking back towards her car.

"But I need to see the photo of Macey again," added Tennessee.

Cooper unlocked her phone, opened the photo app and handed it over. As Tennessee studied the photograph Pearl had sent her, her mind drifted back to the night she and Kenny had met at the Metallica gig. Catching herself feeling all warm and fuzzy, she vigorously shook her arms out as if to free herself from such ridiculous thoughts. As Tennessee handed the phone back to her, she pushed Kenny from her head and glanced at her messages to see if Justin - sweet, intelligent Justin - had been in touch. He hadn't.

"What did you need the photograph for?" Cooper asked.

"I thought I remembered Macey being fairly slim, but I wanted to check. There was a bra in Aaron's room, under the bed. The label said thirty-eight D."

"There's no way that can be Macey's. Far too big."

"So, my theory is that Aaron Quinn and Macey Gallagher aren't as loved up as he wants us to believe."

Cooper raised her brows and looked up at Aaron's flat. Aaron's face was pressed against the glass, watching the two detectives on the street below. As soon as he made eye contact with Cooper, he disappeared behind the curtain.

Tennessee patted Cooper on the shoulder and pointed across the Metro bridge that connected Heaton with the ward of Byker. A pasty man in board shorts with scrawny, lily-white legs poking out of them reached into his pocket before shaking hands with a greasy-haired girl with a terrible bout of the shakes. "Look what the cat dragged in."

- Chapter 7 -

"Well, well, well," Tennessee smirked. "If it isn't my old acquaintance, Mitch Logan. How's my favourite petty criminal?"

"Oh, bugger off, will ya?" Mitch Logan stood no more than five-foot-four and wouldn't weigh more than eight stone if he was fully dressed and soaking wet. His shaved head reflected the sun, and his bare, pigeon chest was tattooed with a Sunderland AFC crest; a brave move in these parts.

"Boss, have you had the honour of dealing with this little toe rag?"

"Can't say I've had the pleasure. Mitch Logan, did you say? I'm DCI Cooper."

Tennessee folded his arms over his chest and grinned knowingly. "Did you hear the joke about the skinny chav who robbed a load of tools and paint from a building site?"

Mitch propped himself up on a low wall and pouted. "Oh aye, here we go. Never going to live it down, am I?"

"Well, the dummy dropped one of the tins of paint. It spilt on the ground, he stood in it, and left a trail of magnolia footprints right to his front door."

Cooper chuckled. "That was you? I remember that case. It won the Piece of Piss award at the department Christmas party last year because a three-year-old could have solved it."

"Aye, that was me. Sixty hours community fucking service. So what do you two want?"

"Ah, just a catch-up," teased Tennessee, "and to conduct a stop and search."

Mitch tensed. "You can't do that. I know my rights. You need reasonable suspicion."

Tennessee snorted. "I literally just watched you give something to a girl who was shaking so hard she'd register on the Richter scale. I am *reasonably suspicious* that you are dealing drugs. Now empty your pockets."

Mitch threw his arms out wide. "I gave her a stick of chewy. That's all."

Tennessee glanced at Mitch, his watch, then back to Mitch. "I'm waiting."

"Fine," he grunted after looking left and right and deciding that running wasn't a wise choice. He laid the contents of his pockets on the wall behind him one by one.

"So, what you driving these days?" asked Tennessee. "Still got that rust bucket of a Renault?"

"Nah," answered Mitch, laying a lighter, a ten-pence piece, three sticks of gum, a torn five-pound note, and a key on the wall. "Got a fourth-hand Audi. Nice paint job. Glacier white."

"And how's that handsome fella of yours? James?"

"Haven't seen him in months, mate. Met this six-three Jamaican lad called Harrison on Grindr."

"Good for you." Tennessee assessed the items on the wall and made Mitch turn his pockets inside out to be sure.

"Happy?" he asked with a smug grin.

"Ecstatic." Tennessee couldn't sound more sarcastic if he tried. "Now clear off."

Mitch Logan stuffed his things back in his pockets and sauntered away while muttering about police harassment.

Two large coffees later and Cooper was up to speed on all Tennessee's dealings with Mitch Logan. Having also nicked a load of designer gear from John Lewis, he was caught after bragging about it on Facebook. He'd even posted the links to the eBay auction where he was flogging it all.

"Sounds like he fell out of the stupid tree and hit every branch on the way down." Cooper fished her keys from her trouser pockets and unlocked the Mazda. "What's next on our to-do list?"

"I think it's time we visited the others who were out the night Macey disappeared." He checked his notepad. "Imogen West and Alison Sparks-Forster."

MACEY GALLAGHER'S FRIENDS LIVED in a purpose-built student facility five minutes from Newcastle University. A bald facilities manager buzzed Cooper and Tennessee in and scrutinised their warrant cards. He was about the same height as Cooper, which made him short for a man, and his brown beard was flecked with grey. He pointed the detectives toward the lifts and told them they needed the third floor. On their way to the lifts, they walked past a glass-fronted, state-of-the-art gym and an impressive social room fitted with a full-size pool table, air hockey and - Cooper couldn't believe it - a karaoke machine.

Tennessee's eyes were popping out of his head. "Man. University's changed since my time. I lived in the halls of residence at Sunderland. My room was smaller than a prison cell. Not exaggerating. And man, you should have seen the state of the toilets."

"I didn't go to uni," said Cooper as she pressed the button for the lift. "I had Tina. I needed a job."

Tennessee stole a sideways glance at his chief. Cooper suspected he was shocked to hear that she didn't have a university education, given that it was common knowledge in the department that she'd aced the detectives' exam. At that moment, the lift doors opened and a raven-haired woman in a stylish blouse emerged carrying a baby in one arm and a pile of textbooks in another. She can't have been more than nineteen or twenty. Cooper smiled at her and then at her baby. *Impressive*, she thought, before feeling a pang of jealousy that ripped through her and caught her off guard. If only those opportunities had been there in her day. The subjects she could have studied, the people she could have met. She'd still have wanted to join the force, but a first-class degree in a core subject could put a new recruit on an accelerated course for promotion.

Emerging on the third floor, Cooper knocked on the door to room three hundred and twelve. A Taylor Swift song was playing from within, so Cooper had to knock again to be heard.

"What's the password, *biatch*?" chirped a voice behind the door, followed by hysterical sniggering.

Cooper thought about answering *Northumbria Police* in her toughest voice, but she refused to answer to *biatch*, so instead, she knocked again and waited.

"Come in already." This time, the voice was impatient.

Cooper shrugged and pushed the door open to Imogen West's room. Imogen, whom Cooper recognised from the photos Pearl had shown her, was an hourglass of a woman with a waist so much smaller than her hips that Cooper suspected she'd fallen prey to the Kardashian-inspired trend of waist trainers. She was sitting at her desk doing her makeup in a magnifying mirror, and a curtain of long red hair flowed to her lower back. She clocked the detectives in the mirror and span on her swivel seat.

Her eyebrows lowered as she surveyed them with a mascara wand held delicately between manicured nails. "Yah? Can I help you?"

Yah? Cooper's jaw tensed. "Northumbria Police. We're here about Macey."

"Oh, gawd. She hasn't turned up yet?" Imogen turned back to her mirror, finished her mascara and returned the wand to its bottle. She stood, walked to the opposite wall and thudded the side of her fist against the plaster three times. "Get over here, Ali! The police are here," she shouted into the wall.

Thirty seconds later, Alison Sparks-Forster sat on Imogen's bed. She looked like a modern Snow White: sharp black bob, peaches and cream skin, and scarlet lips.

"Ladies," started Cooper, "Macey's been missing for over eighty hours now and we're extremely concerned about her well-being. It's imperative we get as much information as we possibly can. Even the smallest detail could be important."

Imogen and Alison exchanged a look. "What do you need to know?"

"Everything that happened that evening," Cooper said. "Start at the beginning."

Alison picked up a stuffed toy and held it to her chest. "Christ. Right, let's see. Pearl and Macey got the Metro into town and met us at this Greek place for dinner."

"What Greek place?" Tennessee asked. Cooper knew he knew the answer from their interview with Pearl. He was testing that the girls' stories matched. Clever.

"No idea how you pronounce it," shrugged Alison as she pulled her phone out from her pocket. "I can find it on the map though." Her fingers slid across the screen. "Here," she said. "It's this one."

Tennessee made a note. "And how was dinner?"

"Oh, it was fabulous. We had this delightful meze platter—"

"I meant, how was the atmosphere? Did Macey mention anything to concern you? Anything out of the ordinary? Or did her mood seem out of character?"

"Ah," Alison blushed, looking at Imogen who took over.

"Not really. She was as bubbly as ever. She was trying to sweet-talk the waiter into letting her smash some plates. He didn't let us so Macey said we shouldn't leave a tip. But we did anyway. All was forgiven after a glass or two of wine."

"Can you remember the waiter's name?" asked Tennessee.

She shook her head and pouted for a moment. "Another thing, she wasn't talking that much about Aaron. I remember because she's been like a broken record recently with all the lovey-dovey talk, but on Saturday, I remember Alison making a joke, you remember, don't you, Ali? You said it was a new record. That she hadn't said his name in over an hour."

"Do you think they'd had a fight?"

"Who knows? It was probably just a sign of the spark fizzling for the first time."

"Pearl told us that Macey didn't have much to drink on account of her having diabetes. Is that accurate?"

Alison and Imogen traded looks.

"Please be honest," said Tennessee. "If Macey drank more than usual, we need to know."

"It's not that," answered Alison. "Macey didn't need alcohol to have a good time. She had two, maybe three, glasses of wine, and she switched to soft drinks once we left the restaurant. When we met up with Nico, he bought a round of vodka shots. When Macey refused hers, I think, well I'm not certain, and I don't want to get him into trouble, but I think I saw him drop it in her soda." She hugged the stuffed toy harder.

Cooper showed the photo she had of the group on her phone to Imogen and Alison. "This man here," she said, pointing to the man Pearl had referred to as Nick, or Rick. "Is this Nico?"

"Yeah, that's our Nico."

"His full name?" Cooper asked.

"Nicolas Petite," Imogen replied.

"French?"

"Yah."

Yah? Seriously? "Lucky, Nico. Outnumbered four to one by you ladies."

"Alison thinks he likes boys because he's so well dressed, but I keep telling her all French guys dress immaculately. I used to summer in France almost every year, you see. Father owns a château and a handful of gîtes, so I'm fluent in French, and as Nico barely spoke English when he arrived here, I sort of adopted him."

"And the only French I know is *voulez vous coucher avec moi ce soir*." Alison giggled to herself before parting her lips slightly and looking up through her long lashes towards Tennessee.

Give me strength, thought Cooper. "We'll need to speak to him. Does he live in this block?"

Imogen flicked her hair over her shoulder. "Yah, he does. But you're out of luck. He's gone back to Lyon for Easter."

"No problem. We'll get his details from Admissions. Let's go back to Saturday night. What time did you leave the restaurant? And where did you go afterwards?"

"About half eight, maybe nine-ish? Right, Alison? Yah. Nine-ish. We went to Jalou for about an hour and a half, then Tokyo, then Feisty's because Pearl wanted to dance."

"When did you notice Macey had gone?"

Imogen pulled a face. "I'm not sure exactly. I was having fun. I wasn't checking my watch every five minutes."

"By *having fun*, she means she was getting frisky with Colin the Cockney."

"Shut up, Alison." She threw a hairbrush at her friend and turned back to Cooper. "It was after one. Before four."

"Didn't you look for her?"

She shrugged and glanced at Alison, but Alison was leaning back and trying to get a better view of Tennessee's backside. "We'd queued for ages," Imogen said. It was a shoddy explanation, and she clearly knew it as she added, "We didn't know anything was amiss. We thought she'd snuck off to see Aaron and get her nightly fix of Geordie boy."

Cooper didn't think she would get anything further from Imogen West or Alison Sparks-Forster. Macey's so-called friends were more concerned with making eyes at Tennessee than with her welfare. They let a man sneak her vodka shots and didn't look for her when they realised she'd become separated from the group. Macey's Dad thought the whole thing was a joke and Aaron, Macey's boyfriend, despite his insistence that he loved her, had another woman's bra in his bedroom. Cooper wondered if she, Tennessee and Pearl Baxter were the only people in the world who were worried about the missing diabetic.

Cooper made a quick note to follow up on the waiter at the Greek restaurant and to find Nicolas Petite, the drink-spiking son-of-a-bitch. "Thanks for your time, ladies. If we need any further details, we'll be in touch. I'll leave you to your studying."

Alison snorted. "It's Wednesday, no one studies on Wednesdays. We're off to the new cocktail bar near Grey's Monument. Imogen knows the manager. Don't you, Mo? Said he'd get us some Champers on the house. You can join us if you like," she said to Tennessee while licking her upper lip.

"He's married," Cooper snapped before her DS could reply.

"To you?"

"No."

"Then why do you care?"

Cooper swallowed down her anger. She cared because Tennessee was a new dad, struggling with all the adjustments that came with that huge responsibility. She cared because she was his chief and friend and—

"DCI Cooper cares because she holds her team to the highest standards." Tennessee closed his notepad and stored it in his trouser pocket. "You were two of the last people to see Macey before her disappearance. It would be unprofessional for me to see either of you in a social setting." He moved to the door and opened it for Cooper. "And like she said, I'm married."

- Chapter 8 -

"It's gone five," Cooper told Tennessee when they were back at Northumbria CID. "Get yourself home to that beautiful baby of yours."

Tennessee shut the open browsers on his computer screen and gathered his things. He paused, hesitating.

"What is it?" she asked him.

He shook his head. "It's nothing. Don't stay too late. Follow your own advice and get back to Tina, okay?"

She brought her hand to the side of her head and saluted the DS. "Aye, aye, captain."

As Tennessee left the room, Cooper knew he was right; she should follow her own advice and get the hell out of there. There were two things she wanted to do first, however. One, finish her report of the information gathered from Aaron, Imogen and Alison, and two, find out if Oliver Martin had any luck at the dump. She typed up her last two sentences, shut her computer down and went in search of Martin.

After searching most of Northumbria Police headquarters and ringing Martin twice, only for her calls to go to voicemail, Cooper eventually found Martin coming out of the shower rooms. He was void of styling products and had a face like someone had pissed on his chips.

"There you are. Find that phone for me?"

"No, I bloody didn't." Martin was on the verge of having a tantrum of teenager proportions and as much as Cooper empathised she didn't appreciate being spoken to like that. Not by the newest recruit. She could take a leaf out of Nixon's book and give him a swear-laden dressing down, or she could keep it simple.

"It's *no, I bloody didn't, boss.* Or if you absolutely must, *no I bloody didn't, ma'am.*"

Martin took a deep breath. "Yes, boss. Sorry, boss."

"Want to get it off your chest?"

He took another breath, deep enough for his chest to visibly expand and stretch the fabric of his t-shirt. "Sorry, ma'am. Six hours I spent in that rat-infested stink-hole with flies buzzing about my head and all we found were a couple of iPhones and a duffle bag of Russian rubles."

"You what?" That caught Cooper's attention.

"Rubles. Worked out at thirty grand's worth."

"Hmm. Interesting. Any indication of who or why—"

"Not a thing. Plain black bag, no labels, no nothing. It's intriguing all right but it's also not our problem. I handed it over to Fraud."

"Fair enough. You got the smell out of your nose yet?"

"Not quite." Martin squeezed his nostrils together. "I've tried vapour rub but it's still there."

"I'm not surprised. You live in Gosforth, right?"

"Yeah."

"Nip into Boots on the High Street and buy yourself a nasal rinse. It'll help."

"Will do. Thanks for the tip. Oh, and boss..." Martin ran his fingers through his hair before swinging his backpack strap over his shoulder. "Sorry for being a brat."

Cooper softened. She patted his upper arm and bowed her head. "We've all been there. Just don't let it happen again."

COOPER WAS PLEASED TO get home. She loosened the laces on the cherry Dr. Martens boots she'd been wearing, pulled them off, and wiggled her toes. What she would give for one of Atkinson's foot rubs right now. Cooper checked her watch. It would be almost seven o'clock in Germany. Atkinson would be getting ready for dinner. Probably donning a well-fitted shirt and a smart pair of jeans, maybe adding a squirt of aftershave. He'd sit down to a no-doubt excellent meal and converse all evening with Europe's best and brightest in the field of forensic sciences. Meanwhile, Cooper was about to reheat last night's leftover lasagne and watch the news for any developments in the trial of the Tarot Card Killer.

The kitchen was spotless. Cooper was certain she'd left it as if a bomb had hit it this morning. Tina must have cleaned. *She'll be after something,* thought Cooper, *and whatever it is, it probably costs a fortune.*

A shoebox sat on the kitchen table and scrawled on the lid, in thick marker pen, were the words *Not junk. Do not throw out.* Cooper lifted the lid expecting to see a pair of shoes or a bunch of old photographs. She did not expect to see a baby seagull.

"TINA!"

Tina's footsteps trotted down the stairs. She was wearing a t-shirt of a llama in sunglasses. "Ah," she said when she spotted the lid was off the shoebox. "I see you've met Steven."

"Steven? *Steven?* Christ, you've named it. Why is that disease-carrying ball of feathers in my kitchen?"

Tina walked over to the shoe box and scooped the hatchling into her hands. "He fell off the roof, poor thing. I found him in the backyard. That's why the gulls were making a racket this morning."

"Tina. You can't keep it, sweetheart. You need to put it back in the yard."

"No." Tina's features pinched, and she looked fixedly at her mother. "He won't survive in the yard. All the cats that live on this street? He won't survive the night and he's at least a month away from being able to fly."

"So you plan on raising him? You can't keep a wild animal. It's illegal." She removed the leftover lasagne from the fridge and slid it into the microwave.

Sitting down at the kitchen table and stoking Steven's feathers, Tina shook her head. "Nice try. It's perfectly legal to keep a wild bird if it's unfit for release as long as you meet its welfare needs and release it as soon as it's ready to survive on its own."

Of course, Tina had already formulated her counter-arguments and conducted the required research to back them up. She'd probably printed off the supporting documents and filed them ready for presentation to a sceptical mother.

"Surely you need a licence?"

"Nope." Tina was smug. "The only birds requiring a licence are ostriches and cassowaries. Schedule four birds such as eagles and buzzards need to be registered with the council, but that doesn't include seagulls."

Cooper had been completely outmanoeuvred. "Okay, counsellor. You say you need to meet its welfare needs. How do you plan on feeding it?"

"Steven. Not *it*. I got some scraps from the fish quay, blended them into mush and froze them in an ice cube tray. At feeding time, I defrost one, warm it up, pop it in a piping bag and squirt it into his mouth."

The little genius had thought of everything. "Right." Cooper had lost. There was no point in arguing. "So you're telling me that not only is a seagull now living in my kitchen but that our ice cube trays are full of fish scraps?"

"Yes."

The microwave beeped and Cooper dished two portions onto plates. "Fine. But wash your hands for goodness sake before you give us all E. coli, salmonella and who knows what else."

Tina popped Steven back in his box and went to the sink. She was grinning from ear to ear.

WHEN COOPER LEFT FOR work the next morning, Tina was busy piping fish into the mouth of a greedy gull and reading her physics study notes. Cooper grabbed a Starbucks en route, and upon arriving at HQ headed straight to see The Collector.

The Collector, real name Cedric Bell, was a Local Intelligence Officer whose windowless office was usually ripe with body odour and egg sandwiches. Cooper always tried to send lower-ranking detectives to do this job but as Tennessee hadn't shown up yet she had to do her own dirty work.

"Erica Cooper, what brings you to my lair?" Cedric Bell chuckled from behind his computer. He had sweat patches under his arms and was drinking Lemsip. His desk was cluttered, and as Cooper's gaze scanned over various files and papers, he hastily gathered them into a neat pile.

She was almost certain she'd spotted a porn mag amongst it all.

"I have some updates for you from DS Daniel." Cooper wanted to get out of The Collector's office as soon as possible. The man was creepy. "Mitch Logan. Full name, Mitchell Peter Logan."

Bell's fingers jabbed away at his keyboard. His fingernails were dirty and he had a frayed plaster fastened around his thumb. "Found him. What you got for me?"

"No longer driving a Renault. He has a white Audi now."

Bell entered the information into his database. "Anything else?"

"Yes," Cooper said. "Known associates. He's dating a Jamaican man named Harrison. No surname, but I'm sure it won't be too hard to find out."

More jabbing at the keyboard. "And how about yourself?" Bell asked. "Is it true you're off the market?"

Cooper felt ill. Everything about Bell and this room made her want to run. "I'm off the market, and you're inappropriate for asking." She turned, opened the door and left.

"Don't leave it so long next time, Erica, darling. I've missed you."

Cooper walked past the shower rooms. If she didn't have work to get on with she'd go in and wash Bell off her. Macey Gallagher was still missing. Nico Petite had possibly spiked the diabetic's drink with vodka and was one of the last people to see her. Cooper needed to speak to him as soon as she could. She looked up the number for Newcastle University's Admissions Office and waited for someone to pick up. She introduced herself and explained that she needed the home address and telephone number of Nicolas Petite.

"Oh, I'm afraid I cannot give out that information," replied the woman on the other end of the phone.

"Cara, was it? One of your students hasn't been seen since Saturday evening. She's an Irish national, and the man I want to speak to in connection with her disappearance is a French national. If Macey dies because I can't get insulin to her in time, it will be news across the entire continent, and I will not hesitate to let the press know that you slowed down our investigation. I want his home address and phone number, and I don't want to waste hours getting a warrant."

There was silence. Enough silence for Cooper to wonder if she'd been put on hold or hung up on, but eventually the admissions officer came back to the phone. "Sixteen Rue De Reims, Lyon." She followed with the phone number.

"Thank you, Cara," Cooper said. "You did the right thing."

Cooper wasted no time in ringing the number. With no knowledge of the French language beyond *bonjour* and *au revoir,* Cooper hoped the Petites would speak English. She would have to wait to find out as, despite twenty minutes of trying, no one was picking up.

Cooper typed the address into Google Maps and zoomed in to a pretty, suburban street where it looked as if one in every three homes had a swimming pool. She rolled her mouse back and forth over the surrounding streets until a little orange icon appeared with a knife and fork on it. "Petite Boulangerie," she read aloud. A Google search and a few trips to Google Translate later and Cooper's suspicions were confirmed. The bakery was run by a local family who were named Petite. She found the phone number for the business and gave it a call.

"Bonjour? Madame Petite? Je suis DCI Cooper. Je suis, erm..." That was the limit of Cooper's French. "I need to speak to Nicolas. Is he there?"

"I am sorry. I do not speak English," came the reply, ironically in perfect English.

The line disconnected and Cooper stared at her handset. Rude. She'd try again later. She wasn't going to give up that easily. Besides, she had translators at her disposal. She'd book one for later that day.

"Hey, stranger."

Cooper looked up to see Sam Sutherland pulling up a chair. If Tennessee was Cooper's CID brother, then Sutherland was her CID father. Older than her but junior in rank, Sutherland used slang from the seventies and occasionally dressed like it was still the eighties. His BMI was on the wrong side of twenty-five, but luckily he usually worked with ex-rugby star detective Paula Keaton. If anyone needed chasing, Keaton had it covered.

"How's it going?" asked Cooper, "and whoa! Look at that bling." She grabbed Sutherland's wrist and admired a sparkling Rolex that looked like it was worth more than her car.

Sutherland blushed. "An anniversary present. Twenty-five years. Doesn't seem like two minutes."

"Nice," said Cooper, still admiring the watch. It wasn't her style, but it was still mighty impressive.

"I screwed up, though."

"Don't tell me you bought Sue a new vacuum cleaner."

"Not quite that bad. I got her favourite flowers and these chocolates she likes from a patisserie in Edinburgh and some other small gifts. All the stuff I knew she'd love, but still, nothing on par with a Rolex."

Cooper raised her eyebrows. "So, you're sleeping on the couch, right?"

"Nah, I managed to swing it back by telling her I'd booked us a week in the Maldives. As soon as I stop for lunch, I need to get straight to a travel agent and book it before Sue asks any more details."

"Smooth. And what about Caroline? Has she settled in at Westfield?"

Sutherland loosened his tie. "Truth be told, no, not really. She likes the teachers, and they have a trampoline club which she's loving, but she's not making many new friends. Her grades are up, so Sue's pleased, but I just want her to be happy."

Cooper could appreciate that. She never had to worry about Tina's grades, but she was always worried that the bullying that had plagued her daughter's first few years at secondary school would start again. "We're having a bit of a party for Tina's fifteenth if you want to bring Caroline over. She won't have seen Tina since November. I know she's a few years younger, but it will be nice for them to catch up. Bring Sue. Atkinson will be there."

Sutherland's face glowed. "That's very kind of you, Erica. I'm sure Caroline will jump at the chance. What's the date? I'll have to check with the missus."

"The twenty-third. Easter Sunday."

"Great. Don't think we have anything on. Sue'll probably go to mass in the morning, but it's not my scene. So how's the missing girl case going? Heard it's a tricky one."

Cooper closed her eyes and shook her head. "I'm very worried. My gut tells me she's still alive, but..."

"But you don't have long?"

"I really don't."

"Well, if you need any help just give me and Keaton a shout. The armed robbery was open and closed - Muscovites connected to the Red Skulls - and this matricide in Benwell we were just handed is pretty straightforward. Eight kids. She changes the will to leave it all to the youngest, and three days later, she collapses at bingo. Ingested rat poison." He looked pointedly at Cooper. "We know the little swine did it; we just need to prove it. I'll have him in the cells by the end of the week. So, as I said, if you need a hand, just say."

Cooper gave an appreciative smile. "I might just do that. Oh." Tennessee had just arrived. "You made it in?"

"Yeah," he said with a yawn. "Sorry I'm late. Hey, Sam. Alfie's got a cough. Had to get him to the GP. Then Hayley... Oh, and I saw Nixon on the way in."

He held up some papers. "I have Macey's phone records."

Cooper turned her chair to face him, her interest piqued. "And?"

"And, if you look to Saturday evening, there's a bunch of incoming calls that go unanswered. This number is Pearl Baxter, this is Aaron Quinn and this," he pointed to another number," is an unregistered pay-as-you-go phone. I've called it, and there was a foreign dial tone, but no answer. I also tried Pearl Baxter to see if she recognised the number but she doesn't have it in her contacts."

"Nico Petite?"

"Maybe. I can check with Imogen and Alison but..."

"But you don't want to be sexually harassed?"

He sat down and handed the phone records to Cooper. "Exactly."

"I'll do it."

"Thanks. But here's the interesting thing." He motioned to the records. "All those incoming calls, probably Pearl and co trying to find where Macey had disappeared to, but only one outgoing call."

Cooper ran her finger down the list until she found what she was looking for.

"Recognise the number?" Tennessee asked.

Cooper frowned. Should she? Then she saw it. A double seven, a double three and another double seven. "Matt Walker. The landlord. Now, why oh why did our missing girl call her landlord at three a.m.? And why didn't he mention it when I spoke to him?"

- Chapter 9 -

"So this is Great Park?" asked Tennessee. He wound the window down on Cooper's Mazda and stuck his head out to get a better view as she idled along a suburban street. Given his blonde curls, he was a panting tongue away from resembling a labradoodle. "Bit soulless, isn't it? What's with all the balconies and roof terraces? And is that a palm tree? They know this is Newcastle, right?"

It was a clever move on the part of the developers. Selling the dream of al fresco dining and barbecues in an area with an average temperature of eight degrees. Then there was the promise of a town centre, village stores and community spirit. Eighteen years after the houses went up, there still wasn't a supermarket or restaurant in sight.

Cooper knocked on the door to number eighty-four. Through the front window, she could see a man of average height with shaggy hair watching horse racing on a curved, wide-screen television. He turned to look and reluctantly got to his feet to answer the door.

"Yeah?" he asked, looking at Tennessee and barely glancing at Cooper. He had bright green eyes, a tan and a physique he was obviously proud of, given how tightly fitted his t-shirt was.

"Mathew Walker?" Tennessee introduced himself and held up his warrant card. Cooper did the same.

"You the one I spoke to on the phone?" he said, addressing Cooper with wandering eyes. "You don't look like a detective."

Cooper should have known better, but she took the bait nonetheless, "Then what do I look like?"

"I divint nah. Hair that short and a leather jacket? A neo-nazi? A tattoo artist? Both?"

Cooper's lips pulled inwards and she cocked her head. "I can assure you, I am neither of those things. Now, can we come in, Mr Walker? We have some questions."

Walker shrugged and moved aside. After leading Cooper and Tennessee into his kitchen he opened his fridge and got himself a beer.

Tennessee caught Cooper's eye as Walker's back was turned. "This place is immaculate," he whispered.

"Smells it too," she replied, noting the distinctive aroma of bleach.

As Walker opened his can it made a whooshing noise and foam bubbled from the top. He slurped it off the aluminium and grinned at Cooper. "I'd offer you one but yee lot aren't meant to drink on duty, are ya? That's the good thing about being self-employed. You set your own hours. I think I'll clock off right about now." He popped his hips to the side and leant against a faux marble worktop.

Cooper tried not to scowl. "How long have you known Macey Gallagher, Mr Walker?"

"Since August. All my student lettings run from August to August."

"And are you regularly in contact with her?"

"Nah. Not really. I carried out an inspection in December to make sure they weren't trashing the place, but they keep the flat in good nick. If anything needs doing it's usually the other one who gets in touch."

"Pearl Baxter?"

"Aye, that's her. Hair like she's stuck her finger in a socket."

Cooper's dislike for Matt Walker was growing by the second. She pinched the bridge of her nose and counted silently to three. "When did you last see Macey?"

"Ages ago. Would've been February time. I went round to install a new washing machine."

"And that was the last time you spoke to her?"

Walker took a long drink of beer, burped with his mouth closed and released the gas slowly through pursed lips. "Aye."

"So, then why, Mr Walker, did Macey phone you at three a.m. on the night she went missing?"

There was a palpable change in the atmosphere as Walker stayed motionless for a good ten seconds. "Did she?"

Cooper snorted. "Yes, she did. You know she did. Why did she call?"

"I don't know. I didn't pick up. I put my phone on silent overnight." His voice was quickening and he took brief sips of his drink between each sentence. "Was probably just a pocket dial. I didn't see it until the next morning."

"You didn't return her call?"

"No. It was from three in the effin' morning. I told you, I thought it was a pocket dial."

Tennessee folded his arms and lifted his chin. "Mr Walker. I'm only going to ask this once, so be honest, were you and Macey in a relationship?"

"God, no. Nee chance. I'm single, me." Walker finished his beer, rinsed the can under the tap, squashed it down to a disk using his bare hands and tossed it into a bin marked for recycling. "Would be unprofessional, wouldn't it? Improper. You don't have me picked as the sort of landlord who reduces the rent for sexual favours, do ya?"

"Of course not," lied Cooper. She didn't know what to make of Matt Walker, but a squeaky-clean landlord he was not. She'd bet her right leg on it. "Could I use your bathroom?"

Walker's nose wrinkled but before he could refuse, Cooper added, "Lady problems."

"Ah, alreet. Top of the stairs." He nodded his head back towards the hallway.

Cooper excused herself. As she climbed the stairs she could hear Tennessee asking Walker if he had a cleaner. Walker's bathroom was like the rest of his house, sparkling clean with a whiff of peroxide in the air. Cooper didn't need the toilet, nor did she have *lady problems;* she did, however, want to snoop around. She opened a mirrored medicine cabinet and scanned the shelves. A single toothbrush, a Wilkinson Sword five-blade razor, a box of paracetamols, shaving gel, caffeine shampoo, and a Nivea Men roll-on deodorant. If Macey had been in a relationship with Walker, she hadn't left any trace in the bathroom. No spare insulin kit, tampons or toothbrush. To Cooper, this looked one hundred per cent like a bachelor bathroom. That was until she spotted a Kirby grip on the floor behind the toilet.

Cooper crouched down and took a photo of the hairpin with her phone before pulling a clear evidence bag from her pocket and bagging the grip. It still had a hair attached to it. Dark blonde or light brown, it was hard to tell, but if the lab matched it to the hair sample they'd taken from Macey's hairbrush, it would be proof Macey had been here and that Walker was a lying piece of shit.

"Whose hair grip is this?"

Walker's head whipped around to the doorframe where Cooper was standing. "What?"

"This hair grip." She held the bag up in front of her and jangled it like a child does with a bagged goldfish from the fair. "If you're single, who does it belong to?"

"I divint nah. My sister's, maybe." Walker pushed his weight off the worktop and began walking back to his front door, trying to shepherd the detectives from his home.

"Oh, and one more thing," started Cooper. "Do you have voicemail?"

Walker's jaw clenched. "Yeah. Why? I told you it was a pocket dial. Just muffled night-out noises."

Cooper stood firm despite Walker's attempts to manoeuvre her to the door. "Play it for me."

Walker groaned and looked to the ceiling. "Fine. Don't even know if I still have it." He pushed his phone to his ear and cycled through a couple of messages before thrusting the phone at Cooper. "Here."

Cooper switched the speakerphone on and listened to what did indeed sound like a pocket dial. The message lasted three minutes and Cooper played it four times before giving up. She couldn't make out anything other than the noises of traffic and music. Tech, on the other hand, might be able to salvage something from it.

Cooper walked out of Walker's house and approached her car.

"Hey," he called after her. "My phone."

"You can have it back in a second, Mr Walker." Cooper opened her boot and pulled out a black canvas bag. She unzipped the bag and produced a black device that looked like an old Gameboy from the nineties. She selected an iPhone attachment and plugged the two devices together.

"Hey!" Walker had moved within a foot of Cooper. Tennessee moved within a foot of Walker. "What do you think you're doing?"

"I'm extracting your data," explained Cooper.

A furious look coloured Walker's face. "You can't do that. Not without my permission."

"Actually," started Cooper with half a smile. "I can."

- Chapter 10 -

Mobile phone extraction - more commonly referred to as a digital strip search - required neither a warrant nor a suspect's consent. The devices were a quick and easy way to download a person's call history and messages, as well as their communications using social media and apps. Digital strip searches had hit the headlines in recent times after forces began to use them on victims of crime, particularly in cases of rape, to establish the nature of any prior relationship between the accuser and the accused. Rights groups were campaigning to have this process more tightly regulated, but for now, Cooper had a great tool at her disposal. If Walker had so much as sent a Snapchat to Macey Gallagher, she would know about it.

"Play it again," asked Tennessee as he and Cooper strolled back into Northumbria Police HQ.

Cooper played the recording from the voicemail message again, shutting her eyes to try and focus her senses on the sound.

"You hear that? Like a swoosh and thud?"

Cooper opened her eyes and looked at Tennessee. He was pointing into thin air and swiping his finger in time with the noise. She heard it too, a swoosh and a thud, followed by a swoosh and another thud. "What is that?"

"I'll tell you what that is," said Tennessee. "That's a sliding door on a van or a people carrier."

"You're right." Cooper played it again just to be sure. "So what does this mean? Did Macey take a taxi? We've already sent her picture to all the major firms."

"They haven't all got back to us though. I'll chase them up. Now that we have a specific time of three a.m., they should be able to narrow down which drivers were in the city centre then."

"What if it wasn't a taxi? She could have accepted a lift from someone else?"

"And either that someone, or a taxi, took her to Jarrow and dropped her off at a bus station in the arse end of nowhere? To take a bus to South Shields for no reason that we can work out."

Cooper took a deep breath and thought things through for a moment. Macey Gallagher couldn't just vanish off the face of the planet. She was either hiding somewhere, being held somewhere or - and Cooper didn't like this option - she was lying dead somewhere. "Right," she said, "You follow up with the taxi firms and make some enquiries about the thirty-seven bus that runs from Jarrow Road to

South Shields. If you have time, book a translator for us. Madame Petite is pretending she doesn't speak English. I'll drop the hair grip with evidence and take the extraction device to Tech, see if there's anything to link Walker to this, and then I'll start work on a press release. We need Macey's face in every newspaper. Someone must have seen her after she got separated from Pearl and the others."

Tennessee stifled a yawn. "I'm on it," he said before walking towards the lift. "I'll come and find you when I'm done."

COOPER HAD COMPLETED ALL but one of the errands and was hurrying through HQ on her way to the press office when she spotted a familiar face: Kenny Roberts was chatting to the desk sergeant.

"Kenny," she gasped, a wave of panic threatening to take over her. There was only one reason for him to be here. "What's happened? Is Tina okay?"

Despite his lack of social intelligence, Kenny registered the alarm in her voice. "Nothing's happened, Erica. Tina's fine. Last I heard, she was at the library."

Cooper almost collapsed into his arms. Ever since the Tarot Card killer had taken Tina, Cooper had been on edge. It was exhausting. Just when she thought she was getting over the trauma, something would set her off and she'd assume the worst. She closed her eyes momentarily and placed a hand over her heart. It was beating at over a hundred beats per minute. "Then why..." she opened her eyes and slapped Kenny on the arm, "...are you here? You gave me a heart attack."

Kenny chuckled and held up a paper bag. "I brought lunch. You still love Thai, right? Tina said she was worried you were losing weight with the Science Man being away."

Cooper flashed him a suspicious look.

"And I was in the area," he added.

She kept staring.

"And I thought we could discuss Tina's birthday. It's coming up and I don't have a blooming clue what to get her."

Cooper hadn't realised she was holding her breath until she finally exhaled. Of course he didn't know what to buy Tina. He'd only been around for two birthdays and Christmases. At least he was trying to make up for lost time, she thought, and by God, the Thai food smelled irresistible.

"Follow me," she said, letting her heart rate lower and a smile return to her face. "We can eat in the break room."

- CHAPTER 11 -

HE PULLED THE GIRL to her feet. It was Friday morning, and she was a mess. A whimpering, shivering, snot-dribbling, pathetic mess of a girl. "This way," he growled, and she shuffled her bound feet, struggling to keep up with him. Struggling because she was blindfolded and he was not. The high-pitched snivelling was driving him mad. She sounded like a whippet begging his master for a scrap of lamb fat. It was enough to make him want to slap her.

"No funny business," he said as he cut her cable ties, "or I swear to God, I'll knock you out before you can blink. And you don't want to know what the lads'll do to you once you're unconscious." Her entire body shook like the last leaf of autumn. "Do I make myself clear?"

The girl nodded and squeaked a yes through her gag.

"The bucket's behind you. Be quick about it."

Women and their bloody bladder shyness. The last thing he wanted to do was hang about here for ten minutes while she worked up the courage to piss. If the little bitch didn't go now she'd have to hold it until lunch, and lunch was five hours away. She could piss herself; the other one had. Stunk the whole damn room out. Dirty cow. He'd had to clean her up because he was the only one the boss trusted not to get carried away. It was hard not to do anything that would get him a kicking, given how fucking fit she was. He'd sprayed her with a hosepipe and taken great pleasure in watching her flinch from the cold water. Not as much pleasure as he'd taken in drying her. He'd used a thin towel and could feel everything. He savoured the memory.

"Finally," he grunted when the tinkling came and the girl relieved herself in the plastic bucket. He handed her a few sheets of bog roll and waited while she wiped and dropped the paper into the bucket. Within seconds, he'd bound her hands and was roughly pushing her along the corridor and back to the rat-infested so-called bedroom.

He'd managed to get a syringe yesterday. He was going to prick her himself but he didn't want to fuck it up and kill her by injecting an air bubble into her veins. He'd have got a right hiding for that. Instead, he let her do it herself. He stood behind, so she couldn't see his face when he removed the hood and blindfold and held a knife to her throat in case she tried anything stupid with the needle. She didn't. Of course, she didn't. He could tell she wanted to fight, wanted to try, but she was in self-preservation mode and she wanted to live. To live meant following his orders.

He watched her settle into her corner of the room and try in vain to get comfortable. Impossible on a concrete floor. Maybe he'd bring them some blankets, a reward for not screaming all day. Or maybe he shouldn't. Can't be going soft now. The lads would rip him to shreds. She pulled her knees to her chest and looped her bound arms around them. Then her head tipped forward and she let out a barely audible sob.

He slid the heavy door closed and secured the padlock. The insulin he'd stolen would do for now. It was enough to keep her alive until she wasn't his responsibility anymore. He hoped.

"COME ON, ONE MORE." DS Paula Keaton stood behind the weights bench in the gym at HQ. "Push. You can do it." Her dark hair was scraped back into her usual short, tight ponytail. She was rosy-cheeked from her workout, and from where Cooper lay on the bench, she could see straight up her upturned nose.

Cooper pushed with all her might as she finished the last repetition in a set of bench presses and was relieved when Keaton took the bar and secured it safely in the rack.

"My arms are shaking," she said, watching the tricep muscles on the back of her upper arm twitch rhythmically.

Keaton loaded the bar with an additional twenty-five kilograms and rattled out her set without so much as a gurn. Cooper would ask if she wanted her to spot her but she knew it would be pointless. If Pitbull Paula Keaton couldn't lift it, there was no way Cooper could.

Keaton caught the impressed look on Cooper's face. "I've been lifting weights since I was in primary school."

"I don't think I'll ever be able to lift what you lift," Cooper said.

"And you shouldn't." Keaton wiped her forehead with a sweat rag and took a swig from a metal water bottle. "We train for different reasons. I want to maintain my rugby body and have quads that could kill a man. You though, we're just undoing the shit that cancer did to you. Get you some strength back, a little bit of toning, a little bit of fast-twitch. Baby steps." She held up a palm for Cooper to high-five. "Good workout, boss. I'm going to hit the showers. I'll see you back upstairs."

Cooper was exhausted, but it was a good feeling. A satisfied feeling. Whatever she ate for lunch today, she'd feel like she'd earned it. Cooper had been working out with Keaton for a few months now, and she was already seeing some changes. She was still a scrawny wee matchstick but the first hint of curves were beginning to return to her thighs and her shoulders. The squats and presses were paying off. She could bound up the stairs without huffing and puffing, and she didn't have to ask Justin or Kenny to carry things for her anymore. She was beginning to feel like she had pre-the-big-C.

Back upstairs in CID, showered and dressed in a grey suit and white shirt, Cooper was about to call the Petites, and failing their cooperation, call the local police department in France and have them round Nico up on her behalf. Her plans were scuppered when Chief Superintendent Nixon coughed and called Cooper to his office. *Christ on a bike.* Cooper's stomach lurched and she prayed to herself. *Tell me she hasn't been found dead.* She got to her feet and trotted along the hall, her boots click-clacking on linoleum tiles, and entered Nixon's office only to find Neil Fuller in there, slumped in a chair and picking something from under his nails.

"Before you go off it, it's not my fault," he said with a wary look in his eyes.

Cooper's heart rate instantly raised and she met his eyes with distrust. "What do you mean it's not your fault?"

Nixon coughed again. "Settle down, you two. Nothing to fret about Cooper. Just some reshuffling."

Cooper didn't like the sound of that. If Nixon was about to tell her she'd been partnered up with Fuller, she'd hit the roof. There was no way she was working side by side with that weaselly, coward of a man-child.

Cooper's eyes remained narrowed, and she folded her arms across her chest. The muscles in her chest cried as she did so. In a slow, sceptical tone, she said, "Define reshuffling."

Nixon closed the door to his office and inched his way into the old wood and leather chair behind his antique desk. "I'm taking you off the Gallagher case."

"No."

"Yes," he barked before she could fly into a torrent of reasons why not. "I'm not wasting my best talent on a missing, presumed dead case. Chances are that girl got pissed, got emotional, and jumped in the river. Fuller can handle it."

Fuller took the insult on the chin and said nothing. Cooper, despite being called his best talent, was about to protest. She hated being transferred off cases. She liked closure. Anything less was unacceptable, and as far as she was concerned, Macey Gallagher was worth fighting for. Even if no one else was fighting for that poor girl.

"She's still alive, sir."

"God willing," said Nixon, though his voice suggested otherwise. "But I need you on a suspected hate crime. Keep the PC brigade off my back."

Cooper bristled. PC brigade meant one thing and one thing only. "I'm not your token female," she said, almost snarling.

"Don't forget part Arab."

Cooper's mouth hung open. "I'm like five per cent Persian, sir. Ninety-five per cent white British. You can't parade me as—"

"You need to solve the case before I can parade you as anything. Sit down. Fuller, take Sam Sutherland and Oliver Martin. Sam's suspect in the matricide case made a full confession. Pick up where Cooper left off on the Gallagher case."

Fuller ran a finger and thumb over his moustache and left the room under a cloud of humiliation.

"Question the French boy," Cooper called after him. "Get on the next flight to Paris if need be. It leaves at eleven forty." The door clicked shut and Cooper turned her attention back to the superintendent. "I'm keeping my fingers in that pie."

"Keep your fingers where I can see them," he warned. "Fuller will be fine. Too many cooks and all that. Anyway, this case." He dropped a file on the table. It was light and clearly new. "Omar Ali, Egyptian national, brought into the RVI this morning," he said, referencing the Royal Victoria Infirmary that resided in Newcastle's city centre. "A dozen stab wounds and beaten half to death. Left for dead in Weetslade."

"Weetslade? That's the park just off the A189, right? Former colliery."

"Aye. That's the one. Found by a dog walker in the early hours. Given the recent marches from the English Defenders and the White Rights Party, there's been an increase in violence against Muslims. Not to mention that far-right prick from Manchester bringing up the Rochdale sex abuse ring every five minutes."

"You mean Dominic Jefferson, acclaimed Member of Parliament?"

"Indeed I do. Specky, chinless, Mancunian twat."

Cooper hid her astonishment.

Nixon thrust the file into Cooper's hand. "You get Daniel and Keaton. Now get your skinny arse down to the RVI and speak to the victim before he bleeds to death. I want a UKIP-voting skinhead in custody before the loony lefties string me up by my left bollock."

Cooper took the file and closed her eyes for a moment. At least, she told herself, at least Nixon was equal opportunities when it came to offending people.

- Chapter 12 -

Cooper dodged a team of paramedics wheeling a patient into the trauma centre of the Royal Victoria Infirmary. A robust woman with tension alopecia at the temples was sat astride the patient, the heels of her hands thrusting into his chest as a pale, panicky-looking man squeezed a bag valve mask and tried to keep pace with the trolley. Cooper waited for the commotion to die down before she approached the young man monitoring the main desk. He was a pretty boy with lipstick smudges on his neck and a twinkle in his eye. His face hardened when she presented him with her ID and he escorted her to the room that housed Omar Ali.

Cooper's step faulted as she took in the scene. Doctors and nurses buzzed around the bed at such speed that Cooper could barely see Omar. The movement of their blue and indigo scrubs moulded them into a sea of bodies. Machines beeped, wires and tubes protruded in all directions and pads of white gauze blossomed with red blood. She approached the bed cautiously, not wanting to get in the way of the people doing the most important work right now; keeping him alive. She caught Omar's eye. His mouth and nose were covered with an oxygen mask and his dark eyes were wet with fear and confusion. His lips quivered and his finger twitched.

"Omar," she whispered in his ear. "My name's Erica. I'm a detective with Northumbria CID and I'm going to do my very best to find the people who did this to you." She didn't want to question him while he was in this state. Her intention was only to let him know she was on the case, that the police knew he'd been attacked and that they cared. She moved out of the way while a doctor applied pressure to a wound on Omar's chest. His finger twitched again, beckoning her back to the side of his bed. "What is it, Omar?" She leant in as close as she could.

"Ba— Da—"

She didn't understand.

His arm was swollen and bruised with great grazes along the length of his forearm and blood oozing from his elbow. He managed to lift it, hook a finger under his oxygen mask and try again.

"Bad dog," he said.

"Bad dog? What do you mean, Omar? Were you attacked by a dog?"

Omar's eyelids flickered, and his irises rolled back into his beaten skull. The rhythmic beeping of the machines turned frenetic and all hell broke loose.

"We're losing him."

A pair of electrodes were pressed to his chest.

"Clear."

As Omar's body convulsed, a nurse with blood-stained scrubs dragged Cooper from the room.

"Will he make it?" she asked.

The nurse sucked her lips in and looked to the floor before answering. "He's in a terrible way. But he's tough. We revived him once already."

"Before he..." Cooper couldn't find the word. "He said bad dog. Those wounds on his chest. Are they bite marks?"

The nurse shook her head. "No. They're definitely stab wounds. Scissors, he told us when he first came in."

"Scissors," she repeated to herself. Then what did *bad dog* reference? "What else did he say? Was it a gang attack?"

"Sorry." The nurse shrugged. She didn't know any more than that. "I'd better get back in there."

Whoever attacked Omar, they had left him for dead and Cooper worried that when word got out he was still alive, they might pay him a visit to finish the job.

"Sir," she called her superintendent. "Omar Ali flatlined. They're working to revive him, but it looks touch and go. I want a uniform stationed at the RVI, outside our assault victim's room. As far as I'm concerned, this is attempted murder. If Omar wakes up and the perp comes to finish what he started—"

"Say no more. I'll have two uniforms in rotation outside his room."

"Thank you, sir. I appreciate it."

Cooper waited at the hospital for an hour. The nurse was right about Omar being tough. They'd brought him back, but he was in a coma. She watched doctors and nurses come and go. Watched them stitch up the stab wounds, clean and dress the grazes and ice the bruises. She couldn't do anything for Omar sitting around waiting for him to wake up so she thanked the man with the lipstick-covered neck and walked out into the brilliant sunshine of a chilly April day in the north. She might not be able to do anything for Omar Ali right now, but she was in town, and she could perhaps do something for Macey Gallagher. Feisty's, the last bar Macey was definitely in, was only a fifteen-minute walk away.

A Greggs bacon butty later and Cooper was hammering on the door of Feisty's.

"We're not open," came the reply.

"Northumbria police," Cooper stated. It was an answer guaranteed to get a response, and within seconds the door was yanked open and a woman with rollers in her hair and a dripping mop in her hand greeted her with an up-and-down stare.

"There's no drugs dealt in here, love. The doormen are top at keeping the dealers out," she said in a rough local accent.

"I'm not here about drugs," Cooper reassured her, "but I would like a quick chat. Can I come in?"

The mop was shoved back into its bucket and the door opened enough for Cooper to squeeze through.

Nightclubs without people and music always seemed sad to Cooper, like a seedy ghost town. Without the disco lights and foggy vision of alcohol consumption, the cracks of the place showed. Stained floorboards, peeling wallpaper, and rips in the upholstery. In the harsh light of the day, the roped-off area that she had been led to looked more DIY than VIP.

"Misha Rudd," the woman extended her hand. "I'm the owner-manager of this money pit."

"Business not good?" Asked Cooper.

"Not since the bar next door was featured on Geordie Shore. Now every Charlotte Crosby wannabe has to been seen in there instead of here." She sighed and adjusted a roller that wasn't cooperating, pinning it back in place.

"I'm here about Macey Gallagher." Cooper brought up a picture of Macey from her phone.

Recognition showed on Misha's face. "She was on the news last night. Missing?"

"That's right. She was here the night she disappeared. The eighth. This was the last bar we know she visited. Could I speak with anyone who was working that night? And I'll need to take a look at your CCTV."

Misha looked in two minds but pointed to a girl polishing glasses behind the bar. "Dora was in. You can speak to her, but," she paused, "our cameras are on the blink. Have been for weeks. I can't afford to have them fixed. I know it's not proper, but it's that or be able to pay the staff their wages."

Cooper seethed. Camera footage could have been key. She thanked Misha through gritted teeth and approached a mousy girl in huge round glasses. "Dora? I'm DCI Cooper with Northumbria police. Your boss tells me you were working on Saturday the eighth."

Dora nodded. "I work most Saturdays. Is there a problem?"

"This is Macey Gallagher, she went missing last Saturday and was last seen in here." She displayed the photo of Macey and her friends and zoomed in so that Macey's image filled the screen. "Do you recognise her from that evening?"

Dora nodded and her glasses slid down her nose; she pushed them back up with her middle digit. Cooper hoped that wasn't her veiled way of giving her the finger. "She's been in a few times. I recognise her friend. She was... yeah she was in a bad way, like. Wobbly on her feet."

"Did you see anyone hassling her or looking at her funny?"

"She's a pretty girl in a little dress. Lots of guys were looking at her."

Cooper picked up a hint of resentment. "Tell me more."

"There were some guys in the club that night playing pub golf. About forty of them, all in golf jumpers. They looked like right pillocks. Anyway, I think I saw her chatting with four or five of them for a while. She stumbled about a bit, and they had to help her stay upright. I think one of them fetched her a glass of water at one point, but I didn't serve him, it might have been a gin and tonic for all I know."

"Did you see her leave?"

"Yeah, she was hurled out."

"Hurled out?" Cooper leant in.

"She was sick on herself. Not a lot. Not like projectile or owt. More of a hiccough that turned into a little bit of spew. Anyway, the bouncer saw, and he had her outside in under a minute."

When Cooper got her hands on Nico Petite, she was going to wring his— Nixon's warning rang in her head. She shouldn't even be here. "Who was the bouncer?"

"Tiny McGown. He works a day shift outside the jewellery shop on Pilgrim Street."

Cooper tried her best to get descriptions of the boys playing pub golf from Dora but they all sounded alike. Preppy, barely old enough to drink but acting like they ran the entire city.

Back in the daylight of the main road, Cooper put a call into Neil Fuller.

"Erica?"

"You in France yet?" A snorting noise confirmed he was not. "I just spoke to a barmaid from Feisty's who was working the night Macey went missing. "She was chatting to some guys who were playing pub golf."

"The barmaid?"

"No, you idiot. Macey was. They might have plied her with more alcohol. Find them and see what the deal is." Cooper's temper was being tested. "And get to Newcastle Jewellery Co. on Pilgrim

Street. Speak to a security guard named Tiny McGowan. Something tells me he's not so tiny. He was on duty at Feisty's that night and he chucked Macey out after she threw up on herself."

"Erica..."

"Yes?"

"Thanks for the intel, but Nixon warned me you'd do this. This isn't your case anymore. Let me get on with it and let it go."

Hanging up and thrusting her phone into her pocket with unexpected aggression, Cooper marched up and down the street, avoiding the wrath of mums with pushchairs, commuters dragging wheelie cases towards the train station, and death-wish delivery cyclists who shouldn't even be on the bloody path. She scanned the street until her eyes came to rest on a camera bubble above a doorway to an office building. A few minutes of sweet smiles and Cooper was sat in front of an accountancy firm's security footage.

"Perfect," purred Cooper. The image was grainy but it clearly showed Macey leaving Feisty's, trying to re-enter and being denied. As predicted, Tiny was easily six-three. Cooper watched Macey walk along the street, stumble and continue. It was a chaotic Saturday night and it was hard to keep track of Macey in the crowd. Cooper tried to take in all the details. Countless Uber cars, an ambulance whizzing by, a topless man dancing in the middle of the road, a dark van driving past, a skinny boy losing his pizza to a bald man with a beard. The bald man getting into a fight. The bald man approaching Macey before she ran down a side street. "Who is this prick?" she muttered, thinking he looked familiar. "I need a copy of this."

A most obliging man with pink cheeks and even pinker ears burnt the footage onto a USB stick and handed it over. Cooper thanked him with the sort of smile that would last him all day and headed for the side street she'd watched Macey disappear into. A cat café selling crepes and overpriced coffees to people wanting a side order of fur with their food had a camera over the door. The Japanese waitress wasn't sure if the owner would want her letting someone into the office but Cooper had her call the boss in question. She let him know that as his camera pointed onto the street, she was entitled to look at it and if he made her come back with a squad car and a bunch of uniforms it would be very bad for business.

Scanning the files for the previous Saturday, Cooper clicked on footage that had been taken between two thirty and three thirty and sat back in her chair and waited until she spotted Macey run into the arms of a woman who resembled Pearl Baxter. She was a little taller and a little paler, and though the footage was in greyscale, she appeared to be wearing some form of worker's vest over a jumper. They chatted for a little while. The ambulance was visible in the distance; it appeared at the end of the street for less than a second as it made its way to its destination. A van slowed as it passed the two ladies, and the bald guy came back into the frame. He walked behind Macey, keeping his distance. The woman with the curly hair pointed further down the street. They linked arms and strolled out of shot, followed by the bald guy. Cooper rewatched the footage four times, pausing and playing, pausing and playing. She was sure she recognised the bald man with the beard, she just wasn't sure where from.

IN A LAY-BY OFF the A696, Cooper avoided paying for airport parking as she waited for Justin Atkinson's flight to land. Man, she had missed her favourite scene of crime officer. Missed his conversation, missed his warmth, his humour, his tender kisses that made her giggle like she was five years younger. Whilst she'd been in town, after visiting Omar Ali and viewing CCTV of Macey Gallagher, she'd let off steam by nipping into John Lewis's lingerie department and picking up a lacy bra and knicker set from Elle McPherson's collection. It fit perfectly, and she couldn't wait to slide out of her clothes and show them to her man. She heard her phone buzz, and she reached into the Mazda's glove box to retrieve it. Her hopes that it was Atkinson saying he was at baggage reclaim were dashed when she saw the message was from Fuller. *I'll follow up on Curly and Baldy. But seriously, Erica, stop stepping on my toes. Don't make me go to Nixon.*

Cry baby. Cooper checked her reflection in the mirror. Her make-up was on point, and she didn't have to check her hair. Since clipping it, she knew there was nothing to check. Heels, skinny jeans and an AC/DC t-shirt with rips up the sides. She was ready for a night on the tiles with the man she adored.

The flight was late and Cooper waited in the lay-by for over an hour until she finally got the text she'd been waiting for. Thank God, there were only so many times a woman could scroll through the BBC news or check the Newcastle Evening Chronicle for updates on the Tarot Card Killer's trial. Apparently, a scuffle had broken out in the viewing gallery between Hutchins's brother and the first victim's father. Igniting the engine and pushing the gearstick into first, Cooper joined the duel carriageway, turned right at the roundabout and made her way into Newcastle International Airport. She found a space just as Atkinson emerged from arrivals, pulling his suitcase behind him. He looked handsome in the sunshine in cargo pants and a designer t-shirt with his glasses tucked into his breast pocket. His silver hair accentuated the slight tan on his early forties skin. Cooper leapt from the car and into his arms. Her heart swelled as she felt the reassuring but understated strength in his arms.

"Oh, how I've missed you," he whispered, his hand folding around the back of her head and holding her into his chest.

"I missed you too. Woo. Even if you do smell like a brewery. Must have been a good night?" Cooper beamed at him and took the case, guiding it to the car. "And boy, do I have a night planned for us." Atkinson slid into the passenger seat and let out an almighty yawn. Cooper jumped in the driver's seat and headed for the barriers before her parking rate increased. "There's a taxi booked at seven, a table for two at Blackfriars... Four quid? Are they having a laugh? Bloody airport parking. Anyway, Blackfriars. If you've never been, get the pork belly. Then we're off to The Cluny. Hush In Hell have a set at nine. And..." she turned to wink at Atkinson before telling him about her new underwear, only Atkinson was covering his mouth with his hand and all the colour had drained from his face.

"Pull over," he urged.

Cooper hit the hazard lights and drew the car up on a grass verge just before the duel carriageway. Atkinson opened his door, leant over and emptied his stomach. He spluttered and heaved again for round two, round three, round four.

"Jesus, I'm sorry, Erica." He wiped his mouth with his hand. His glasses had slipped from his pocket and into the puddle of vomit. He bent to retrieve them, only to bring up round five.

Cooper shook her head. "How much did you have?" She felt all her excitement fall away; there was no way he was going anywhere near a bar or restaurant that evening.

"Not that much. Shared a few bottles of wine. I think the chicken was underdone."

Cooper felt like slapping him around the head. The chicken, indeed. He'd wanted to let off steam after all those days at the convention. It was understandable he'd want to socialise, network, and have a good time. But throwing up on the junction to the A696 and filling Cooper's Mazda with the stench of bile? No. That was not okay.

"I'm sorry, Erica, darling. I think I need an early night. Could you just drop me at mine?"

Cooper didn't know what to say. The night she'd planned was ruined, and although it might be childish, she felt abandoned. He should have wanted to spend time with her, his girlfriend.

"Fine," was all she could muster.

The drive back to the coast was spent mostly in silence. Atkinson only broke the awkwardness to mumble that maybe it wasn't just wine he had had, that he had a vague memory of drinking shots of Sambuca.

"Sambuca? Why would you drink that stuff? It's deadly." It was hardly his style.

"Kenny recommended it last time I saw him."

"Kenny? My Kenny? Well, not *my* Kenny, but you know what I mean. Why would you listen to him? He's a flat-Earther, for goodness sake."

Atkinson managed not to vomit for the remainder of the journey. He apologised profusely when Cooper dropped him at his home. Cooper was too sad to be angry. This wasn't the Atkinson she was expecting to meet at the airport.

It wasn't long until Cooper was home alone, all dressed up with nowhere to go. Tina was at Kenny's. She'd shipped her daughter off to her father's - along with that bloody seagull - so that she wouldn't have to keep the noise down when they'd returned to the bedroom, but as that wasn't happening either, Cooper was at a loss.

"Sod it," she said aloud. She'd have her own party. Cooper stripped to her pretty new underwear, grabbed a cool beer from the fridge and played

Hush In Hell's latest album on her phone. She danced the night away in her bedroom. Bouncing and waving her arms around her head, occasionally stopping to admire herself in the mirror. Her body anxieties from the previous year were beginning to fade away, and it was about time too. She peeked under the lace fabric of the bra and found the small blue dots that had been tattooed on for the oncologist to target her radiotherapy treatment. It wasn't the most rock and roll tattoo in the world. Although Tina would no doubt tell her that it was a symbol of her survival and that was as badass as it could get, sweet thing that she was. Between the lumpectomy scars and the blue dots, Cooper had felt reluctant about taking her top off in front of Atkinson. Unless the lights were off, she kept her top on in bed. That was until tonight. Tonight, she'd been ready. But he'd been hungover. She took another swig of beer, removed her bra and checked out her reflection. For the first time in a long time, she didn't look away or immediately cover up. Maybe it was the beer talking, or maybe it was the fact that the lead singer of Hush In Hell was tattooed from top to bottom, but Cooper fancied some artwork.

- CHAPTER 13 -

ATKINSON USED HIS CULINARY skills to work his way back into Cooper's good books over the weekend. A mammoth Sunday roast for her and Tina had done the trick. Besides, Cooper rarely stayed mad at anyone for long, Fuller being the exception. Atkinson had been a perfect partner up until that point. He'd been reliable, patient, and had got to know Tina at a pace that had suited her. As Cooper mopped up the last of his delicious gravy with a crisp Yorkshire pudding, she decided he was more than forgiven.

Tina cleared the plates away. "Can I introduce Steven to Justin now?"

Cooper nodded. "If you must."

Tina's face spread into a wide grin. "Great." She raced up to her room and returned with the shoe box.

Atkinson looked curious. "Been getting a hamster?"

"Not quite," Cooper said as she started the dishwasher. "Doctor Doolittle here rescued a seagull hatchling that fell off the roof."

The three of them crowded around to look at the fluffy bird. Cooper didn't want to admit it, but he was rather cute. About the size of a tennis ball, with big black eyes and pale brown feathers. He plodded clumsily about on his stick-thin legs and looked up at them expectedly. She'd been impressed with Tina's dedication. She was an excellent seagull mother and hadn't complained once about Steven cheeping away in the middle of the night when he was hungry.

Atkinson reached down and scooped the little bird into his hands. "Hello, Steven Seagull. Oh! I get it. Steven. Sea. Gull. Very witty, Tina."

Tina blushed and Cooper bit her lip. She didn't get it. She was about to ask when Steven pooped all over Atkinson's hand and sent the two Cooper ladies into fits of giggles. As Atkinson furiously scrubbed his hands at the kitchen sink, Tina set about feeding her surrogate chick his evening meal.

"Did Mum tell you she wants a tattoo?"

Atkinson and Cooper's eyes met. She hadn't told him. Last night, she and Tina had scoured the internet for ideas. Hours they'd spent on Google Image Search, saving their favourites into a folder as they dipped crisps in a fancy beetroot dip that she'd bought from Marks and Spencer. There were some amazing floral designs, and Cooper had narrowed it down to three.

"No," answered Atkinson with heavy brows. "She didn't tell me that." He moved closer to Cooper. "Erica?"

Cooper opened her laptop and brought up the images. "To cover my scars."

His face softened. "Your scars? You don't need to do that. You're perfect just the way—"

"I know I don't *have* to. But I want to." She wrapped her jumper around herself without thinking. "It's not like I hate my body. I'm happy with how I am. But... but I could be happier. They really are works of art. Look at this one." She brought up an image of an intricate bouquet of black and grey flowers formed from mandalas.

"Hmm." Atkinson's mouth twitched from side to side, running the inside of his lips over his teeth. "I'm not sure that's a good idea. Shouldn't we discuss this? You should think it through before you permanently—"

"It's Mum's body," said Tina in a defensive tone. She squeezed the pipette and deposited fishy mush into Steven's beak. "She can do with it what she likes."

Cooper maintained a poker face.

"I mean, Mum doesn't tell you to dye your hair, does she?" The poker face slipped and try as she might, Cooper couldn't put it back. Her laughter had put an abrupt end to the conversation. *Thank you, Tina.*

ON MONDAY MORNING, COOPER called the Royal Victoria to check on Omar's status. She was told by the prim-sounding lady on the phone that he was still in a coma and the doctors were working to reduce the swelling on his brain. She then called PC Frankie Ingram, currently on guard duty, to check that no one had come to visit the victim or that no one had been lurking around his ward. So far, they had not.

"Right," she said, addressing Keaton and Tennessee. "The dream team, back together again. Let's find the bottom feeder who did this to Omar Ali." She pinned a picture of the victim to the board.

Tennessee leant over his desk and flipped through his notepad. "Here's what I have so far. Forty-four years old. Lives alone on Kendal Street in Byker. His landlord describes him as being a great tenant. Bills paid on time. No complaints from neighbours. No problems with the property. Has lived there for a year and a half."

"Family?" Cooper asked.

"A wife, Salwa, and two sons back in Cairo. His boys are fourteen and twelve. The wife's flying out tomorrow morning. I've arranged for an Arabic speaker to meet her at the airport."

"Good. Have the translator meet us at the hospital, too. I want to know what she knows. Did he have any enemies, any debts?" She turned to Keaton. "Work?"

"An eye doctor. Works in the opticians on Shields Road. The branch manager had only good things to say about him. Said not turning up to work was highly out of character. Apparently, the bloke never took a sick day, boss. He was a no-show on Wednesday, so they called his flat, but there was no answer. They put it down as an irregularity and called in someone to cover for him. The same thing happened on Thursday. This time they called the number of his next of kin but the number was disconnected. On Friday morning, they reported him missing, and that's when he was discovered at Weetslade."

"So he's been gone since Tuesday night or Wednesday morning?"

Keaton nodded. "Looks like it. Lives and works in Byker but was found six miles away, covered with stab wounds."

"And what was that bad dog reference about?" Tennessee asked.

Cooper looked at the photograph on the board. "No idea," she sighed. "The nurse was adamant he didn't have any bite marks."

"Bad dog?" Keaton brought up a map of Weetslade on her computer. "Yeah, I thought so. There's a doggy daycare centre a stone's throw from where he was found. My mum leaves her greyhound there sometimes."

Cooper got to her feet and looked over Keaton's shoulder. "Huh. Well, I know where I'm starting my inquiries. Can you two arrange some door-to-doors?" It wasn't really a question. "Tennessee, you take Byker. Talk to his neighbours. See if there's been anything suspicious going on or if they heard any commotion, especially Tuesday night or Wednesday morning." He saluted. "Keat on..."

"Around the park, boss? The roads leading into it and the surrounding businesses? I'll check traffic cams too."

"Perfect. Let's reconvene at lunch."

SCENE OF CRIME OFFICER Hong Evanstad met Cooper at the entrance to Weetslade Country Park. A North Korean by birth but Norwegian by adoption, Hong had the looks of his motherland and the accent of his adopted parents.

"Good morning, DCI Cooper," he greeted her, removing his gloves to shake her hand. "Are you looking for Justin? He's not assigned to this case."

"No, no. I came to see you," she assured him. "Justin's up near Rothbury today. Two poor souls were found drowned in the bogs up on the Simonside hills."

"Might be the duergar." Hong chuckled to himself and handed Cooper some white coveralls so she could join him beyond the police tape that marked the area where Omar Ali's dying body had been discovered. With over forty hectares of walking trails, woodland and wildflower meadows, Weetslade was a tranquil oasis and a far cry from its former life as a colliery. Atop the hill at the centre of the park, three giant drill bits paid homage to the park's past and on a brisk, bright day like today, they sparkled like beacons.

"What's a duergar when it's at home?" Cooper asked, struggling to wiggle into the paper outfit.

"Us Scandis aren't the only ones with tales of magical creatures roaming the countryside. You Brits have some folklore of your own. The duergar are dwarves that live on Simonside and use their lanterns to lure travellers to their deaths. Either by pushing them off the cliffs or into the bogs."

"Fascinating," said Cooper, truthfully. She'd never heard of the duergar; her knowledge of local folklore extended no further than the Lambton Worm.

Beyond the tape, Hong gave Cooper a quick rundown of his findings so far. There were no signs of the scissors used in the attack or any weapon for that matter. Some dirty needles and blackened spoons were found beneath some nearby trees. There was an extensive amount of disturbance to the meadowland, indicating that Omar had either been dragged through the area or had crawled through it on his knees, probably trying to reach the car park to find help.

"Over here," said Hong, "we found a wallet. Don't get your hopes up though. I'd say it's been there months given the water damage. Belongs to a Bryce Morton of Hayes Walk in Wideopen."

"That's just on the other side of the park. I'll have a couple of uniforms swing by and question him. If he walks here regularly, there's a chance he noticed something or saw something."

Hong nodded. "Worth a shot. There were a lot of footprints around here, as you might expect. A lot of hikers, dog walkers and bird watchers come through here. I ran some of the clearer prints through the database and found a match that was rather interesting. A pair of Yeezy Boosts."

Cooper looked blankly at him.

"That's Kanye West's brand. People queue up for days when new designs are launched. Even second-hand, a pair can fetch over two grand."

"Two grand? For trainers?" Cooper's eyes almost burst from their sockets.

"I know. Ludicrous. Now what sort of person would wear trainers worth that kind of money through a muddy country park?"

"An excellent question," mused Cooper. What sort of person indeed? One with more money than brains at the very least. Cooper gave the area one last look over, bid Hong Evanstad farewell and asked him to call her if anything else came up. She left the scene and took a walking trail towards the doggy daycare centre. A row of trees protected Cooper's head from the spring sunshine, and she took a moment to appreciate the birdsong surrounding her. Her boots crunched on patches of dry grass and without realising it, Cooper was taking deep inhalations of clean air.

When the smell of woodland gave way to the smell of traffic, Cooper had reached her destination. Dolly's Place was built on the border between the park and some industrial land. A cartoon of a small, black, fluffy dog greeted clients at the entrance and Cooper watched as a woman in kickboxing shorts and a vest wrestled an overly energetic Welsh terrier into her car.

After introducing herself to a minuscule woman whose ponytail almost reached the back of her knees, Cooper asked if she was aware of the assault that occurred in the park on Thursday night.

"Oh yes," she replied. "Word travels fast around here. The lady who found him, Patty, she brings her dogs here when she needs to pop into town for a few hours. Never likes to leave her babies unsupervised, you know. Very responsible dog owner."

Cooper's eyes wandered over the reception area as the loquacious manager continued.

"We've known Patty since this place opened. Dolly - my girl - loves her. She's a poodle cross. Just the most affectionate creature I've ever met. Would you like to meet her? She's playing with her friends in the outdoor area."

"No, thank you," said Cooper, hoping not to offend but registering the look of disappointment in the woman's eyes. She certainly loved her dog. "I'd rather know more about those cameras." Cooper motioned to a television screen that showed four different camera angles around the centre.

"Ah, our webcams. When clients leave their dogs with us, we give them a code, and they can log in and watch their dogs from work or wherever they happen to be. Builds trust, you see. I know when I'm not here, I'm always logging on to see what Dolly's up to."

"Do they capture any footage from outside the centre?"

"No, I'm afraid not. Just the inside of the enclosures. Besides, they're turned off when we close at half six. Turned back on at seven in the morning."

Cooper let out an audible sigh. That wasn't good news. She'd been hoping for otherwise, hoping to spot a clue. A man in mud-covered Yeezies sniffing around after dark with a pair of scissors in his hands might have been wishful thinking, but any clue would have done.

"Do you recognise this man?" Cooper showed her a photo of Omar that Tennessee had sent over from his place of work. It showed Omar in a shirt and tie, a wide smile and eyes that crinkled in the corners. It was a far cry from how Cooper had last seen him.

She shook her head. "No. Is that him? The man who was attacked?"

"Yes," said Cooper. "I'd like to talk to your other staff, see if they recognise him, or have seen or heard anything suspicious around here."

She pulled on a gilet and tidied her desk. "Follow me," she beamed, beckoning Cooper towards an indoor enclosure labelled *Puppy Playroom*, "hopefully someone can help. Just awful having something like that happen around here. I hope you catch them. Hope he gets what's coming to him. Okay, watch your feet. The young ones aren't toilet trained. The dogs, I mean, not the staff." She sniggered to herself. "Oh, hello Archibald. This is Archibald, our German shepherd pup. And little Cookie the Lab, and oh, isn't Buddy the cutest pug you've ever seen?"

Cooper found herself surrounded by eight to ten puppies all scrambling up her jeans and sniffing at her boots.

"I'll go find Leslie. He was working all last week, and Beth as well, our work experience girl. Perhaps they can help you generate a lead. Pardon the pun. Ha!"

She trotted off, and Cooper was certain that if the woman had a tail, it would be wagging.

- Chapter 14 -

Keaton proudly held up three brown paper bags as she sauntered into the lobby of HQ. The unmistakable aroma of a McDonald's takeaway floated over to Cooper's nostrils.

"Diet of champions," Keaton said with a grin.

"Darts champions, maybe."

"Oh?" Keaton forged a look of mock insult. "So you'll not want any? More for me and Tennessee in that case."

Cooper laughed and took a bag from Keaton. "Nice try." She opened it up and had a handful of soggy fries in her mouth before they'd even reached the lifts.

"Six o'clock," said Keaton and Cooper spun a one-eighty to look back at the glass doors. Detectives Neil Fuller, Sam Sutherland and Oliver Martin escorted a man into the building. Cooper recognised him as Aaron Quinn.

"That's Macey Gallagher's boyfriend," she explained to Keaton, her eyes never moving from Quinn. "Tennessee and I thought he was a bit twitchy when we went to see him."

Quinn's jogging pants were once again halfway down his backside and his cream-coloured hoodie was speckled with yellow stains. Curry, most likely. His face had the sheen of someone who hadn't washed so far today and his stubble was coming through in patches.

"Fuller," Cooper called. Neil Fuller broke away from the group and instructed Sutherland to get the young man into a cell until an interview suite became available. "What's going on?"

Fuller blew his nose on a tissue and looked to his left for a moment. Cooper wondered if he was considering telling her to mind her own business.

"I stopped by his flat with Sutherland. We were asking some routine questions, you know, following up where you left off, and we spot a baseball bat hidden behind his sofa. Not a big deal I thought at first; he's a sporty kid, might be on the university team, or maybe he wants it in case his flat gets broken into, but when we asked him about it, he freaked out. Started demanding a lawyer."

"That's a bit of a red flag." Cooper's gaze flicked back to Quinn; he had dark circles under his eyes and was demanding someone call his mother.

"Exactly. So we brought him in and asked forensics to take a closer look at the bat and his place."

"Christ," said Keaton, before taking a large bite of her burger and getting mayonnaise all over her chin.

Cooper shook her head. "All those posters. All the canvassing. He was the one really pushing the search for her."

"Aye, well, he wouldn't be the first guilty party to play the role of concerned lover. We'll see what the labs come back with." Fuller shrugged and walked away.

Cooper's heart was heavy as she pressed the button on the lift to take her to CID. She didn't like Quinn, didn't trust him, but she hoped he hadn't killed his girlfriend. She was still hoping Macey was alive somewhere.

Tennessee must have smelled the McDonald's coming because he was at the lift waiting for it to open. "Sweet," he said, taking a bag and tucking in without pausing for breath.

Cooper made space on one of the desks in the incident room and the three spread out their feast, sharing chicken nuggets between bites of burgers.

"Right." Cooper clapped her hands together when they had finished. "Tennessee, clear the table, and Keaton, you're up first. What you got?"

Tennessee crunched the rubbish into a tiny ball while Keaton opened her notepad. "Not a lot, to be fair. Door-to-doors are still ongoing. Seeing as we have no witnesses, I figure the attack happened in the middle of the night. I don't think he was lured to the park and then hit with a surprise assault because Omar was missing for a few days prior to his attack. So, I figure he was either staying with someone or was being held by someone during that time."

"That's what I thought," confirmed Cooper. "But we don't know if he was brought to the park then attacked, or if the attack occurred elsewhere and he was dumped in the park. Hong's taken soil samples to assess the blood content around where Omar was found. If the content's high, it's likely the attack occurred in the park. How are the door-to-doors coming along so far?"

"We started on the side of the park where the car park is. Around Clarks Terrace and Weetslade Crescent."

"Good shout."

"But no one has anything for us so far. A few of the older residents have pointed the finger at each other. Baseless, of course. Number twelve leaves his wheelie bin out, so he's obviously an axe murderer, and number thirty-two's conifers cast a shadow into number thirty-four's garden, so she's worse than Hitler."

"Traffic cams?"

"Well, as you can imagine, the roundabout on the A189 is stupidly busy. Always has been. But I've started with cars exiting the roundabout for Great Lime Road between one and four a.m. We can extend the time frame if nothing comes from what I have so far. Only three cars took that exit: a red Vauxhall Astra, a dark green Honda Civic, and a black Nissan Qashqai. I have the names and addresses of the registered owners and can give them a visit."

"Good start, Paula. Jack?"

Tennessee sat up straight in his chair. "I have footage of him getting off the Metro at Byker at eleven p.m. on Tuesday and heading towards his home. However, none of his neighbours can recall hearing him come home, including a busybody who lives next door on the left and seems to know everyone's comings and goings. According to her, Omar Ali stuck to quite a rigid schedule. Left for work at seven forty-five on the dot and returned between six and six thirty each day."

"This neighbour, did you get a stalker vibe at all."

"She's like ninety years old. She's not stalking anyone and certainly too frail to do what was done to Omar. She's just bored."

Cooper wiped the residual grease from her fingertips with a serviette and mulled it over. "He broke his schedule on Tuesday then. Where was he coming from so late? Tennessee, can you contact Nexus, try and find out where he got on the Metro? Cheers. Now, what happened after he got off the Metro? We can assume he never made it home. Was he taken? Lured away? What other cameras are in the area?"

Tennessee shrugged. "Frighteningly few. The climbing centre might have one. I can check and take a look for cars matching the ones Keaton described."

"Great."

"What about you, boss? What you got?" asked Keaton. "Do we have Omar's phone? And, did you get anything useful from the kennels?"

"No phone, unfortunately. And as for the kennels, no one's seen anything, no one's heard anything, no one knows anything."

Keaton blew a raspberry. "Balls."

"I had a good snoop around once I'd finished questioning the staff, but there were no signs of trouble. Still, I've asked Hong to sweep along the walking trail that links Dolly's Place with the park."

"Shame," said Keaton. "I really hoped *bad dog* was a reference to there."

"You mean..." Tennessee paused for dramatic effect. "We're barking up the wrong tree?" He laughed at his own joke until Keaton clipped him on the back of the head.

- CHAPTER 15 -

MARGOT SWANSON STUBBED HER cigarette into a metal grate atop a bin and waved a perfectly manicured hand at Cooper as she approached the main gates to the Royal Victoria Infirmary. A group of junior doctors gave the Scottish pathologist an admiring look as they passed. Margot glanced down at her outfit, smiled, and undid another button on her blouse. Happy with her adjustments, she pulled out a compact mirror and checked her ruby-red lipstick.

"Margot." Cooper tried to disguise the tension in her voice.

"Great to see you, Erica. So, why have you summoned me into enemy territory?" Margot chuckled. She usually worked at the Freeman Hospital in Heaton.

"I have an assault victim. Omar Ali. He's in a coma..." Cooper's voice trailed away as she spotted the mountainous engagement ring on Margot's left hand. When she and Fuller had gone their separate ways, he had got together with Margot suspiciously quickly. Cooper was certain the pair had been having an affair behind her back. It didn't matter now. She was pleased to be shot of Fuller but the memory still stabbed at her and brought up all the feelings of inadequacy she'd tried to overcome. "Erm, where was I? Yes, he's in a coma and suffered multiple stab wounds. The nurse said he'd been stabbed with scissors, but I wanted your opinion on his wounds and other injuries."

With a dramatic click, Margot closed the compact mirror and dropped it into her designer handbag. "Well, I prefer to work with the dead. But I'll help if I can."

Cooper led her to Omar's room and introduced the pathologist, with her perfect hourglass curves, to the PC stationed on the ward. *Bless him*, thought Cooper, as Margot ran her eyes over his chest and arms. She'd have probably asked to squeeze his biceps if Cooper weren't standing next to her.

"Shall we?" Cooper opened the door and took a moment to steady herself. Besides the subtle rise and fall of Omar's chest, he barely looked alive. His bruising had developed further, mottling his skin with purples and greens and an IV fed nutrients into the crease of his elbow.

Margot took in a sharp inhalation of breath. "My goodness. They did a number on him."

"He has severe head trauma," said Cooper, "the doctor told me it's the swelling in his brain that's keeping him in the coma. They hope he'll regain consciousness when the swelling goes down. But the longer he's in a coma, the less chance he has."

"That's right," Margot said, in a tone that made Cooper think of a primary school teacher congratulating a child on reciting the alphabet for the first time. As if her tiny, detective brain couldn't comprehend a little medical knowledge. Margot put on some latex gloves, approached Omar and walked up and down both sides of his bed. As she examined him, Cooper glanced at her phone, hoping for news from Tennessee or Keaton. She had four missed calls from Tina from over an hour ago. *What's up?* She typed, with one eye on Margot. *Nothing. Doesn't matter now,* came the reply.

"He's been tied up at some point." Margot pointed to his ribs and arms. "He has friction burns over these linear bruises. I'd be inclined to suggest he was bound around the torso with his arms pressed to each side of his body. See the bruising stops at his flanks and continues onto the arms." She carefully lifted one arm to examine some of Omar's back. "It continues around his upper back. A rough rope by the looks of it."

Cooper quietly made notes, allowing Margot's thoughts to flow uninterrupted. A nurse assigned to Omar flinched as Margot rolled him further.

"It's okay, sweetheart. I won't interfere with his tubes," she assured her in her sweetest Highland accent. "The bigger wounds are on his back rather than his front. If he were dead I'd be able to get in there and estimate the depth, but as he isn't - thank goodness, of course - I only have the width to go on." She laid Omar flat again and peeled back a dressing on his chest. Again, the nurse flinched but Margot ignored her. "Not necessarily scissors, but most likely. Do you have photographs from when he was brought in? Before they stitched him up?"

"Yes." Cooper opened a file, pulled out a series of A4 photographs and handed them to Margot.

Margot's attention moved back and forth between Omar and the photographs. "There's a symmetry to most of the wounds. Ovoids with bruising around each one. Here, look. The attacker needed a lot of force to puncture the skin as the cutting blades are contained. These wounds aren't clean; they're ragged at the edges. But here, look closer. These parallel sets of puncture wounds are from when the scissors are open. The wounds are fishtailed in opposite directions and the entry points are much smoother. Yes. I'd say scissors with a shaft of, say ten to fifteen millimetres across. Probably just your everyday kitchen scissors."

Cooper straightened up from peering at Omar's wounds and rubbed her lower back. "Thank you, Margot."

"Oh, I'm not done yet." Margot moved to the top of the bed and examined Omar's neck.

Cooper put the gory photos back in her file and addressed the nurse. "Do you have the clothes he was wearing when he was brought in? We need them as evidence."

The nurse looked confused for a moment. "Clothes? No. He was naked when he was brought in."

"Naked?" Cooper's eyebrows lifted an inch, and she checked her notes. "No one told me that."

"His knees were caked in mud, his hands and feet too," said the nurse.

"He might have crawled away after the attack," Cooper mused. She scribbled down a note reminding herself to check with Hong about any clothing that had been recovered.

"This bruising is interesting," Margot said, capturing Cooper's attention once more. She pointed to Omar's neck.

"Strangulation attempt?"

"No. No, I doubt that. These aren't finger and thumb bruises."

"Rope? Like his arms?"

Margot's eyes narrowed. She straightened up, removed her gloves and placed a hand on her hip. "No, something smooth. Heavy too. It's been there a while, feasibly over forty-eight hours, and it's been pressed down on his clavicles and left bruising there as well. I don't know what, but he's had something clamped around his neck."

Cooper met her eyes. "Like a dog collar?"

"Yes," Margot said, "only much heavier. I suspect it was made of metal."

Cooper gulped and turned her head away. Margot had described a slave collar.

BY THE TIME COOPER negotiated city-centre traffic, picked up Atkinson, and made it back to the coast, dusk had arrived and Tynemouth's sky was an inky blue. Cooper took Atkinson's hand as they walked up to her front door. It felt nice. Warm. Soft but strong. After a day looking into Omar Ali's case and seeing the worst of what one human could do to another, it was grounding to feel the simple pleasure of walking hand-in-hand with the person she loved.

The smell of shepherd's pie hit Cooper before she'd even closed the door behind her. Tina was scrubbing a pan in the kitchen sink. She didn't look up when Cooper and Atkinson greeted her. She wasn't being rude. She was just being Tina.

Kenny raised a hand as he joined them in the kitchen. "Erica, Science Man."

"Of course he's here," muttered Atkinson, only loud enough for Cooper to hear. "He's always here."

Cooper huffed and looked up at him. "He's Tina's father. Play nice."

Oblivious, Kenny opened the fridge and handed Atkinson a beer. "Erica?"

Cooper nodded. "Hell, yes." She took a long drink of the cool IPA and savoured the refreshing flavour before peering into the oven to look at a layer of grated cheese bubbling atop creamy mash. "This looks amazing, Tina."

Tina still said nothing.

Kenny continued to busy himself in the kitchen, setting the table and humming a tune to himself. It was vaguely familiar. "Why can I smell peat?"

"That'll be me." Atkinson sniffed the shoulder of the fleece he'd been wearing and hung it up in the porch area. "A long day working in Simonside."

"Was it the duergar?" asked Cooper, her mouth curling at the corners.

"The what?"

"The dwarf things that live on the hills. Hong told me about them. Some local legend."

"Erica, two people lost their lives. They died awful deaths—"

"Jeez, just trying to lighten the mood." Cooper put her beer down and folded her arms over her chest.

Kenny began to dish up and continued to hum through the tension. Then it hit Cooper where she knew the tune from.

"That's Cerberus by Hush In Hell," she said, pointing a finger at Kenny. "That's so weird. I was just listening to that song the other night."

Kenny beamed. "No way? Spooky. Well, great minds think alike."

Tina slammed a cupboard door shut. "And fools seldom differ." She picked up her plate. "I'll eat in my room."

Her eyes were wet and her face painted with fury.

Cooper's mouth fell open. "Whoa. Tina, what's wrong?"

"Nothing you need to worry about."

Tina marched past her mother and headed for the stairs.

"Is it Steven? He's okay, isn't he?"

"Of course he is. He's a stupid bird. Looking after him isn't rocket science."

The sound of footsteps running up the stairs and Tina's door slamming left the three adults in stunned silence for a moment. They took their seats and Cooper turned to Kenny.

"What's going on?"

Kenny looked longingly at his forkful of food, put it down and ran a hand over his forehead. "Tina was at Josh's this afternoon."

"Oh God, Kenny. What did you do? You didn't give Josh a hard time again, did you?" She thought they'd worked past the over-protective-Dad stage. The man had been completely overbearing when Tina had started hanging out with Josh, and understandably, Tina thought he'd had no right.

"Me?" Kenny's eyebrows shot upwards. "I did my best. That's what I did. Tina called me after trying to get through to you for an hour."

Cooper's heart sank. "I texted her back. She said everything was fine."

"It wasn't. She was doing homework at Josh's house. Sat on his bed and she got her period. I don't know much about these things, but she was crying, said it came from nowhere, wasn't supposed to be that day and was super heavy. Niagara Falls, she called it."

Cooper rested her forehead in her palm. Her poor girl.

"She didn't know what to do. She'd bled through her clothes, so I came here, picked up a change of clothes for her and called in at Boots. Didn't have a clue what sort of, err, products she needed so I bought applicator, non-applicator, regular, super, towels, liners... You know they have organic tampons? What's that about? Anyway, I took them over with a box of chocolates and showed Josh how to use the washing machine." He took a sip of beer and shook his head. "I thought I'd done everything I could, but she's still upset."

Cooper reached across the table and patted Kenny's hand. To her left, Atkinson prickled, but she ignored him. She didn't have the energy for insecure egos right now. "You did do everything you could. She's not upset with you. She's embarrassed."

"But she didn't do anything wrong?"

"That doesn't matter. Being a girl... It's complicated. Look, we're only a generation or two away from when women were called dirty or unclean for having periods. In some parts of the world, it's still that way. That sticks with you."

Cooper covered her face with her hands. She hadn't been there for Tina when she needed her. She'd wanted her mum and she hadn't been there. Cooper had thought being a single, working mum would get easier as Tina got older. She'd been wrong. It was just going to get harder.

- CHAPTER 16 -

THE MAZDA'S ENGINE WARNING light illuminated just as Cooper slammed the brakes and brought the car to a stop in a car park on top of a cliff in South Shields. She'd narrowly missed a young girl of five or six who was carrying three pink balloons and holding hands with her mother. *Don't let it be her* she pleaded to the heavens as she emerged from her vehicle and raced to the cliff edge. *Don't let it be her.*

Down on the sand below her, uniforms were extending the police cordon as scene of crime officers worked to maintain the integrity of their evidence amidst a growing crowd of onlookers. Cooper ran as she descended the steep stone staircase that zigzagged down the cliff face, connecting green fields above to the grotto below. Her breath was haggard, and beads of sweat instantly formed on her forehead. Her feet maintained a steady rhythm, tip-tapping down the stone steps as fast as she dared. She didn't know how many steps there were, but she knew they weren't as many as Ropery Stairs in North Shields or King Edward's Bay in Tynemouth. When Tina was younger she would always count the stairs. It was a habit, or rather an obsession, that Tina must have grown out of at some point. Cooper was unsure when that had happened, and she felt sad for not noticing it sooner.

Marsden Beach was stunning. Ochre sand peppered with shells and pebbles faded to umber where the water lapped the shore. The odd piece of sea glass shimmered in the sunshine, and a towering monolith, the famous Marsden Rock, dominated the scenery. The rock stood one hundred feet tall and during high tide was completely cut off from the beach. Home to thousands of kittiwakes and cormorants, the rock had once been much bigger. Erosion had caused a large chunk of the rock to collapse into the sea, forming an impressive arch. It was postcard-perfect until the limestone above also fell victim to the saltwater.

Cooper continued running until she reached the police tape. Here, she found someone else who had fallen victim to the cruelty of the North Sea.

Atkinson met her at the tape as she flashed her identification at the officer in charge of logging all attendants.

"I had to call you," said Atkinson. He was dressed in the usual white coveralls. "I know it's not your case any more, but I know how invested you were."

"Thank you," she gasped, trying to regain her breath. "Is it her? Is it Macey?"

His eyes darted to the floor. “We’re not certain. The water, well, you’ll see for yourself, but I think so. She’s female, the same height and hair colour. Approximately the same age.”

Cooper felt like she’d been punched. The wind was suddenly gone from her sails. They were too late. “Can I see her?”

He paused for a moment. Cooper wasn’t supposed to be there and he knew it. “Here,” he said, “put these on. And be quick.”

Cooper tried to lower her heart rate and steady her breathing before she entered the forensics tent. This wouldn’t be the first victim that Cooper had seen pulled from the sea, but they never got any easier. She took a deep, slow breath, firstly to calm her nerves, and secondly, to fill her lungs with clean sea air.

“Shit.” Cooper bowed her head in respect, and though she didn’t consider herself religious, she hoped Macey was at peace and her soul was taken care of. The body was grotesque. She was bloated and barely recognisable as the smiling girl whose photograph Cooper had studied. She turned her head away to hide the tears forming in the corner of her eyes. It might not be professional, but dammit, she was sad; she’d let Macey down. “She’s so swollen,” she said in a voice so quiet she didn’t even know if Atkinson had heard her. “Her face.”

“That’s the gas. When a human dies, the bacteria in the body, the gut especially, can go on living for some time, feeding on the sugar and protein in the body. As decomposition begins, gas is produced and the body swells.”

Speaking of unrecognisable, Margot Swanson looked a shadow of her usual glamorous self. The white coveralls hid her curves, and the face mask she wore no doubt covered plump ruby-coloured lips. At least she couldn't pout at Cooper's man, not that she was ever interested in men over forty. "Erica," she greeted. "I'll have her transported from here as soon as possible. I'm sure Neil will arrange for the family to make a formal identification."

Cooper shook Margot's hand and forced her eyes back to the naked body of Macey Gallagher. "Who found her?"

"A boot camp coach," explained Margot. "He was setting out his cones and kettlebells when he spotted her in the shallows."

Cooper swallowed.

"She's been in the water at least thirty-six hours," said Atkinson, taking over. "Marine creatures had started to feed on her. That's why her eyes are gone, and parts are missing from the flesh on her stomach and thighs. Her hands were fastened together with a cable tie, and I think her legs had been as well."

"Jesus," hissed Cooper, her gaze moving down her legs as Atkinson spoke. "She's missing a foot. Someone cut off her foot?"

"I don't think so," said Atkinson.

"Me neither." Margot moved towards what was left of Macey's right leg. "She has marks on her left leg, around her ankle. And the way the flesh is pulled over here," she pointed to the stump, "I think her ankles were also bound with cable ties and that something heavy had been attached to them to weigh her down. They wanted her body to stay submerged for longer. But with the level of bloating and gas accumulation observed here, it's possible the upward force of her body caused the detachment."

Cooper was choked up but tried not to show it. Why would anyone want to do this? Why would anyone want to harm a beautiful girl who by all accounts was happy and friendly to everyone she met? "Was she alive when they did this?" she asked.

Atkinson shrugged. "We don't know. She has no gunshot wounds. No stab wounds. No signs of being beaten. And other than the missing foot she has no broken bones that we can tell. You said she was diabetic?"

Cooper nodded. "That's right."

"That might explain why her body bloated so quickly. If her sugar levels were elevated, it would be perfect conditions for the bacteria to feast. It's near impossible for us to know if she was killed by drowning or if she was already dead when she was dumped in the water. If she'd been discovered sooner, we might have been able to tell, but after being submerged for so long, her lungs would fill with water either way."

"There are tests," said Margot, "But they're unreliable. I might, however, be able to run some blood work and establish her insulin levels. It won't be perfect as the bacteria will have used the glucose in her body, but it might give us an idea of whether she slipped into a diabetic coma before this happened."

"Cooper," the voice was unmistakable, and it was angry. "What in the blue blazes are you doing here?"

"Sir," said Cooper, her voice squeakier than she would have liked.

Superintendent Howard Nixon's face was hard and his eyes furious. "You know damn well you were taken off this case. Fuller and Sutherland are on their way, how do you think they'll feel finding you crawling all over their crime scene?"

"I'm hardly crawling, sir." Cooper knew she was in the wrong, but her intentions were good. She just wanted to help. That was all she ever wanted to do.

"Hold your tongue, young lady. I'm not finished."

Cooper practically choked. "Young lady? Sir, human resources—"

"Fuck human resources."

"Hey!" Atkinson's voice was lower than Cooper had ever heard it. "Do not talk to her like that. Don't *ever* talk to her like that." He'd moved within six inches of Nixon, who looked like he was about to blow a fuse. He was visibly shaking and Cooper didn't know whether to love Atkinson for standing up for her or to hate him for, well, standing up for her. She almost always held her own with Nixon. Their relationship had never been the best, but she usually handled him okay.

"And just who do you think you are, addressing me like that?"

Atkinson pulled his shoulders back and lowered the mask covering his mouth. "I'm the senior scene of crime officer, and I have jurisdiction. No police, no detectives, no no one unless I say so. So get out of my tent and stop crawling all over *my* crime scene."

Nixon's mouth twisted. Cooper didn't think anyone had ever thrown his own line back at him before, and he couldn't argue with Atkinson's logic. He left the tent, giving Cooper a look that meant her life wouldn't be worth living.

"Bugger it," she sighed, throwing her hands up. "Bugger it all. I shouldn't be here. We both know that." She spun on the spot, hoping Nixon wasn't waiting outside the tent. "Here goes nothing. I'll see you at dinner, Justin." Cooper blew a kiss into the air and left.

In the few minutes she'd been in the tent, the crowd had grown exponentially, and television cameras had appeared on top of the cliffs. Out at sea, the Newcastle to Amsterdam ferry looked immune to the swell as it headed to the continent. Beyond it, on the horizon, storm clouds were moving in. Fast.

- Chapter 17 -

THE OIL WARNING AND brake system lights illuminated orange. The power steering began playing silly buggers. Cooper didn't have time for this, but she didn't have much choice. She dropped the car at her local Kwik Fit and took an Uber into HQ.

The image of Macey's body wouldn't leave her. As she threw her handbag down next to a desk, she remembered the swollen, grey stump that was Macey's left leg. Exposed flesh, nibbled away at by fish and who knows what else. Cooper gagged. She clamped a hand to her mouth and raced to the toilets, desperately hoping to make it in time. She pushed open the door to the first stall and dropped to her knees. The top of her tibia slammed against the tiled flooring and she yelped in pain. She retched over and over again, but nothing came up. Panting, she placed a clammy hand back over her mouth and closed her eyes, but the image was still there. Cooper sat in the stall for over ten minutes.

Only when she was certain she wasn't going to vomit over anyone did she emerge, red-eyed and pasty-faced.

Returning to her desk, she switched on her computer and began searching the database for crimes involving scissors or heavy collars until Tennessee arrived looking both harried and distracted. Cooper glanced at her watch. What time did he call this?

"I just passed Nixon in the hall. What's up his arse?" he asked, joining her at the desk.

"Me, mainly," she replied. She rubbed her eyes and turned back to the screen. "Margot confirmed scissors as the weapon used on Omar Ali. I'm looking for any matches in MO. We think he had some sort of heavy collar fastened around his neck too."

"A collar? Is that what the dog reference was all about?" Tennessee looked confused.

"We won't know until he wakes up." Cooper hesitated and added, "*If* he wakes up. He was probably delusional with pain. He could have said anything, but for now, it's a..." her voice faded away.

"You were going to say *lead*. Admit it."

"It's a line of inquiry."

After a few minutes of searching, Tennessee tapped his monitor. Nine years ago, homicide in Sunderland. Murder weapon was a pair of scissors. Toby Cresswell convicted... Oh, never mind, he's still in the can."

"Seamstress, Alba Fitz, attempted rape. Stabbed her attacker with sewing scissors. Self-defence. The assailant almost bled to death."

"Hmm." Tennessee leant back in his chair. "You don't think this could be something similar?

Maybe Omar isn't the victim here. Maybe he's the perpetrator and some woman defended herself?"

Cooper snorted. "Omar attacks some woman and instead of running away, she somehow overpowers him, holds him captive for a few days, then beats him up and stabs him?"

Tennessee's posture shifted. He slumped forward in his chair, propped his elbows on the desk and rested his chin on his hands. "Sorry, stupid idea. Forget I said it."

He wasn't making eye contact. Cooper knew he wasn't right. He hadn't been right in days. "Jack," she said tentatively, "what's going—"

"What about this guy? Khush Patel. Convicted of GBH for stabbing someone with scissors. Served four years and now living in, would you believe it, Byker?"

Whatever it was, DS Jack Daniel didn't want to talk about it. Cooper bit her lower lip, and she bobbed her head. "Good. Let's shortlist him. We'll send a car over. In the meantime, keep looking."

Cooper kept scrolling and came across a case from ten years ago. "James Blake," she said. "Arrested after threatening a steward at St. James' Park with a pair of scissors. Blake and his girlfriend had turned up to the game in goth gear, and get this, the girlfriend was on a leash."

"No way?"

"Yes way. The stewards wouldn't let them in. Health and safety. Blake kicked up a fuss, said the collar and leash were a sign of trust and guardianship in the goth subculture. The stewards wouldn't budge, a scuffle broke out and Blake lunged at one of them with a pair of scissors he had in his pocket."

"Definitely on the shortlist."

The sound of Keaton's heavy boots plodding the corridors preceded her arrival. She greeted Cooper and Tennessee and shook her coat, leaving a small puddle by the door. Cooper turned to the window; the sky was black. Rain pelted the asphalt and paving outside.

Tennessee took in the state of Keaton. "I guess it's raining," he said sarcastically.

"You guess correctly." Keaton squeezed her small ponytail, adding more water to the puddle around her feet. "You know, with observation skills like that, you should be a detective."

"Now, now, children." Cooper picked up the phone and dialled for maintenance. She requested someone with a mop, a bucket and a wet floor sign pay a visit to CID. "Right, Paula, what's the latest from Weetslade?"

"The door-to-doors on the eastern side of the park aren't getting us any further forward, boss. On the western side, I've got a farmer who woke up at two a.m. on Friday when a car went past his house."

"Traffic cams on the western side?"

"None. But to get to the farm track you need to pass a retirement home. I have an appointment to view their CCTV later today."

Tennessee got to his feet and began pacing.

"What else, Paula?" Cooper asked.

"Well, I've contacted the owners of the cars we picked up on the traffic cams from the A189. The Astra owner, Vince Shepherd, Clarkes Terrace, was driving home from Bournemouth where he's been working. Was a crash on the M18 just south of Doncaster. Hence he was home so late. Checks out."

Cooper made notes while Keaton spoke. "And the Qashqai?"

"The Qashqai's owned by seventy-three-year-old Alice Faith. She'd been at a friend's bedside as she passed away." She made a sympathetic face before continuing. "And the Honda I traced to sixty-three-year-old Deanna Morton, who had no knowledge of her car being used at that time. She called her son who lives next door and apparently borrows it from time to time. He confirmed he'd gone for a drive because he couldn't sleep."

Tennessee scoffed. "He lives next door to his mother and uses her car? What are the odds she still cooks him dinner every night?"

"He's probably still breastfeeding," said Cooper. "What's the son's name?"

"Bryce." Confirmed Keaton.

Cooper tapped a finger on her lips three times before massaging her temples. "Bryce Morton," she said quietly to herself. "Hayes Walk, Wideopen?"

Keaton nodded. "That's the one. How'd you know?"

"Hong's team found his wallet near where Omar suffered the worst of his attack."

Keaton and Tennessee turned to look at her with furrowed, serious faces.

"Don't get excited. It had been there a long time. Doesn't prove anything, but that alibi was wishy-washy at best. We definitely need to speak to him."

Tennessee looked disappointed. He resumed his pacing and glanced at his phone again. He frowned, moved his thumb over the screen, and then frowned some more. "Sutherland says we should turn on the BBC."

Cooper, Keaton and Tennessee gathered around a small television in the corner of the room and Cooper scrambled for the remote. "How," she asked, "can this building be less than ten years old, but the television's from the Jurassic era?"

"Cutbacks," laughed Keaton. "Nixon probably bought it from Oxfam."

The screen flickered and eventually formed the red and white familiarity of the BBC news. The studio cut to a reporter at Newcastle International Airport sheltering under an umbrella that repeatedly threatened to turn inside out. "This morning a body matching the description of Macey Gallagher was discovered on Marsden Beach. Her parents, Sean and Iris Gallagher, are due to arrive in Newcastle shortly and are accompanied by their daughter, Katherine, as well as members of the Irish press and a representative from the TD of Dublin South-Central. They have issued the following statement: We are heartbroken at the thought of losing our beautiful baby girl. Macey was the sunshine in our lives and now that light has been extinguished. We are struggling to come to terms with what has happened to Macey, and we have many, many questions for Northumbria

Police and Detective Neil Fuller. We ask for privacy during this difficult time."

"Oh, shit," said Keaton, "Fuller's in for it."

Cooper blinked back a feeling of shame. "He barely had that case two minutes. He never stood a chance. I failed that girl as much as he did, and now the press are going to tear him to pieces."

Tennessee placed his hand on Cooper's shoulder but she shrugged him away. "No one had seen her, Coop. No one had any clue where she'd gone or what had happened to her. We did our best. And as for her parents, they're redirecting their guilt. Her father didn't give a monkey's that she'd disappeared and now he feels shit about it so he's going after Fuller."

He might be right, but it didn't raise Cooper's spirits. She had questions of her own: Where was Nicolas Petite? Did the hair grip at the landlord's house belong to Macey? Why did Aaron Quinn get so upset when asked about the baseball bat? Was he released?

Tennessee's phone rang. He pressed it to his ear, pressing the volume button so neither Cooper nor Keaton could hear the other side of the conversation. "It's okay. I promise it'll be okay." He ran a hand over the back of his neck and spoke so quietly Cooper could barely make out his words. "I'm at work... I'll call Dr Worthington. Slow down and breathe. I'll call him. Is your mum there?"

While Tennessee hung up, Cooper and Keaton's eyes met. Keaton shrugged. She was as clueless as Cooper.

"Jack?"

Tennessee shook his head and looked away. "It's nothing, ma'am. It's fine."

"It's not fine." Cooper rose to her feet and approached him. His eyes had reddened, not that he would look at her. What had happened to the pristine man she once knew? She searched his face and asked again, "Jack? Talk to me."

"It's Hayley." His voice was barely audible. "She's struggling. Ever since Alfie was born. She loves him, I know she does but they're not bonding, and she's depressed, and sometimes she just stares into space for so long. It's like she's a statue of Hayley. She looks like her but isn't her... It's like she doesn't do anything for herself anymore, nothing that brings her joy. And... and I'm just worried she's going do something, you know, like hurt herself, or..."

"Jack." Cooper took Tennessee's phone from his hand and laid it on the desk. She took his hands in hers and looked at him until he finally looked back. "Go and be with Hayley and Alfie." Between not finding Macey in time, not being there for Tina when she'd needed her and not noticing what was going on in Tennessee's home life, Cooper's guilt levels were killing her. She squeezed his hands. "Go home. Take as long as you need."

"But Omar's wife, Salwa—"

"I'll take care of it," said Keaton.

"What about Morton and the others we shortlisted?"

"I've got it covered, Jack. Give Alfie a kiss from me."

A lightning bolt illuminated the sky and highlighted the worry lines on Tennessee's forehead. He nodded once, picked up his coat and left without saying goodbye.

- Chapter 18 -

The incident room remained silent for several minutes after Tennessee's departure. No matter how hard Cooper tried to focus on her work, her brain kept returning to her failures. She was failing as a chief, as a detective, and as a mother. Eventually, without giving any explanation to Keaton, she got up and left in search of caffeine and a backbone. Feeling sorry for herself wouldn't do anyone any good, least of all the people she cared about.

The drinks machine at the end of the hall gurgled and spluttered until a plastic cup was full of cappuccino, or what was supposed to be cappuccino. Having tasted it, Cooper wasn't so sure. She blew on the frothy top as she walked up and down the corridor, cupping it with both hands and taking sips until she finished the drink. There was no backbone or magic cure in the bottom of the cup, but she'd used the time to give herself a pep talk, and by the time she got back to the incident room, she was ready to roll.

Keaton and her soggy coat were gone. She had initiative and didn't need Cooper to direct her every move. She'd be on her way to the retirement home on the western side of Weetslade before heading to the hospital to check on Omar and his wife. Cooper sat down in front of her computer and searched for James Blake. Nothing. She pouted and tried again, this time for Jimmy Blake. Again, the search didn't produce anything of use. There was a kinesiology lecturer in California by the same name and a managing director of a screen printing company in Alberta, Canada. Finally, she tried Jamie Blake.

"Bingo."

Jamie Blake worked as an art dealer and was based out of a gallery with the unusual name of The Biscuit Factory. Cooper zoomed in on the photograph of his face and squinted. She flicked back and forth between that and the photo she had on file from the incident at St. James' Park. They could be the same person, she concluded. His hair was lighter now; it must have been dyed black in his goth days. The earrings were gone, and he looked broader. But there were still many similarities: the thick brows, the shape of his ears and lips and the intensity in his eyes.

She wrote down his name, along with Khush Patel and Bryce Morton before reluctantly heading downstairs to visit the Collector.

"Erica. Two visits in the space of a week? I am a lucky boy."

Cedric Bell had half an egg sandwich open on his desk. The plaster on his thumb was now a disgusting shade of grey.

"And I am not a lucky girl," Cooper muttered, not caring if he heard or not. "I need you to bring up all known members of far-right groups within a thirty-mile radius of the city. I'm looking for Bryce Morton, James Blake and Khush Patel."

The Collector raised his eyes. "You think there's a Khush Patel in the White Rights Party?"

Cooper was silent. It was - admittedly - highly unlikely, but weirder things had happened.

"Suit yourself." The Collector shrugged and began typing with only his index fingers. After a minute or so, he printed a list of names and handed it to Cooper.

She scanned the list. "I don't see them. Can you run a separate search?"

His typing was painfully slow and Cooper hoped he wasn't intentionally dilly-dallying to keep her there longer than she needed to be.

"The only Bryce Morton I have in here lived in Hexham, was convicted on drug offences and died in HMP Haverigg. That your guy?"

Cooper shook her head. "Patel?"

"GBH? Four years?"

"That's the one."

"Living on Chirton Wynd, Byker. Arrested for drunk and disorderly in September 2016, but nothing else of note. No connections to radical groups on the left or right. Works as a refuse collector for Newcastle Council. As for Blake, his file hasn't been updated since his release." He picked a bit of green veg from his teeth, inspected it, and then ate it. "I have his address from the time and known associates. But it's ten years old. Shall I print it anyway?"

Cooper nodded and held out her hand with all the patience of a five-year-old. As soon as she had the printout, she was out of there.

AS THE GARAGE WAS still performing open-heart surgery on the Mazda, Cooper borrowed a panda car and headed to Shieldfield. The Biscuit Factory was a converted warehouse from the Victorian era. Bare brick and white plaster, combined with glass and metal fixings, created a light and airy venue with a very modern vibe.

Unable to get a parking space at the gallery, she parked around the corner on the street. One of these days she'd sell her old girl and get herself an upgrade. Sutherland had recently got himself a shiny new BMW, and Nixon's Mercedes had caught her eye. It wasn't that she couldn't afford a new car; the Mazda had memories. She'd driven that rust bucket for over twelve years now. She hadn't been able to drive when she first joined the police but the walk to North Shields police station, where she'd been posted at the time, was only fifteen minutes at most. Once Tina was three and ready to go to nursery, Cooper bit the bullet and learnt to drive. She and the Mazda had been together longer than any relationship she'd been in. For richer, for poorer. In sickness and good health.

Despite the full car park, the art gallery appeared to be empty. A hum of excitement was coming from the brasserie, and Cooper concluded that some sort of function was going on. She wiped her boots on the mat, removed her wet coat and slung it over her arm. She cast a look around the place and decided to have a browse. A little culture would do her good.

An exhibition of animal heads on human bodies wasn't to Cooper's taste, but some humungous charcoal drawings of the local area took her breath away. What skill, she thought, until her mind turned to Brian Hutchins. The art teacher had been sketching with charcoal when Tina had made a joke that ultimately put her life in danger. Her stomach twisted as the memory of searching Tynemouth Academy for the Tarot Card Killer returned to her. She set her jaw and moved on to some sculptures made of old motorcycle parts. Some were vast and filled their alcoves. Others were small and set on pedestals. One in particular caught Cooper's eye. It was about the size of her fist but was made to look like a dragon. It would look great in her living room, or she thought it would until she saw the price tag.

"Quentin Herbert's work is masterful, don't you think?"

Cooper jumped and turned around. He was tall, just shy of six feet, and muscular too. He clearly worked out but not to bodybuilder standards. His eyes were the brightest green, his hair tidy and the colour of sand. A sling supported one arm, and he was, without a doubt, Jamie Blake.

"Very talented," she replied.

"Are you looking to make a purchase today?" He smiled at her with a mouth of bleached teeth and stood closer than Cooper was comfortable with.

"Oh, I was just browsing," said Cooper, "and sheltering from the rain." She gave him an innocent shrug. "Besides, I can't afford six grand on a tiny sculpture, no matter how masterful the artist is."

She wasn't sure if she should show her cards and introduce herself as a detective. All she had to connect Blake to Omar Ali was a pair of scissors and a mumbled comment about a dog by a man about to slip into a coma.

Blake chuckled and seemed to move even closer. "Well, I can't blame you for seeking shelter. It's teeming down out there." He touched her upper back and guided her to the left. "And six grand is pretty steep. Although, we did have Xanthe Lewis in here last week. You know, the girl who won Love Island a few years back then went on I'm a Celeb? She spent over ten grand on a single painting. Hideous thing."

"The painting, or Xanthe Lewis?"

He laughed too loudly for the empty gallery, and his voice carried around the room. "The painting, of course. Although, those lip fillers... Here," he stopped manhandling Cooper and pointed to a stack of prints. "I might not be able to tempt you with a six-grand Herbert sculpture, but perhaps one of these prints will capture your heart."

Cooper felt very small, and there was something in Blake's eyes that she didn't like. It was as if he saw straight through her and knew exactly who she was. She wished Tennessee was here. Or Sutherland. Then she wished she hadn't had such an unfeminist thought. It was all in her mind anyway. A simple case of height-envy. "Thanks," she told Blake, "I'll take a look."

He was about to walk away, but Cooper couldn't help herself. "Your arm looks painful," she said.

Blake's eyes darted to the sling. "Car accident," he explained, though Cooper noticed he didn't walk with a limp or have any cuts and scrapes. What she did notice were the bruises on his knuckles.

With a print of North Shields's fish quay that cost her thirty quid, Cooper nodded goodbye to Blake and got the hell out of the gallery. She'd come back with Keaton once she'd collected more intel. Keaton could provide just as much muscle as Tennessee, probably more.

For now, time was getting on and she wanted to get home at a reasonable hour. After what had happened with Tennessee, she wanted to spend some time with her daughter, and she hoped Tina would like the print. She'd bought it for her and thought they could name the seagull in the top right-hand corner after Steven. She was going to make it a girls' night. Neither Kenny nor Justin were staying for dinner, so they'd get a takeaway and go on a Netflix binge. She'd pick up some ice cream on the way home and— "You're effing kidding me!"

Some toe rag from parking enforcement had slapped a ticket on the windscreen of the panda car.

"Cheeky swines."

- CHAPTER 19 -

COOPER HADN'T SLEPT WELL. She'd checked the time on her phone at least eight times since three in the morning when she'd awoken. It was now a few minutes past six, and she thought it was a good time to act as Bryce Morton's wake-up call. She left twenty pounds on the dining table, along with a note, telling Tina to take Josh for lunch and to have a great day. Last night had gone well; Tina had loved the king prawn pathia and coriander naans she'd ordered and all appeared to be forgiven. Two things had kept Cooper awake. The first was a feeling of dread for her DS. Tennessee hadn't texted or called, and Cooper didn't want to pry or invade his personal space by checking up on him. But every time she'd drifted off she dreamt of bad news coming in the form of a text message and awoke with the phone gripped in her sweaty palms. The second thing keeping sleep at bay was a thought she didn't want to consider. A nagging threat at the back of her mind that ate away at her and distracted her every attempt at focus.

HISTORICALLY, WIDEOPEN WASN'T THE wealthiest of areas, but Hayes Walk had a sense of pride to it. Well-presented semi-detached houses with bay windows stood proudly behind perfectly manicured lawns. The scent of flowers carried down the street, and not one piece of litter could be seen.

Without even checking her notes, Cooper knew which houses belonged to the Mortons. A set of semi-detached houses, painted in the same shade of jasmine white with sage masonry, had identical lawns with stone hedgehogs and other woodland creatures scattered around them. A Honda Civic was parked on one driveway. Cooper gave it a once over as she approached the neighbouring doors. The car had mud splatter on the hubcaps and a nasty dent on the front bumper.

She knocked on Bryce Morton's door three times and waited. Silence. She huffed and knocked again. When there was still no response she pushed her face to the letterbox, and using her fingers to hold it open, called, "Mr Morton? Wakey, wakey. It's Northumbria Police. I'd like a word."

"Can I help you?"

A fragile woman in her sixties was standing in the neighbouring doorway. She wore a thin nightgown and was barefoot.

"Deanna Morton? I'm DCI Cooper. I'm looking for your son."

"He's already spoken to your lot," she answered, folding her arms over her flat chest.

"I understand he's spoken to a colleague of mine, but I have a few questions of my own."

Deanna rubbed her hands on her arms. Goosebumps were forming on her pale skin. "Guess you'd better come in then. He's in the kitchen having his breakfast."

Of course he is, thought Cooper. She was expecting a man-child and she wasn't disappointed. Bryce Morton, in his late thirties, had slim shoulders and wobbly pipe cleaners for arms, but his hips and thighs were wider, giving him a pear-shaped frame that would be more suited to a female. A pair of Harry Potter style glasses had slid down his nose, and he wore plaid pyjama bottoms with a t-shirt sporting Marvel's Avengers.

"Mr Morton, Bryce, I know you already spoke to my colleague, but I need to ask you about Thursday night and Friday morning, specifically why you turned off the A189 in the direction of Weetslade Country Park."

He looked at his mother before answering. "I told the officer who was here. I told her I have insomnia and when I can't sleep I like to go for a drive. I find it peaceful when it's dark and the roads are clear."

Cooper hadn't been offered a seat but she took one anyway, sitting opposite Morton. His mother's kitchen was old-fashioned with floral tiles and beige-coloured units and worktops. The kitchen table was covered with a plastic tablecloth and on the windowsill, a framed photograph of a portly man was surrounded by fake flowers and battery-operated candles. A small plaque read: Rest In Peace Derrick Morton. Cooper crossed her legs and made eye contact with Bryce. "What keeps you awake?"

"Oh, you know. The usual." He gave a brief chuckle. "Work stress, money worries, this and that."

"You obviously know about the assault that occurred in Weetslade on Thursday night?"

He nodded and ate a spoonful of Sugar Puffs. A drop of milk dribbled down his chin. "The officer who was here last time told me about it. She wanted to know if I'd seen or heard anything."

"And had you?"

"No."

"It was a very serious assault, Bryce. Weapons were used and the victim may not survive. In that case, this investigation will escalate to manslaughter, maybe even murder."

His eyes flicked to his mother's and they exchanged a look that Cooper wasn't able to interpret.

"I didn't see anything," he added, taking another mouthful of cereal.

Cooper opened her notepad and asked Morton to describe the route he had taken that night.

"I drove south and left the estate to join Sandy Lane. Then I went up Great Lime Road, past Weetslade and then along Dudley Lane and back into Wideopen."

"That can't have taken very long." Cooper was visualising the route in her head. In rush hour it would be a nightmare, but in the middle of the night, it wasn't more than a fifteen-minute drive.

"No," he agreed. "Twenty minutes maybe. Just long enough to zone out. Driving can be a form of hypnotherapy, you know. People get into a sort of autopilot."

"Did you stop off in the park?"

He shook his head. "No. I told you, I just went for a drive."

"Did you see any cars in the car park when you passed it?"

"No. I don't think so."

"No one hanging about?"

"It was pitch black beyond the road. If there was, I wouldn't have noticed. I'm very sorry that that man got hurt but I can't help you. I don't know anything about it."

"So, the forensics teams won't find your tyre tracks in the car park?"

He looked from Cooper to his mother and back again. "I go into Weetslade a lot. My car, I mean Mum's car, is often there."

"When was it last there, Bryce?"

"Last night," he said, the colour seeping from his pasty face. "Around six. The park's open again now, all the tape's been taken down. I went for a walk." He patted his belly. "I wanted some exercise. Got to get ten thousand steps a day."

Cooper knew many perpetrators liked to return to the scene of the crime. Some got a kick out of it by reliving the moment in their heads. Others liked to snoop around, see if the police were still there. The most audacious would seek out the police, pretend they witnessed the event or saw someone suspicious. Bryce Morton seemed a bit wet, a bit too much of a Mummy's boy to overpower a man, hold him captive and beat the living shit out of him. Still, she didn't rule out the idea that this weak man-child thing he had going on was a convincing act.

She tilted her head to one side. "Did you hear we found your wallet near to where the attack occurred?"

"My wallet? I— I lost that months ago. Months." His eyebrows inclined towards each other and his chin tucked in, merging into his neck.

Cooper said nothing.

"I cancelled all my cards. There was eighty quid in it though. Do you know if the cash was still there?"

"I don't. I can ask forensics."

"Forensics? It's not, I mean, you're not using it as evidence, are you? I said I wasn't in the park on Friday night. I didn't hurt that man. That wallet's been missing for ages. Am I in some sort of trouble?"

"We're just trying to establish who was in or near the park at the time of the assault." She put her card on the table and slid it across to Morton. While his eyes watched the card, she scanned his knuckles and forearms; he had no defensive wounds or bruises to raise Cooper's suspicions. "Have a think, Bryce. If you remember anything. No matter how insignificant it might seem, call me."

She got to her feet and excused herself. She had somewhere else she wanted to be.

Cooper had the Mazda back, and eight hundred quid later, it had been given the all-clear. She put it into first gear and headed north. Once she joined the A1 she put a call into Keaton using speaker-phone.

"Boss?"

"How's it going, Paula? Any news?"

"I've got Omar's wife settled in at the RVI. She's a mess, poor thing. Imagine not seeing your other half for almost a year and when you do see them, they're in a coma and... well, you know what he looks like."

"Have you heard from Tennessee?"

"Nothing. You?" When Cooper didn't answer, Keaton pressed again. "Boss?"

"Sorry, Paula. I'm a bit distracted. Driving. Erm, no. I haven't heard anything. I'm giving him some space."

"I'm feeling pretty shitty about not realising something was up."

"You and me both, Paula. Postnatal depression's a terrible thing. I hope Hayley gets the help she needs. Tennessee too. Seems like he's been shouldering this for a while. I wonder why he didn't talk to us sooner?"

"Because he's a bloke. And blokes aren't exactly the best at opening up, are they?"

"Times are changing. Mental health seems to be at the forefront of people's minds these days. Hopefully the next generation won't be as closed off as we are." The irony of what Cooper had just said wasn't lost on her. She wasn't distracted because she was driving. She was distracted because of something else, and she bit her bottom lip for a moment as she pondered sharing her own feelings.

"I heard from Nexus," said Keaton before Cooper could decide. "Omar got on the Metro at Monument in Newcastle. I followed the CCTV backwards and traced him to Times Square. He was coming out of The Eagle."

"The Eagle?" Cooper racked her brain as she drove. "I don't recognise the name."

"It's a gay bar."

"Huh." All this time, Nixon had thought the attack on Omar was racially motivated. Perhaps this was a hate crime of a different sort. Was his attack down to homophobia? "Does the wife know?" she asked.

Keaton snorted. "If she doesn't, I'm not telling her. Besides, you don't have to be gay to go to a gay bar. Maybe he was meeting a friend? Maybe he just likes the music. He was only in there for an hour."

As Cooper continued north, she left Newcastle's northern suburbs and her world became very green. Sheep and cattle grazed in open pastures. Copses of conifers stood tall on either side of the dual carriageway.

"We don't know of him having any friends," Cooper mused, mainly to herself. "His work colleagues said he kept to himself and from what the neighbour said, it didn't sound like he had much of a social life. Can you nip into town, Paula, and talk to the staff? See if anyone remembers anything or recognises him. Then take another look at the cameras. We know he was fine when he got on the Metro at Monument, and we know he was still fine when he got off the Metro at Byker. I want to know if anyone followed him. See who got on at the same station. Did anyone approach him?"

Keaton confirmed she'd follow those lines of inquiry and hung up. It was an overcast day and the sky was stony grey. The darkness above made the colour of the fields pop in vibrant shades of green, punctuated occasionally with the bright yellow of rapeseed. It was the sort of day made for baggy jumpers, hot tea and a good book but Cooper stood little chance of engaging in that sort of behaviour; she was approaching Morpeth.

No one agreed on where Morpeth got its name. Some said it was derived from Moor Path as the road, which was the main route connecting England and Scotland, traversed the Northumbrian moorlands. Others said it was derived from the more sinister Murder Path, after a brutal killing that had occurred on the road. What everyone could agree on was the fact that Morpeth was a beautiful market town with many structures still standing from the 1500s. Cooper was especially fond of a cuboid clock tower that dominated the town centre. She slowed the Mazda as she drove past to get a better look and to cast her mind back to days out with her parents. Morpeth Castle had always fascinated the feminist in her; it had been handed down the female line of numerous powerful families, until the 1980s when, disappointingly, it became a holiday let.

Cooper continued until she reached the opposite side of town and followed a quiet street lined with plush, detached homes that Cooper would describe as half mansions. Finally, she reached her destination. An impressive house stood at the end of the road, separated from the nearest homes by at least a hundred metres of scrubland on either side. It was Jamie Blake's house.

"So, this is what you can buy on an art dealer's salary?" she whispered to herself. She was in the wrong profession. Cooper looked left and right and couldn't see any other cars. Blake should be at work by now, but she wasn't taking any chances; the man was creepy and she wanted to make sure no one was around. She waited in the car for several minutes, watching the windows for movement, and when none came, she dialled the number for The Biscuit Factory.

"Hello, The Biscuit Factory. Leanne speaking, how may I help you?"

Leanne's voice was prim and fast.

"Morning, could I speak to Jamie Blake, please?"

"He's not in yet." Cooper's heart quickened. "Could I take a message?"

Cooper hung up and waited several more minutes before sliding into the back seat of the Mazda to change her clothing. She dispensed with the smart trousers and blazer she had worn to speak to Bryce Morton and pulled on a pair of baggy jeans, an unflattering hoodie and a pair of worn Nike trainers. It wasn't her greatest look. Frankly, she could pass for a prepubescent boy, but if the goal was to not look like a detective, she'd achieved it.

Exiting her vehicle, Cooper locked the car and wandered up to Blake's house. Immediately, a sign above the letterbox caught her attention: Beware of the dog.

Bad dog? she wondered, peering through the living room window and seeing a stylish, modern interior. Not a piece of chintz or clutter in sight. There was also no sign of the aforementioned dog. Not able to hear any barking or scratching, Cooper squeaked the front gate back and forth on its hinges for a few seconds. No German shepherds came running at the door and no Jack Russells thinking they're German shepherds came either. The sign might just be a decoy to dissuade potential burglars. Not that Cooper had any intention of illegally entering Blake's property. As long as she stayed on the public land that surrounded his house, she wouldn't be doing anything wrong.

Cooper followed the start of a bridle path that ran down the side of Blake's house and casually cast her gaze through his kitchen window. She couldn't see much, being on the short side, but she could see two ornaments on the windowsill: a matching set of porcelain cocker spaniels. Blake's garden was vast and shielded from view by seven-foot-tall fences. Cooper had no chance of being able to see over the top, but she could just see through the gaps between some of the slats. The lawn was well-maintained, short and neat. There were no flowers but there were numerous pots of herbs, including mint, thyme and chives. She couldn't see any rosemary, but she could smell it. A garden path with night lights on either side snaked towards a two-person sauna, a hot tub and an outdoor shower. Jamie Blake had some serious wealth. This was a man who could afford Yeezies.

Near the far end of the garden, but still at least three or four metres away from the back fence, was a green shed. The shed was reinforced with sheets of hardwood that had been nailed to the sides. A series of heavy padlocks secured the door.

It was protected like Fort Knox.

Having recently studied a case file on David Parker Ray, the American known as the Toy Box Killer, the shed gave Cooper an uneasy feeling, but before she could take a closer look, the sound of an approaching car made her jump. She pulled up her hood and did her best *boy walk* back towards her car, never looking back for fear of making eye contact with Jamie Blake.

It took twice as long as it should have to drive back to Wallsend. Some numpty had left a gate open and a flock of sheep had wandered onto the A1. Thankfully, no sheep or humans had been harmed. Back in Wallsend, Cooper stopped at the local McDonald's drive-through to pick up an Egg McMuffin and an Americano hot enough to melt glass. She struggled to eat the breakfast sandwich while she was parked outside the restaurant; her mouth was dry and no matter how much she chewed, each bite was difficult to swallow. Eventually, she gave up, throwing the remaining sandwich in the bin and heading back around the corner to HQ.

As she exited the car and slung her handbag over one shoulder, Cooper looked to the sky and saw the sun beginning to break through the grey. A beam of sunlight shone down upon her car. Perhaps it was a good omen for her afternoon? Or, maybe it was the patron saint of cars trying to take her old Mazda off to the afterlife? She picked up her coffee in one hand and her suit in the other and strode into the building only to be immediately clocked by Nixon.

"Cooper."

"Sir." She hoped he wasn't about to rant at her for being at Marsden Rock yesterday.

A line appeared between his brows as he scrutinised her. "Why are you dressed like a twelve-year-old chav?"

Cooper's jaw tightened and she held up the suit she was carrying. "Don't worry, sir. I'll be suited and booted before you know it."

"What's the latest on the Weetslade assault case? The Chronicle ran a story last night, and there was something on Look North about women being too scared to go jogging or walk their dogs because of the attack. Now the blinking RSPCA have released a statement about how terrible it is that dogs are being denied the exercise they need because we're not making the streets safe."

"What a load of old tosh," said Cooper. "Statistically, Northumberland and Tyne and Wear are—"

"No one cares about statistics, Cooper. They care about headlines and selling papers. So, what's the latest?"

"The net's closing in, sir." Cooper took a deep breath and could smell the aroma of her coffee as it drifted up to her nostrils. It might have been a cheap cuppa from the local drive-through but it was causing her to salivate. Even just the smell of it was waking her up.

"The victim was last seen on Tuesday the twelfth. He finished work at the usual time and in the evening he visited a bar near Times Square. He got on the Metro at Monument at ten-forty and alighted at Byker shortly after eleven p.m. None of his neighbours can recall hearing him come home, and he never made it to work the next day. We believe he was either taken on Tuesday night or was lured away somehow. The bar he visited is a gay bar, so we're considering that the attack could be homophobic in nature rather than racially motivated. Keaton is speaking to the staff today."

Nixon glanced at his watch but urged Cooper to keep going.

"The wounds suffered by the victim indicate he had some sort of metal collar attached to his neck and had been bound by ropes around the torso. He suffered multiple stab wounds, which are consistent with scissor attacks. I've found some previous cases with similar MOs. Cases involving collars or scissors. One of whom is of particular interest. James Blake. I've checked with local intelligence and have found no connection to far-right groups."

"Sounds like you've made a good start, Cooper. I need it wrapped up as soon as you can though. We're stretched beyond belief at the moment." He checked his watch again. "Anything else?"

Cooper could have gone into more detail. She could have mentioned the cars caught on traffic cams and the wallet found at the scene. She could have asked why she'd been taken off the Macey Gallagher case and enquired about the latest developments. Instead, she fished the parking ticket she'd received yesterday from her bag and thrust it into Nixon's hand.

"Yes, sir. Can you make this go away, sir?"

- Chapter 20 -

When Cooper entered CID in the early afternoon, she spotted Paula Keaton playing a game of rock, paper, scissors with Oliver Martin. Apparently, in this version, every time someone lost they had to do five push-ups. Cooper watched Martin do fifty push-ups before asking if they had work to be getting on with.

Martin, whose complexion was now somewhat dewy, scurried away. Presumably, he still had his tail between his legs after the scalding she'd given him over his attitude. Keaton dusted her hands on her trousers and picked up some files from her desk.

"Boss, I'm just about to head over to Byker. Going to check in with the guys canvassing the area and see what they have. See if Khush Patel's name has come up. He served time for attacking someone with scissors, and I think it's a good idea to find out where he was on Tuesday evening and Wednesday morning. The climbing centre returned Tennessee's call. They have a small camera that covers a stretch of the main road directly in front of the centre. I'm going to go and see if it's picked anything up."

Cooper's face lit up. This was good news. Hopefully, the cameras caught something of use. "Excellent," she said. "Keep in touch and let me know how you get on. I have somewhere I need to be later, but if I don't pick up, just leave me a message."

Keaton nodded and moved towards the door. She hesitated and then turned back. "Boss, I'll be near the big ASDA in Byker. Thought I might nip in and pick up some things for Tennessee and Hayley. Some posh fruit? A load of vitamins might do them some good. There's a couple of herbal teas from Clipper that might help them sleep. Their organic nettle infusion's the bee's knees." She tipped her head from side to side. "Or, do you think I'm best staying clear and keeping my nose out of things?"

"I think that's a lovely idea, Paula." Cooper wondered why she hadn't considered the idea herself, but she knew the answer, deep down, she knew the answer. "Tell Tennessee I'm thinking of him and give Hayley my best. I have something to take care of this evening but I'll give him a call tomorrow, see how things are."

Just as Keaton left, Neil Fuller and Sam Sutherland walked in.

The men tipped invisible hats to Cooper with perfect synchronicity and Cooper was at a miss as to when the two had become so close. Sutherland, like Cooper, had always considered Fuller a bit of a cowardly wet blanket, and now, Cooper wouldn't be surprised if Sutherland put his arm around Fuller's shoulders in a display of uncensored bromance.

"Erica," they said in unison before taking a seat on either side of her.

Cooper was sceptical. "Gentlemen," she said with a rising inflection. "What can I do for you?"

"Two things," Sutherland said. "Firstly, Caroline said she'd love to come to Tina's party."

"Excellent. It'll be lovely to see you all."

"Sue asks what we should bring."

Cooper itched the back of her head as she thought. "We're just ordering food in but something with a percentage would go down a treat. What's the second thing?"

"We thought you'd want to know the latest from the Gallagher autopsy," said Sutherland.

"Margot's finished already?"

"She put a rush on it. Put it to the top of the queue, given all the press."

"And why are you coming to me with this?"

Fuller shrugged. "Because you're Erica Cooper, and whether Nixon approves or not, you'll find out one way or another."

She tried not to smirk. "Well?" she asked. "What did Margot find?"

"The glucose levels in the DB's urine and blood were perfectly normal."

"Meaning wherever Macey was, she had access to insulin?"

"No. Meaning, whoever washed up on Marsden Beach, isn't Macey Gallagher."

Cooper leant back in her chair and folded her arms. "What? You're shitting me?"

"I shit not," said Fuller. "The visual ID from the parents was negative as well. Macey has a large scar on her right thigh from being burnt as a toddler. Add to that, the DB is an inch too short and had clear braces. Macey's dentist sent over her latest X-rays. They don't match and she wasn't undergoing orthodontic treatment."

Cooper didn't know what to think. There was a chance Macey was still alive and that gave her hope. But who the hell was this other girl? Why did they look so similar? Questions raced through her mind so quickly she hardly knew where to begin.

"Holy Shit. Where's Macey? Who's the DB?"

"We don't know," Fuller said. "Missing persons are trying to find a match. Her braces have a serial number. They're in touch with the manufacturers. They should be able to match the brace to the victim."

"She looked so similar to Macey. Do you think this is somehow connected?"

"Who knows?" Sutherland yawned. "Margot's doing what she can. We have fingerprints from the body, so between those and the dental work we should be able to get an ID sooner rather than later."

"I'm completely blindsided." Cooper shook her head. She didn't know what to think. "Speaking of Margot, I noticed the massive rock she was sporting on her ring finger. Congratulations."

Fuller shared a look with Sutherland before getting to his feet and walking towards the window.

"Something I said?" Cooper asked Sutherland.

Sutherland picked at his lip, gave Cooper a meaningful look and slightly shook his head as if to say, *it's a sore subject*.

When Fuller turned around, his eyes had a slight sheen to them. "I didn't put that ring there," he said. "Some other bloke did that. I was traded in for a younger model."

"Jesus," said Cooper, more out of shock than pity. "Well, that sucks. Sorry to hear that, Neil."

"It was so out of the blue," he sniffed. "One minute we're in love, the next minute she's telling me it's over and she doesn't see a future for us anymore. Within days I heard she was seeing some twenty-something, tanned, steroid muncher with a waxed chest. Apparently, he's besotted with her. Proposed within a month. Dumb fuck."

The saying *what goes around comes around* flashed in Cooper's mind's eye. Part of her felt sorry for the man, it just wasn't a very large part. No wonder he'd latched onto Sutherland. Fuller was craving a father figure in his time of crisis and Sutherland was always capable of playing that role.

"I told him to keep his head down, get stuck in at work and keep his mind busy. The pain will pass, but until then, he might as well direct his energy into something productive."

She shot a sideways look at Fuller and lowered her eyelids halfway. "Wait," she said. "Is that why Nixon put you on the Gallagher case? Because he wanted to keep you busy?"

"No," he said, stretching the vowel sound for several seconds. He looked deeply insulted. "I don't talk to Nixon about my love life, for goodness sake."

"Okay, okay, I just wondered." Cooper held up her hands.

"I don't. Whatever reason he had for the reshuffling, it's as much a mystery to me as it is to you."

Sutherland interjected, "I think Nixon's just trying to utilise his resources appropriately. My case was cut and dry, Fuller didn't have much on, and this Gallagher case was always going to end in tears. Nixon probably thought it made sense to free you up. You're his golden girl."

Cooper blew out a raspberry. "Golden girl indeed. You wouldn't be saying that if you heard the bollocking he gave me yesterday."

Fuller placed his hands on his hips. "Yeah," he said, "I heard you were down at Marsden."

Cooper gave a guilty shrug but didn't apologise.

"I also heard that forensic investigator of yours gave Nixon a piece of his mind." The left corner of his mouth curled up and he raised one bushy eyebrow into a dramatic arch. "Quite the set of balls he must have. Don't think anyone's spoken to Nixon like that since he was in a nappy."

"To be fair, the whole thing was my fault," conceded Cooper. "So where does your investigation go now? Did the SOCOs uncover anything of use?"

"We haven't heard yet but the lads who were playing pub golf on the night of Macey's disappearance have come forward."

"Yeah?"

"Yeah. The night out was organised by Northumbria University's Student Union. They were all first years. Bussed in from the dorms on Coach Lane and all bussed back out again at the end of the night. All present and accounted for. No one was missing according to the student union rep. We chatted to a few of them. Barely anyone can remember much from that stage in the evening. There was one lad who wasn't drinking, a Damien Blethens. He remembers seeing Macey take her shoes off to rub her feet before putting them back on. He said she seemed tipsy but otherwise fine. She complained about being really hot and some of the blokes made a joke about her being, well, hot in the other sense of the word. Blethens went to the toilet and when he came back, she'd gone. He assumed she'd headed off with her own group."

"Did you follow up with the men who called her hot?"

"Of course we did." Fuller's tone was tetchy, and if Cooper wanted to continue receiving information on the case she had to be careful. Handle him with kid gloves.

"Sorry," she said. "Of course you did. You really don't have much to go on though, do you?" asked Cooper. "It's like she vanished into thin air."

Sutherland let out a small sigh and Fuller shook his head. "I'm hoping the lab turns up some evidence on the baseball bat we found in the boyfriend's flat. Quinn claims he only has it for self-defence. Says the student flats are always targeted by thieves and he wanted the bat in case anyone who broke in was armed."

Cooper knew student flats were a hot target for criminals. Four to a flat often meant four laptops, four mobiles, four televisions and sometimes, four game consoles.

"What really got our attention," Sutherland started before being interrupted by his belly loudly rumbling. He rubbed his palm over it as if to soothe it. "Was Quinn's flatmate coming to see us. I don't know if he and Quinn fell out or what, but he told us Aaron Quinn and Macey Gallagher regularly had blazing rows. He also said he passed out on the sofa at around quarter past one in the morning, so he couldn't vouch for Quinn's whereabouts when Macey went missing at three.

"Sounds like he's your guy," Cooper said.

Sutherland's shoulders lifted and fell. "Might well be. You know as well as I do that the most logical explanation is usually the right one. It's almost always the partner or ex-partner. Time will tell. How about you? Your case progressing nicely?"

"Getting there. I have a theory, but I need a warrant before I can go any further... and I need a bit more evidence if I'm going to get the warrant."

A HALF-HOUR LATER, COOPER arrived at Denewood in the village of Forest Hall. Denewood branched into several cul-de-sacs like bronchi branching into bronchioles. Detached new builds with spacious gardens and off-road parking made Cooper crave more space at home. Her home in

Tynemouth wasn't small, but it was a terrace, and the backyard wasn't suitable for much more than hanging out laundry. Sure, she was close to the sea, but a house like one of these would give Tina her own bathroom and space to study outdoors. She considered as she watched a young boy whiz past on a scooter that she might not be able to afford it on her own, but she and Atkinson together certainly would. Not that they were ready to move in together. He couldn't handle the idea of her getting a tattoo and still resented Kenny's presence in her life.

Kenny had acted like an idiot during the first twelve years of Tina's life; in total denial of the fact he had a daughter. But Cooper had to admit, now Kenny was back and had got his act together, he had made things a lot easier for her. He did the school run when she couldn't, even stocked the fridge when he knew she wouldn't have time. And the little gifts were sweet too. She smiled at the thought of the Metallica poster hanging in her bedroom with its bizarre pin button frame. Atkinson would have to deal with his feelings towards Kenny before they could even contemplate living together full-time.

Cooper pressed the doorbell on a midnight blue front door. Beyond the door, she could hear the sound of children playing and a radio broadcasting the weather forecast. It took a while, but eventually, a woman with poker-straight, red hair cut into a stylish bob answered the door and looked quizzically at Cooper.

"Georgina Hibbert?"

"Yes," she answered, her eyes looking beyond Cooper into the street and the afternoon sun.

"I'm DCI Cooper. Northumbria CID. I know you must be very busy but I'd like a minute of your time."

Georgina's body stiffened and she manoeuvred herself so that the door was half closed between her and Cooper. "What's this about?" she asked.

"It's about James Blake."

"Bloody hell," she exclaimed. "I haven't heard that name in forever." She manoeuvred herself again, this time moving towards Cooper and partly closing the door behind her so that it was only open an inch.

"You were his girlfriend? Back in 2009?"

"Yes, that's right."

"And you were with him the day he was arrested at St. James' Park?"

Her cheeks coloured a rosy pink and she cast a glance back over her shoulder before turning back to Cooper. "Yes, that was me, but I don't understand why you're here now, ten years later."

"I'm investigating a crime where a man was restrained by a dog collar of sorts. He was stabbed several times with a pair of scissors. The only other incident I can find of a crime taking place involving scissors and a collar is the one involving James and yourself. I was hoping you could talk to me about it. Tell me the significance of the collar and leash."

Georgina blew out her cheeks very slowly and quietly clicked the door into place. In a hushed voice, she said, "My husband's home. He doesn't know about that and he doesn't like hearing about ex-boyfriends. He gets jealous, you know, and he really wouldn't want to hear about how James treated me."

Cooper lowered her voice to match Georgina's. "How did he treat you?"

"Great at first. We were both in the goth scene. He was more traditional: leather trench coat, pale face, black eyeliner. I used to like the gothic Lolita look." She laughed at herself and ran her fingers through her hair. "God, we thought we were so cool. A few couples in our group used to do the collar and leash thing. I thought it was just a fashion thing when James first suggested it but there's much more to it than that. It's a symbol of commitment and trust. Like a wedding ring, I guess. If you're collared, you're taken."

"Owned?"

Georgina shook her head. "That's more the BDSM community. It wasn't an owner-slave relationship. More an *I trust you not to tug on this leash too hard and not to lead me anywhere I don't want to go* sort of thing." She sucked in her lower lip and looked at the floor.

"But?" asked Cooper, suspecting Jamie Blake hadn't maintained Georgina's trust.

She sighed. "But... he did lead me places I didn't want to go. He liked taking me to non-goth places just to... I don't know, be stared at, ruffle feathers."

"Like St. James' Park?"

"Exactly. The pub, the library, anywhere for shock value. He said all football fans were saddos whose weekly happiness depended on the success of eleven over-paid jocks, and if we turned up to a Newcastle game in our best goth attire, we'd blow their narrow, little minds."

"You didn't get the chance though. Security stopped you from entering the stadium."

Georgina nodded. "I'd say it was probably for the best, but you know how it ended up. Actually, I broke up with James after that, so it was for the best in the end." She looked down and to the right as if recalling a memory.

"Would you say he made you uncomfortable, Georgina?"

"More than uncomfortable. I didn't trust him at all in the end, but I was too weak to say anything until he was arrested. If I broke up with James I'd be cast out of our circle and that meant losing my friends too. I was scared of being alone and I think that's why I let him..." She wrapped her arms around her chest and hugged her hands into her armpits.

"You can tell me," Cooper said. "I just want to get a feel for James. Work out what he's like."

"He had a violent streak. Most of us were meek and quietly spoken, but he was like our leader. He had an aura about him and he... he slapped me a few times. He had fetishes, too. God, I don't think I can...I'm not like that anymore, you see. I've moved on." She checked that the door was still closed behind her before whispering. "He made me bark, you know, during sex. Like a dog."

WHEN COOPER TURNED INTO the Freeman Hospital in Heaton, her mind was somewhere between gay bars, BDSM and the possibility that Omar went with Blake voluntarily as his submissive. He had been naked, after all. Only, something must have gone wrong, they fought, and he lost. Badly. It didn't really make sense, she told herself as she directed the Mazda towards a multi-storey car park at the rear of the hospital. Missing work was out of character, and why was he at Weetslade? Neither Omar nor Blake lived anywhere near Weetslade Colliery. Either way, she needed to have a chat with Blake. She'd call Keaton when she was done here and have her find out what sort of car Blake drove. She wanted to know where his car was when Omar disappeared and the night he was attacked.

Cooper turned off the engine when she found a space on the roof of the car park and sat quietly for a moment. Her hands had left sweaty prints on the steering wheel. She wiped them on her trousers before exiting the car and approaching the lift.

"Out of order? Unbelievable." She growled and slammed her palm into the metal doors. She was on the sixth floor and her heart rate was fast enough as it was.

She gripped the railing as she walked down over ninety stairs, crossed the road and entered the sliding glass doors to the Northern Centre for Cancer Care.

- CHAPTER 21 -

"WE'RE GOING TO DIE."

"We're not going to die. Don't say that." Macey Gallagher tried to soothe Nina, the girl to her left. She spoke quietly, fearing their keeper was just on the other side of the door. "Everything's going to be okay."

She didn't believe her own words. How could she believe them? She didn't have a bloody clue if they would be okay. She thought of her family, wishing she'd never left Dublin and stayed home to study. What were her mother and father doing now? Did they know she was missing? She ached to be back home with them. It was the simple things she missed, like watching her mother hang laundry on a windy day, laughing as her father got too invested in a game of Gaelic football, and braiding Kate's hair while they watched a film. She made fists to stop her hands from shaking as she wondered if she'd ever see them again.

"They killed Elin," Nina whispered.

"Elin tried to escape."

Elin had nibbled at the cable ties all through the night, slowly weakening them until they snapped. She removed her blindfold but kept her hood on so their keeper wouldn't suspect anything when he brought them their breakfasts. When he was bent over, laying the paper plates of unbuttered bread on the floor, Elin made a run for it. She reached the door only to be dragged back into the room. Unable to cover their ears, Macey and the other girls had to listen as Elin was kicked to death less than two metres from where they sat. They'd heard her last breath. He didn't have to kill Elin. He'd done it to set an example. *This is what you get if you mess with us.*

"Listen, Nina, as long as we do what we're told and we don't piss them off, we'll be fine." Her words were forced and laced with artificial positivity because Macey was worried she'd be next. Kicked to death for asking for insulin one too many times? The irony being, that if she didn't ask for it, she'd be dead regardless.

Macey fought back tears. Last night, she'd heard their keeper on the phone when he thought they were sleeping. She hadn't heard everything, but she had an idea of their intentions and a small voice at the back of her mind kept calling out, *You know, death might be the better option.*

"ERICA COOPER?"

Cooper looked up into the warm face of a young nurse with a glowing complexion and a pregnancy bump of at least seven months.

"This way, Erica. I'll take you to Dr McDermott."

The nurse made small talk, but Cooper was barely listening, and when she reached Dr McDermott's consulting room, she noticed her hands were shaking and she was suffering from dry mouth.

"Good Morning, Erica," boomed Dr McDermott. He was a large man who seemed to fill up most of the room, though not in an intimidating way, more in a Santa Claus sort of way. His thick white beard certainly helped contribute to that image.

"How have you been in the three months since we last spoke? This is your six-month checkup, correct?"

Cooper nodded. "Yes. Six months now. I'm doing okay. Busy but okay."

"Yes, yes, I've been following the news. Dreadful thing that happened last November. Dreadful. They're sentencing him tomorrow, aren't they?"

"It's the verdict tomorrow," Cooper said, not really wanting to think about The Tarot Card Killer right now. "Sentencing is usually straight after, but the judge might delay. We'll have to wait and see."

He nodded and looked at his notes. "So, today's plan, Erica, is to have a mammogram, an ultrasound, and we'll take some blood to run a few tests. He paused and tapped his pen on the desk for a few moments. "I think we'll book you in with one of our dieticians, too. I don't have to ask you to pop on the scales to know you're still underweight, and I'd have expected substantially more hair growth by now."

Instinctively, Cooper's palms went to her scalp. She ran her fingers through the super short strands. "Oh, this?" she said. "This is a choice. Turns out I actually like it short."

Dr McDermott's face brightened. "Yes, I can see why."

"And it certainly saves time. No drying, brushing, straightening..."

The doctor, who happened to be bald as a coot, ran his left hand over his head. "I quite agree. Though my hairstyle is not through choice, it's through age." He chuckled. "Now, tell me, have you noticed any changes such as redness or swelling?"

Cooper shook her head.

"Any dimpling or changes to texture?"

"No."

"Any discharge or pain?"

Cooper shook her head again. "No, nothing that I've noticed."

"And you examine yourself regularly?"

"Yes," she said, though if she were honest with herself, she didn't do it as often or as thoroughly as she should.

"Good, good. Right, let's take some blood and then Alexa here will walk you to the radiographers for a mammogram."

Cooper rolled up her left sleeve. She was wearing a white shirt, and her first thought was that she didn't want to get bloodstains on it.

Dr McDermott tied a band around her arm and readied a needle. "I suppose you're used to the sight of blood in your profession. I don't expect you to faint."

Cooper gave an empty laugh. "You'd be surprised, doctor. Detectives aren't as hardened to the sight of gore as you'd expect. If you don't mind, I'll stare out the window while you stab me."

"No problem at all," he replied. "You'll feel a small scratch."

You'll feel a small scratch was bullshit. Cooper had been a human pincushion during her treatment, and a *small scratch* always felt like someone shoving a needle into her, which of course, they were.

It wasn't until Dr McDermott said, "There, all done," and he'd popped a cotton pad over the ruby droplet forming over the puncture site that Cooper turned her head away from the window. He took a few inches of micropore tape and secured the cotton pad in place. "Now, Erica." He sat back in his chair and folded his hands in his lap. "Do you have any questions? Is there anything you're concerned about?"

"No," she answered him. In her head, however, she had a million concerns. She didn't understand how a nineteen-year-old girl could vanish without a trace and her double wash up on a beach. She was worried Hutchins would somehow be found not guilty and would begin roaming the streets again. She was concerned about Tennessee, his wife and their beautiful baby boy. Insecurities told her Tina hadn't fully forgiven her, and part of her wondered if she'd ever find a way of balancing her daughter's needs with her career. Dark thoughts kept swirling in her mind until Dr McDermott broke the silence.

"Excellent. You know you can call us anytime if you're worried about anything or have questions." He reached a hand over the desk and Cooper shook it. "Take it easy. Don't overdo it."

Cooper let out a more genuine laugh. "I don't always have a choice, doctor. There's never a quiet day at CID."

Alexa showed Cooper back into the airy atrium and guided her towards the rooms used for mammograms. Being in the building made Cooper feel sick. Her body felt like she was back in chemo. It wasn't the doctors or nurses or the volunteers who fundraised in the gift shop. Everyone here was lovely. The facility was famous for its high level of cancer care. It was simply Pavlovian. The building itself made her feel ill.

Once the door was closed, Cooper removed her upper garments. She knew the drill. She adjusted herself in front of the machine and the upper plate lowered onto the top of her breast. It wasn't painful, but it was uncomfortable and Cooper would ache for a few hours afterwards. Once the radiographer had taken her x-rays, Cooper dressed and was moved on for her ultrasound, where she needed to undress again. She lay down and a cold gel was applied. As she stared at the ceiling, Cooper had a nagging doubt. She was ninety per cent sure her results would come back clear, but the remaining ten per cent was playing havoc with her. She hated the thought of taking more sick leave and being out of the game. And what about Tina? She was becoming a young woman; she should be enjoying her life, not caring for her mother. And, God, what if she died? Cooper was still in her mid-thirties; death wasn't something a normal thirty-something had to consider. What would Tina do? Would she move in with Kenny? Or, go to the Canaries and live with her grandparents? Cooper had no idea what the school, college and university standards were like in Lanzarote, or if there even was a university. It was a morbid thought, but she should probably plan for it. It had been foolish of her not to plan last year.

The sonographer handed Cooper a paper towel to remove the excess gel. "I'll finish my notes and hand them to Dr McDermott. Your results will be ready in a day or two. You should expect a call."

Cooper indicated that she had heard and began to pull her bra and shirt back on, careful not to disturb the padding on her arm. She thanked Alexa as she left and began the walk back to the sixth floor of the car park. She shouldn't feel tired; she'd done very little physical exertion that day, but her stress hormones had leaked into her muscles, and her legs felt like lead.

Up and up she climbed, holding her phone to her ear and listening to the two voicemails she'd received. The first was from Tina, who asked what was for dinner because she could call into Co-op on the way home from the library and pick up the tortellini they both liked. The girl was an angel.

She paused on the fifth floor to listen to the second message. This one from Fuller.

"Erica, it's Neil. Nixon said I should keep you in the loop so you don't feel you need to keep poking about. His words. Anyway, three things. First, the hair grip in the landlord's bathroom wasn't Macey's. Second, I have to meet with the Gallaghers tomorrow. Wish me luck. Christ, it's going to be a nightmare. And three, Macey's phone was switched back on."

Cooper's heart jolted. She grabbed the handrail.

"We have the coordinates. We're moving in on a flat in Byker. Rented by Tennessee's favourite waste of space, Mitch Logan."

Cooper almost had a heart attack. What the fuck was Mitch Logan, the pigeon-chested, toe rag of a dealer doing with Macey Gallagher's phone? She pocketed her phone. She wanted to make calls, ask questions and get answers, but it was after six and her daughter came first. She was going home to eat pasta, catch up with Tina and be grateful for being alive. Pushing open the door to the rooftop car park, Cooper filled her lungs with fresh air and looked at the sky which had an almost imperceptible hint of dusky pink to it. She wiped her still sweaty palms on her trousers and fished in her pockets for her car keys.

"Boo."

Cooper jumped. She turned to see who was behind her, but before she could do so, her arms were pinned to her sides and she was being manhandled towards a Ford Connect. She jerked her body right and left, thrusting her head backwards in an attempt to head-butt her assailant. It was useless. He was too tall. Her head only banged against his chest. She tried to scream, but just as in her nightmares, no sound escaped her mouth. She could only manage weak gasping noises. One of his arms was long enough to hold her still, and as she finally found her voice, his free hand pressed a cloth to her face.

Ether, she could smell ether. Panic filled her and she held her breath, kicking the back of her heels into his shins as he continued to push her forward. Her left shoe fell to the tarmac. Her body spasmed as she fought against her instincts to breathe. She shook her head, trying to angle for fresh air but only inhaling more anaesthetic. "No! No!" The chloroform took hold and darkness moved in. She tried to fight once more, one last feeble kick of her foot and desperate jolt of her head. Her eyes closed and the Ford's door clicked into place.

- CHAPTER 22 -

SAM SUTHERLAND LOOSENED HIS belt a notch as he waited outside a flat in Byker. He must start that diet soon. For all his well-intended promises to Sue, he still hadn't shifted even a single pound since they'd had their little chat. His wife was a fine-looking woman: slim and toned. She looked after herself with regular trips to the hairdressers and he knew there'd been the odd bit of filler here and the odd Botox injection there. But her body, that was all-natural. She ate her five portions of fruit and vegetables per day, never snacked between meals, never ate pudding and was in the gym at six thirty every Tuesday and Thursday morning. He didn't think he was in any danger of losing her. He knew she loved him, but he wasn't so sure that she was attracted to him any more. He didn't blame her. His coping mechanism for stress was to eat his feelings. He could always drown his sorrows in chocolate cake or a multi-pack of crisps, and boy did he have some sorrows and stresses.

The diet starts right now, he told himself. Sue had been quite clear that they should set a good example for Caroline. After her school had been the target of a serial killer last year, he'd seen some of the same behaviours in his daughter. He'd seen the empty chocolate bar wrappers she'd tried to hide in the bathroom bin. They'd moved her to a new school, a posh one in a good end of town and hoped that she'd feel safer there. They had good security, and the staff were vetted to the highest standards. He fastened the button on his jacket so he didn't have to look at his gut. Caroline meant the world to him. If he gave himself a heart attack, he wouldn't be able to provide for Sue or keep Caroline safe. They deserved a better version of Sam Sutherland and he would deliver it to them. Screw it. Tonight, he would do the unthinkable. He would go for a bike ride.

Neil Fuller marched Mitch Logan out of the front door. Mitch wore nothing but a white vest, a pair of Y-fronts that used to be white but were now grey, and some pink flip-flops.

"I asked him to get dressed," said Fuller. "Asked him three times, but he refused, so he's coming to the station like this."

Sutherland opened the back door to his BMW and shielded Mitch's head as he sat down and slid along the back seat.

"This is bullshit," Mitch muttered as Sutherland closed the door.

Fuller rolled his eyes dramatically. "Says he doesn't know anything about Macey Gallagher. Claims he's never even heard of her. Doesn't watch the news, apparently."

"What about the phone?"

"He says he bought the phone off - and I quote - some bloke down the boozer with a glass eye and a gimpy leg."

"This gimpy-legged bloke have a name?"

Fuller shook his head. "Not that he's telling me. We'll ask him again when we get him back to the station. All he's given me is that it was a bargain at fifty quid."

Two minutes ago a uniform had emerged with the Huawei and plugged it into an extraction device. The data would be ready for them to examine as soon as they got back to HQ, not that there would be anything of use. There was no way an idiot like Mitch Logan was involved in this. He couldn't get away with kidnapping. Mitch was the dumbest criminal south of the border. He'd claim the British title if it weren't for some Scottish halfwit who, after killing his wife, forgot to destroy his computer. His search history included, *how to hide a body*, and *how to dismember a body*. In his notes, he had a list of equipment he'd need, including plastic sheeting and a powered handsaw. His GPS tracked him travelling to the nearest B&Q, where he was seen on CCTV buying said plastic sheeting and powered handsaw and paying for them with his debit card. Mitch Logan wasn't quite at that level of stupid, but he wasn't far off. Sutherland knew he wasn't their man.

ONLY FOUR STREETS AWAY, DS Paula Keaton's excitement levels rose as she stared at the monitor. The cameras at the climbing centre had captured Omar Ali leaving Byker Metro station and walking in the direction of Kendal Street. So far, this investigation had been like the build-up to an important game: slow and methodical. But now the whistle had been blown, and the chase was on.

Omar stopped a few paces from the station and bent over to tie his shoelaces. After a few seconds, he stood upright and walked to his left. Behind him, a man called out, approached and said something to Omar. Omar pointed further down the street and signalled right and then left as if giving directions. Keaton watched the man give him a thumbs up in thanks. He checked the directions by mimicking Omar's gestures, then walked with him in the direction Omar had indicated. They left the camera's field of vision.

Keaton slapped her hands together and commandeered the footage. She called Cooper but she didn't pick up. She left a message and told her she'd see her in the morning. Leaning in closer so her upturned nose was a mere inch from the screen, she squinted at the man. He was taller than Omar by about six inches and was slim or athletic in build. It was hard to tell as he was wearing a padded coat. He definitely wasn't overweight. His arms and legs were covered and he wore a dark baseball cap which cast most of his face into shadow. From what Keaton could see of his hands and face she thought he was probably white. Who was he?

Nexus had provided footage from the cameras inside the Metro car Omar had been travelling on. She had taken a cursory glance through it and no one had approached or bothered Omar during his journey. No one had stood too close or appeared to be overly interested in him. But now she had a hat and coat to look out for. Her first task in the morning was to find the mysterious man on the Metro footage and try to get a better image of him. The Metro cars were well illuminated and would have better quality footage.

"Right, you bastard," she said, pointing at the grainy image of the man. "I'm going to find you." She looked at her watch. It was quarter past seven at night. She'd be in the office by seven a.m. "Start running, shithead. I'll give you a twelve-hour head start."

"Oh good, you're awake."

Cooper was stirring. She felt drowsy and disorientated; her mouth was dry and she could feel a draught on her skin. Her feet were icy cold.

"Where are my shoes?" she mumbled, still dazed. A weight pressing down on her clavicles caused her pain and made her hands rush to her neck. The metal slave collar was cool, heavy and tight. Cooper's eyes sprung open and she clawed at the edges of the terrifying thing around her neck. She searched for a release button, a catch, or a weak spot. She found none.

A thick metal chain was attached to the collar via a D-ring. Cooper's hands followed it to the wall where it was drilled into a breeze block. She thrashed at it, pulling the chain with both hands, wrapping it around her arm for a better grip as she threw her weight away from the wall, hoping to free herself.

"Careful you don't tire yourself out," came a drawling voice from the darkness. "You'll need your energy for later."

Cooper's breath came in short, sharp gasps. She could feel her vocal cords seizing up with fear. She tried her best to keep the surging panic at bay, but it hit her like a spring tide. At that moment she realised she was not only restrained, but she was naked.

She kicked at the floor, her bare heels bruising against the concrete as she backed herself into the corner of the room. She pulled her knees as tight to her chest as she could, one arm hugging them and the other fighting relentlessly at the collar around her neck.

"Relax," came the voice. "I don't want your body. Not in that way, anyway. You know, it's quite interesting having a female here; all my other pets have been males."

"I'm not your pet," she snapped.

"The female form is very different to that of the male. You're much smaller, weaker, too. You carry less muscle, but your waist-to-hip ratio isn't as pronounced as I would have expected."

Cooper looked around the room, trying to grasp where she was being held. A single spotlight illuminated her corner of the room. The rest was in darkness. She estimated one wall to be approximately ten feet. She had no idea of the other dimensions. Fluorescent tube lights were fixed to the ceiling, but they were switched off. Sheets of foam padding, shaped into peaks that reminded Cooper of the bottom of egg cartons, covered the breeze block walls.

"Where am I?" She demanded.

"Oh, darling. Isn't it obvious? You're in the doghouse." He chuckled and the sound of his laugh gave him away.

"Bryce Morton." It wasn't a question. It was a statement. She knew who her captor was. "Where am I?" she asked again, forcing a brave tone to her voice that she did not feel inside.

"I told you. You're in the—"

"No. Not the doghouse. Where am I? What part of the city? What part of the country? Am I even in Newcastle? How long was I unconscious?"

"So many questions. You need patience. You'll get to explore your surroundings later when I take you for your walk. I hope you walk better than my last pet did. He did not walk nicely at all."

"Why me?"

There was a shuffling as Morton moved in the shadows. "Because you were getting too close."

"Why Omar?"

"No family, no friends. No one was going to go looking for him."

"Was Omar the first?"

"Oh goodness, no. There have been others."

Cooper's mind raced through missing person cases. "How many others?" she asked.

"My favourite pet was Benji," he continued, ignoring her question. "He was such a good boy. A border collie. I trained him myself when I was just eight years old. He was my best friend. My only friend really. The other children at school didn't like me; they thought I was an oddball and wouldn't play with me. But every day I'd come home, my face streaked with tears, and Benji would be pleased to see me." His voice was soft as he reminisced about his childhood pet.

"What happened to Benji?" asked Cooper. She was stuck in this prison with a madman, but she hoped that in talking to him she could understand him and perhaps put herself at an advantage.

There was a deep, sorrowful sigh. "My father was a hard man. I was always a disappointment. He wanted a son who could box and play football, who he'd be proud to take to the match or down the social club on a Sunday after the game. But I was a gentle boy. I prefer books to sports. He'd get so mad, finding me with my head in a comic. Benji never got mad at me."

"Bryce," Cooper's voice was cautious. "Did your father hurt Benji?"

"One day, he came home in a foul mood. I hid in my room, but I could hear him yelling at Mother. He was drunk and slurring and slamming things."

Cooper heard him sniff. "I couldn't hear what he was saying, but I heard Mother scream when he struck her."

"That must have been awful."

"Then Father dragged me from my room and said he didn't have a job any more and that he could barely afford to keep me, let alone the dog. He told me to walk as far as possible and lose Benji. Make sure he didn't follow me home."

"That's terrible." Although Cooper was terrified and hated talking to shadows, she somehow sympathised with Morton's childhood self.

"I pleaded, but he beat me with his belt. Then I wandered the streets for hours in the rain until it got dark. It took all night to lose Benji. He didn't want to leave my side. He loved me, you see. He was a loyal friend."

He appeared to be softening. Cooper hoped that boded well for her. She knew childhood trauma played out in adult life. Usually, it affected a person's relationships, such as how they communicate or how deeply they trust. She'd never witnessed or read of a case like this though. She suspected he was trying to recapture the days of his kinship with Benji through the bizarre means of kidnap.

"Bryce, you're an adult now. Why don't you get another dog?"

"I have you."

That turned Cooper's stomach but she tried to continue. "No. I mean a real dog, like Benji. Maybe even another collie? If you untie me, I could take you to a rescue centre I know."

"Mother won't let me have a real dog. She says I was too upset after Benji."

"But you don't need your mother's permission, Bryce. You're a—"

"No." His voice was firm, and it scared Cooper. "I have you. I don't need another pet as long as I have you." He took two steps forward and was, for the first time, illuminated in the spotlight. He wore a padded Barbour jacket and heavy walking boots, and most concerning, in his left hand, he twirled a pair of silver scissors with pointed blades. "Are you thirsty?"

Cooper wanted to say no, but she couldn't deny her dry mouth and fatigued body. She nodded to say yes. There was an awful screeching noise as something was pushed along the concrete floor by Morton's foot. To Cooper's horror, it was a metal dog bowl filled with water. She hesitated, but her thirst was too much. She picked up the bowl and brought it to her lips, only for Morton to snatch it back, spilling water over her face and left shoulder.

He slapped her cheek. "Bad dog! The bowl stays on the floor."

Rubbing her cheek, Cooper looked up at him. "If you think for one second, I'm drinking off the floor..."

"Please yourself." Morton placed the bowl out of reach before returning to her, cupping her chin in his hand and stroking her head. She swiped his hand away with more force than she knew she was capable of, and certainly more force than was wise in this situation. "Feisty," he said with a yellow smile. "I don't usually like it when my pets have an attitude," he paused, "but it does make it more entertaining when it's time to put them down."

A scream caught in Cooper's throat, but her mind returned to sitting in Deanna Morton's kitchen and a question she knew better than to ask formed at her mouth. "How... How did your father die?"

Morton took a step back. "Officially? He died in a house fire."

"And," her voice shook, "unofficially?"

"He was the first pet I had after Benji. He didn't seem so big and scary once I was fully grown. It was easy. It only seemed right after what he did to Benji. I wasn't kind to him, though. I'll be kind to you as long as you behave. Will you behave?"

Cooper's eyes bulged as she tried to take in as much of the situation as possible. She nodded.

"Good." He sighed. "I thought about taking Father to the woods so he'd get lost and feel abandoned like Benji. I should have done it that way. It would have been more fitting. I kept him for a week until I got bored with him, then I held him over the bath and slit his throat. When the blood stopped dripping, I dragged him to his bed, lit a cigarette and put it in his hands. Mother always used to warn him about smoking in bed, but he'd never listen."

How he spoke so casually about killing his father made it all the more real to Cooper that he'd have no qualms about killing her.

"What time is it?" It may have seemed a strange question, but the windows were boarded up; she didn't know if it was day or night, or how long she'd been unconscious, or how far she'd been transported. Would Tina, Justin or Kenny have realised she was missing by now? She hadn't told anyone about her appointment at the hospital, so the police wouldn't know where to begin looking for clues. *Typical, bloody stupid, Erica Cooper,* she chastised herself. *Keeping things to yourself and not wanting to bother or worry anyone and now look where you are. Chained up like an animal and at the mercy of a madman.*

Morton checked his watch. "I'd say it's dinner o'clock. Here you go." He pushed the scissors into a pocket, emptied a pouch of Tesco own brand dog food into a separate bowl and slid it across to Cooper with his foot. "I'll be back later for your walk. Mother's expecting me for dinner." He fished some keys from his other pocket and jangled them in his hand. He approached the wall and turned on a small electric heater. It hummed as it came to life. "If you're still cold, there's a blanket to your left. Oh, and don't bother screaming. I had this place soundproofed."

Shivering uncontrollably, Cooper reached for the blanket and wrapped it around her shoulders. Morton unlocked each of the bolts and padlocks that secured the door and turned back to Cooper. He gave her an appraising look, then pulled a cord attached to the ceiling. There was a click, and the spotlight went out.

- CHAPTER 23 -

JUSTIN ATKINSON HAD SUFFERED a long day. It started at dawn when he dragged himself out of bed for a morning run along Whitley Bay beach. He put in a good seven miles and hated every step before showering and heading off to work. Work that day consisted of a morning in the labs to examine the samples Margot had sent from the Freeman following the mystery girl's autopsy. In the afternoon, he'd been squatting in the rain, sifting through the remains of a gruesome pile-up on the A686 involving an articulated lorry and three cars carrying six children between them. There were five deaths, three of which were children. The deaths of children always hit him particularly hard, and he was grateful each day that his sons were fit, healthy and living life to the fullest.

Atkinson was painfully aware that his striking girlfriend hadn't returned his text messages all day. It was understandable. She was under a lot of pressure from that berk of a superintendent to crack her current case and make himself look better in the eyes of the good people of Tyneside, Wearside and Northumberland. But now the workday had ended and he still hadn't heard from Cooper. He donned his favourite jeans and a smart shirt, dabbed some aftershave on his neck and went in search of the Wine Chambers and a beautiful bottle of Valpolicella. They hadn't argued much of late, but Atkinson feared she was slipping away from him. Cooper was cool, far cooler than he was, though she'd never say it or even think it. She wore leather jackets and rocked out to bands he'd never heard of. She was happiest being tossed about a mosh pit, and he was happiest with a glass of brandy, a knitted jumper and a good book.

It was dark when Atkinson walked up Cooper's driveway. He rang the doorbell and was surprised when Tina answered the door.

"Hi, Justin," She said in her quiet voice. "Mum didn't say you were coming over." Her natural curls were held back in a bun by a couple of pencils. She had ink on her lip, and in her left hand, she held a copy of Astrophysics For People In A Hurry.

Atkinson apologised for dropping in unannounced; Tina wasn't a fan of the unexpected. He held up the bottle of wine, "Thought I'd surprise her." Then he held up a chocolate bar, "And for you, the future of British science."

Tina smiled and took the chocolate. She stood aside and let Atkinson in. "Thanks, Justin. Mum's not home yet, but you know you're welcome to wait. I've just put Steven to bed and was going to watch Stranger Things; I have a few episodes to catch up on."

Atkinson's brows lowered, and he looked at his watch. "Your mum's not home? It's gone nine."

He was concerned. If Cooper was ever late, she had Kenny watch Tina. She didn't like to leave her alone for too long after the events of last winter.

"Really?" Tina looked at her phone. A look of amazement formed on her face. "Wow. That's late even by Mum's standards."

"Have you called her?"

Tina scrunched up her face. "I texted her earlier to see if she wanted tortellini. She didn't reply, but these days, she doesn't always."

There was a moment of awkward silence as they both remembered Tina's outburst from dinner the other night.

Atkinson reached into his pocket, pulled out his mobile and called Cooper. It went straight to voicemail. He sat at the kitchen table while Tina made him a cup of turmeric tea and told him how she'd had to get Steven a bigger box as he'd grown so much under her care. After ten minutes, he called Cooper again. Still no answer. She could be on an important call, or her phone may have run out of juice. Atkinson didn't want to be the sort of boyfriend who checked up on his woman every time she didn't answer the phone but Cooper wasn't the sort of woman who left her fourteen-year-old unsupervised at this time of the evening. He paused for a moment, then called Paula Keaton.

WHEN BRYCE MORTON LOCKED the door behind him, Cooper sat frozen, waiting for the sound of the Ford Connect to start up and drive away. When no sound came, she put it down to the soundproofing. She counted to one hundred, then burst into action. She grabbed the chain that attached her to the wall and heaved with all her might, trying to tear it from its fixing. It was no use. She pushed her bare feet against the wall and yanked at the chain until it nipped at the skin on her palms. Blood blisters formed and seeped their warm liquid down her hands.

She pinched her fingernails against the screws, trying to loosen them but they were fastened tightly. She pushed her thumbnail in the groove of one screw and twisted, breaking her thumbnail down to the raw flesh that had never been exposed to air before. She tried the padlock that secured the collar to her neck, but the result was, excruciatingly, the same.

Cooper must have thrashed like a horse that refused to be tamed for over an hour. Eventually, she collapsed and began to cry. She cried angry tears for less than a minute, but it was enough time to release the pent-up fear and frustration that gripped her. It was time to focus.

She lifted the water bowl and drank all she could, hoping and praying that Morton hadn't laced the water with poison or sleeping pills, then she moved the bowls to one side and crawled around her surroundings. The room was dark, save for a dot of light coming through a keyhole in the door and an orange light indicating the electric heater was turned on. She found the blanket and wrapped it around her bare shoulders, tucking the edges under the collar to protect her neck from the weight of it. Her fingers crept along the floor, finding a magazine that she couldn't read in the dark. She prized the staples from the spine and stored them in her mouth. They had little use as weapons unless she could stab them into Morton's eyes. She was desperate, and it was an option.

Her best hope was to find her phone, but she doubted Morton was stupid enough to have brought it here. It had probably been switched off and tossed from the van's window. Still, she searched in the blackness until the sound of a key in the door made her insides turn to ice. She had time for one quick movement before Morton entered the room.

"How's my favourite girl?"

"JACK. I'M SORRY, I know this is shitty timing, but have you seen Cooper? I think something's happened to her."

Tennessee was in a dressing gown and slippers. He held baby Alfie to his chest and moved aside to let Keaton into his hallway.

She wiped her boots on the mat. "How's Haley? How are you?"

"She's sleeping. I'm... coping. What's going on?" He bounced the baby gently, making cooing noises and planting light kisses on his head.

"She hasn't been seen since shortly after one this afternoon."

Tennessee carefully manoeuvred Alfie and lifted his sleeve to take a look at his watch.

"She was following up on the cases you two shortlisted. She told me she had something to take care of this evening but didn't tell me what. Atkinson doesn't know where she is. Tina hasn't heard from her since this morning, and her ex, Kenny, he's none with wiser."

An older woman with long, silver curls and reading glasses poked her head around the doorframe to the living room. "Jack?"

"Mum, this is Paula, my colleague."

"Nice to meet you, dear," she said with a glance that swept over Keaton from head to toe.

"Mum, I need to go out. Can you hold the fort?"

She looked concerned. "Jack, Hayley—"

"Hayley's asleep. I'm sorry. It's important." He handed her the baby, kissed him on the head again and kissed his mother on the cheek. "I'll stay in touch. I promise."

Keaton waited in her car while Tennessee changed out of his dressing gown. She needed to stay calm and think rationally but was beginning to fret. Cooper could go rogue occasionally, going dark if Nixon was overseeing her work so closely she felt smothered or if she didn't have time to wait for the relevant paperwork and permissions. This was out of character though; she would usually divulge any plan to her or Tennessee. Where could she be?

Tennessee slid into the passenger seat. "Who else knows?"

"Nixon. He's putting a team together. I'm to brief them as soon as I get to HQ."

"Do you think it's connected to our case?"

Keaton pulled away while Tennessee was still fiddling with his seatbelt. The dark streets were emptying and traffic was light. "Maybe. There's the Gallagher case, too. She was still looking into that one. But let's be honest, mate, Cooper's put some dodgy people away in her time. There'll be some folk out there with vendettas against her."

"Right." Tennessee lowered the visor and checked his reflection in the vanity mirror. He tutted and tried to tame his hair. "First things first, we need to follow the breadcrumbs. Work out where she's been and who she's seen. I'll make a list of everyone involved in the shortlisted cases involving collars and scissors. We can take it from there."

Keaton's hands clenched around the steering wheel as she shifted lanes.

Morton closed the door behind him and padded around in the dark, the sound of his footsteps only slightly louder than the sound of Cooper's heartbeat. She swallowed, using her tongue to pin the staples she'd found to the roof of her mouth. In her hands, she held her only chance. She had to get this right.

"Are you ready for your walk?" he asked. Cooper estimated him to be two metres away. She needed him to be closer.

He took two steps. "I said—"

Now, she told herself. *Now or never.*

The three prongs of the plug dug painfully into her palms as she swung the electric heater with all her might. There was a whooshing noise as it missed Morton the first time but not the second. The heater crashed into his temple with an almighty thump, his knees buckled, and he crumpled to the floor. Cooper could barely see him. He was a black blur on a floor of darkest grey. His shoulder twitched. He was still conscious but only just. Cooper didn't have much time. She grabbed him by the ankles and dragged him closer to her. She pounced on his body, turning him face down and binding his hands behind his back with the electrical cord.

She patted him down like airport security, searching for his keys. When she found them, she tried each key in the padlock that held the collar around her neck. None of them worked. Tears began to spill down her face again. If this plan failed, she would surely be Morton's next victim. She took the keyring and tried the keys in the padlock that held the chain to the wall.

Success. The key fitted but was stiff and wouldn't turn. "No. Come on," she pleaded. Below her, Morton began to stir.

She tried to force the key but could feel it beginning to bend. Cooper tried to calm herself and gently jimmied the key back and forth, her hands slippy with blood and shuddering with adrenaline. The lock sprung apart. She was free. Cooper grabbed the blanket and wrapped it around her naked frame. She didn't dare stop to look for her clothes or phone. Morton was deceptively strong and could free himself at any moment. She burst from the door to Morton's compound and tried to get her bearings. She planted her feet for a moment and looked around what appeared to be an industrial lot. The sound of a car engine caught her, and she sprinted in its direction. She sprinted as fast as she could in bare feet, cursing every time her ankle rolled or her skin ripped against stones and pebbles.

"Please," she screamed. "PLEASE STOP!"

Cooper ran into the road, waving her arms and letting the heavy chain drag and clatter behind her. Her blanket wouldn't stay fastened; she was partly exposed in the moonlight. It didn't matter. What mattered was that the car would stop. It had to stop. She ran further into the road, blocking its path and as the car screeched to a halt, Cooper collapsed on its bonnet.

"Police. DCI Cooper, Northumbria CID. I need your vehicle," she demanded of the driver.

He was a pale man, sporting a flat cap above a lined brow. His concerned gaze wandered over Cooper, and she knew she looked like a lunatic.

"DCI Cooper. Northumbria CID," she repeated. "Where am I?"

Behind the windshield, he spoke with a thick Geordie accent. "Sandy Lane."

Cooper stopped and looked around. She knew exactly where she was.

"What— What happened? What's with the chain?"

Cooper didn't think he'd believe her even if she told him. "I need your vehicle. Call the police. Tell them I need assistance apprehending a suspect."

The man cautiously got out of his car. "I think I need to take you to hospital, miss. You're bleeding."

"No." She wobbled and placed her hands on his shoulders. "Killer. Dangerous man." Her voice shook. "Dangerous. We need— Call the police."

Her legs gave way.

- Chapter 24 -

Two hospitals in two days. It was Good Friday, and from what Cooper could tell, it was a beautiful spring morning. She could see a perfect blue sky and every time the wind blew, a branch covered in pink and white blossom moved across the window. She longed to be outside, basking in the fresh air and soaking up vitamin D. Instead, she was trapped in the Royal Victoria Infirmary. Her wounds had been cleaned and a doctor had checked her for signs of shock. He was happy for Cooper to go home, but the ward sister refused to discharge her until the slave collar had been removed from her neck. A locksmith had been called but so far he was a no-show and the longer the collar remained on, the more claustrophobic Cooper felt.

At some point during the night, a ginormous bunch of roses arrived and a nurse had placed them in a vase with some water. They smelled heavenly and Cooper couldn't wait to thank Justin. She'd given him and Kenny strict instructions to look after Tina and under no circumstances let her visit Cooper while she still had the metal monstrosity fastened to her neck.

"Knock, knock."

Cooper knew Tennessee's voice anywhere. "Come in, Jack."

Tennessee peaked around the curtain before entering Cooper's little corner of the ward. He didn't look as rested as she would have liked, but his posture had straightened, and some colour had returned to his cheeks.

"Bloody hell." His eyes swept over the collar and to a yellowing bruise on Cooper's cheek. "May I?" he gestured to the collar.

"Knock yourself out."

Tennessee examined the lock and felt the metal with his fingertips. "Fuck. This thing weighs a tonne. Is this what he used on Omar?"

"Yeah. And who knows who else? He said there had been others."

He shook his head in disbelief. "Freak. I spoke to Nixon. He wants you to take some time off."

Cooper snorted. "Nixon? *Howard Nixon?* As in, our boss Howard Nixon?"

"Yes, that Nixon. Come on, you know deep down he cares. I mean... really, really, really deep down."

"There's work to be done."

"There's recovery to be done."

Cooper let out a reluctant huff. He was right, and Cooper wasn't averse to being told what to do by her sergeant, not when he was right.

"Here," he said, holding up a bag. "I called at your place. Atkinson dug out some clothes for you. Didn't think you'd want to go home in a hospital gown."

Cooper took the bag and Tennessee moved to the other side of the curtain while she buttoned up a shirt and pulled on a pair of leggings. From behind the curtain, he added, "Someone handed your phone in at the Freeman. No sign of your handbag, though."

"Shit. Oh, well, at least I have my phone. I'll cancel my cards. You can come back in now."

Tennessee threw the curtain back. "Ma'am—Coop, They said it was handed into the Centre for Cancer Care. Erm, you can tell me to mind my own beeswax, but is everything all right?"

"Everything's fine. Just my six-month check." Cooper didn't know if everything was fine or not. She'd call the centre in a couple of days to find out the results, but she didn't want Tennessee worrying in the meantime. "Now, shall we get down to business?" She nodded at the chair next to the bed. Tennessee took a seat.

"You're on the sick," he said.

"And you're starting to push your luck. What's the latest?"

"Morton's done a runner. He's not at his home, his mother's home, or the industrial unit he rents next to Weetslade. There's an all ports warning out for his arrest, and ANPR are tracing his mother's Qashqai in case she knows where he is and decides to pay him a visit. The Ford Connect wasn't in his name. It's registered to the man who rents the next unit down. Keaton's grilling him as we speak."

Cooper nodded and adjusted some pads of cotton wool that she'd placed under the collar to stop it from hurting so much.

"Oh, and you're under protection until Morton's caught." Tennessee flinched in anticipation.

"What? I'm not going to be babysat. Who gave that order? Nixon? Give me my phone, I'll sort this out—"

"Actually, I gave the order, and Nixon agreed. I'm to stay with you until the cavalry arrive. You shouldn't have been chasing James Blake and Bryce Morton alone. I should have been with you."

"It wouldn't have made a difference, Jack," she said to appease his ill-placed guilt. "He grabbed me at the hospital."

"I know, but if I'd been with you the past couple of days, you would have told me where you were going, and then the alarm would have been raised sooner."

Cooper rubbed a clammy hand over her face. "I didn't tell anyone, Jack. And you had better not be feeling in some way responsible. Your priority is not me. Your priority is Hayley and Alfie, and it always should be, okay?"

He lifted his chin to acknowledge the point and looked away.

She nudged his arm and held out her open hand. "I'd still like my phone."

Light returned to Tennessee's face as he handed over her mobile. She ignored the umpteen missed calls and texts and dialled Fuller's number. "Hey, it's me. What happened with Mitch Logan? Yes, I'm fine...Yes, I know I'm supposed to be resting."

Cooper could hear the clinking of crockery in the background. "We arrested him. Sutherland and I spent all night interviewing him. He denies ever meeting Macey. Says he bought the phone from a man in the pub."

Cooper rolled her eyes. "Of course he did."

"Well, we have a name and Sutherland and a couple of uniforms are bringing him in. We'll soon find out."

Cooper hung up and filled Tennessee in on Fuller's half of the conversation until a worried-looking Atkinson turned up with a uniformed officer who saluted and positioned himself at the entrance to the ward.

"That would be my babysitter," said Cooper. "Get yourself home, Jack. Enjoy Good Friday. Go via the fish quay. It's not Good Friday without fish and chips."

"And mushy peas," he added, getting to his feet and shaking Atkinson's hand. "I'm going to nip over to intensive care first. Omar's awake."

"Really?" Cooper's face burst with emotion. She sat up in the bed. "That's brilliant."

"He's still in a bad way, so I'm not going to press him on giving a statement just yet. But I'll let him know that we know who hurt him and that we're after him."

Tennessee left, and Atkinson flooded Cooper with kisses and inspected her head to toe. "Oh, Erica," he said, tears in his eyes as he tugged at the collar. "Haven't they got this thing off you yet?"

"A locksmith's on his way. Apparently. I'd rather wait for him than have the fire brigade cut me out of it."

Atkinson slid into bed next to her and peppered her with more kisses. "I'm so glad you're safe. I don't know what I would have done..." He was quiet momentarily, squeezing Cooper's hand so tightly it hurt. "I've been an insecure idiot of late, and I'm sorry. It's coming up on my *divorceaversary*." He made air quotes with his fingers. "I haven't been feeling myself. Doesn't help that Elspeth got remarried to that barely-legal Spaniard, and she posted pictures all over Facebook bragging about it. I unfriended her. How juvenile does that sound? But the boys are tagged in all the pictures, so they just keep popping up on my feed. Bloody Elspeth, honestly. He's a step-dad to boys only two years younger than he is."

Cooper didn't resent Atkinson's ranting. In fact, she appreciated the subject matter being something other than what had happened to her last night. She'd given him the basics last night when she'd been telling him to stay with Tina. Obviously, he wanted to know exactly what she'd been through but she was too tired and traumatised to go into any detail. She was glad he was respecting that. She'd speak about it when she was ready.

She rested her head on Atkinson's chest. "Thank you for the flowers, by the way. They're gorgeous."

"Flowers?" Atkinson's head craned around to the side table. "Erm... They are gorgeous, but they're not from me."

"Oh." She paused awkwardly. "I just presumed. The department might have sent them."

"I got you a fridge full of pastries, and there's a bottle of wine on your kitchen bench."

"Even better," smiled Cooper, and she meant it. "You can't drink roses. Now, how about we watch some television while we wait for this locksmith?"

Atkinson pulled the television around, handed Cooper the remote and wrapped his arms around her as they got comfortable.

On the screen, a smartly dressed woman held a microphone to her mouth while chaos erupted behind her. "Amelia Clarkson, reporting from Newcastle Crown Court where The Tarot Card Killer, Brian Hutchins, has been found guilty of four counts of murder and handed a whole life sentence." Behind Amelia, the parents of two of his victims, Jasmine Lee and Reuben Jones, were escorted past a wall of journalists and press photographers. "In his closing comments, Judge Justice Finch addressed Hutchins, saying 'You are an abhorrent individual who preyed upon those whom you stood in a position of power over. You abused their trust, and I believe you should never be eligible for release.' We're told Hutchins will be transported to HMP Frankland within the next few minutes."

- Chapter 25 -

Cooper was bored. Mind-numbingly bored. It was early afternoon on Saturday and Tina had just brought her yet another cup of coffee. She placed the cup on her bedside table along with two chocolate digestives and jumped onto the end of Cooper's bed and sat cross-legged.

"At this point, if you cut me, I'll bleed pure caffeine."

Tina looked hurt.

"Sorry, T. Thank you for the coffee. I'm just stir-crazy. There's a lot to be getting on with."

"No, there's not," said Tina. She grabbed a handful of her hair and started twisting it around her forefinger. "The laundry's in, the dishwasher's on, I cleaned the bathroom, fed Steven, I got the shopping in—"

"Jeez, Tina. You don't have to do all that. I'm grateful, but you should be doing your homework, not fussing over me."

"Homework's done. Finished it days ago."

"But I saw you studying last night," Cooper said.

"That was just for fun. I was memorising Latin names for different species of birds. I can recite over sixty now. Want to hear some?"

"I believe you," Cooper said with a laugh. Her daughter was so very different from how she had been at her age, and they had vastly different definitions of the word *fun*. It was hard to believe the six-pound bundle of mayhem that she'd brought into the world was going to be fifteen tomorrow. Where had the years gone? Tina turned Cooper's world upside down when she gave birth at just eighteen years old. She'd been scared, confused and lonely during her pregnancy, but Tina turned out to be the best thing to ever happen to her.

"Can I have a hug?" Cooper asked, feeling nostalgic.

"No," Tina replied. She wasn't being rude. Tina had never been one for too much physical contact, and Cooper had made it clear that she didn't have to make herself uncomfortable so that others wouldn't think she was ill-mannered. "You can have a high-five, though."

"Deal." Cooper sat up and slapped Tina's open palm.

"I'm going to take a shower. Do you need anything?"

Cooper shook her head, and as soon as she heard the hot water running, she jumped out of bed, threw on the first suit she found in her wardrobe and legged it out the front door.

"Ma'am! Ma'am!" The babysitter jumped out of his panda car and rushed towards Cooper.

"It's all right, Northcutt. I'm just running some errands."

Northcutt got to her before she could unlock the car. He was young and tanned and sported a unibrow. "You're not to leave unescorted. Superintendent Nixon's orders."

"I'll be fine, Northcutt. I'll be back within the hour."

"We both know Nixon will have my head if anything happens to you."

She turned her gaze upward and growled at the sky. "Fine. Shall we take your car or mine?"

Northcutt gave the Mazda a scathing look. "We'll take the squad car."

Cooper held out her hand for the keys but the young man just laughed and opened the passenger door. "With all due respect, ma'am. Not a chance." He settled himself into the driver's seat, fastened his seatbelt and asked, "Where to?"

"Frankland," she said. "HMP Frankland."

FRANKLAND, HOME TO SOME of the UK's most notorious serial killers and terrorists, was found eighteen miles south of Newcastle in County Durham, an area otherwise known for its prestigious university, picturesque castle and magnificent cathedral. Northcutt had insisted upon not waiting in the car like Cooper had requested and even threatened to call Nixon if she didn't abide by his rules.

"Have it your way," Cooper said, smoothing down the front of her suit jacket, "but if anyone asks, we were never here."

Cooper considered heading towards the visitor's centre, but she wasn't here to hold hands with a loved one and stare longingly across steaming mugs of tea. She directed Northcutt to the main reception.

"They probably haven't even processed Hutchins yet," he said as he parked the car.

"Who said I was here to see Hutchins?"

Northcutt gave her a searching look but didn't press the matter. Cooper held her ID up to a camera and was buzzed into the building where she was immediately funnelled into a metal detector and then forced to stand very still while a drug detection dog sniffed at her shoes, legs, and awkwardly at her crotch.

"Erica Cooper." A guard spread his arms in a welcoming gesture. "Long time no see."

"Bruiser." She smiled and walked towards the desk once the dog was satisfied she wasn't a cocaine mule. She slid the logbook towards herself and signed her name. "I'd like to see Eddie. Nothing formal, he has every right to say no, but I'd appreciate him speaking with me."

"Eddie?" asked Northcutt. "Eddie Blackburn? Newcastle's answer to Tony Soprano?"

"Who's this?" Bruiser asked, examining Northcutt's ID.

"My babysitter. It's a long story," she said with a shake of her head as she'd rather not get into the whole Bryce Morton stripping her naked, chaining her up and keeping her as a pet thing.

Bruiser closed the logbook, picked up a phone and made a call. "Right," he said after he'd hung up. "Room B. I'll show you the way. Someone's fetching Blackburn."

A few moments later Cooper slid into an orange plastic chair like the ones she used to sit on at school. Northcutt insisted on being in the room so Cooper insisted he sit in the far corner and not to make a peep unless she said so.

"Well, well, well." Eddie Blackburn shuffled in. His hands and feet were shackled. Cooper fought not to let her hand go to her neck as the memory of the collar was still as fresh as her bruises. "If it isn't my favourite copper."

"Who's your second favourite?"

Aside from the similar job description, Blackburn also shared an uncanny resemblance to the Italian-American gangsters of Hollywood and HBO. He was a large, barrel-chested man with dark features and a crease down the middle of his nose.

"There are no second favourites. You, I like. The rest of your kind can go fuck themselves. You're the only reason I struck a deal with the CPS and kept my eldest out of here. The rest of those pigs would have sent my whole family down."

"How is Theo?" asked Cooper as Blackburn struggled into a chair that was far too small for his frame.

The guards who had escorted Blackburn mumbled a few words to Northcutt and left the room.

"He's gone back to school, believe it or not. Enrolled in some adult education classes, business and the like."

"Good for him."

"It's brilliant is what it is. Inspired me to, erm..." he waved his hands around, looking for the right phrase, "better myself. Got a job in the library. Can read all day if I want."

"That's excellent, Eddie. I'm glad to hear it."

"But that's not why you're here, is it? You didn't come for a catch-up with ol' Eddie. You need something? Information?"

Cooper cast an eye over her shoulder at Northcutt, then leant across the table and lowered her voice to a barely audible whisper.

"Macey Gallagher."

"The Irish girl? Pretty young thing?"

"Yes. That's her. You know who took her?"

"Nah. Nothing to do with my lot. You know that's not our style."

"But have you heard anything? Whispers on the grapevine?"

Blackburn shrugged. "Sorry, darling. You know I'd help you out if I could, but no one tells me owt these days."

"I heard Fletcher was running the family business. He tell you anything?"

Blackburn propped his elbows on the table and rested his chin on steepled fingers. "The Blackburns run a taxi firm and a chain of pizzerias.

We're just honest entrepreneurs trying to earn a living in today's competitive climate."

"Yeah. And I'm Kim Kardashian." Cooper sighed and looked to the table in disappointment.

"There's something else." Blackburn's eyebrows peaked in the middle as he read her face and took a butcher's into her soul. "What else did you want to ask me?"

Was she that obvious? Cooper leant even further across the table so she was close enough to smell his prison-issue porridge breakfast and considered the ramifications of what she was about to do. It was out of character, unprofessional, and it was criminal.

"Hutchins," she said.

Excitement flickered in Blackburn's eyes. The corner of his mouth twitched. "You want him killin'?"

Cooper quickly shook her head. "No. And I mean it. No."

"But?"

"My daughter was next. He would have killed her..."

He sat quietly for a moment, his eyes darting back and forth, imagining what he would do if someone harmed his own daughter. Not that anyone would dare. "And you want his stay at this fine, five-star establishment to not be the most comfortable?"

Cooper's hands gripped the edge of the table between her and Blackburn until her knuckles turned white. She wasn't a perfect detective, the sort who never broke the rules or slipped into the grey area between moral and immoral. She was human.

"I want him to know what fear feels like."

Blackburn surveyed her face. She was serious.

"Consider it done."

"WHERE HAVE YOU BEEN?" Tina had a face like a bulldog chewing on a wasp. She was standing on the front step as Cooper and Northcutt pulled up. Her hair was wet from the shower and she was dressed in pyjama bottoms and a vest.

"I just had to nip out, sweetheart. No need to worry?"

"No need to worry?" Tina's voice was so high Copper wondered if all their glassware was about to smash. "You were kidnapped by a madman! Who's still on the loose, I may add."

"It's fine, Tina." Cooper walked past her daughter into the kitchen and poured herself a glass of wine.

"It's NOT fine." Tina's face was red and blotchy, tears were about to spill onto her cheeks. "You, Dad and Josh have made sure I'm accounted for at all times. Never left alone. Escorted here, there, and everywhere. And you know what? It's been a right pain in the arse, but I've gone along with it because I knew it gave you peace of mind... and then..." A tear burst free. Tina wiped it away with closed fists. "And then when something similar happens to you, you just swan off without telling me and it..." Her voice caught in her throat.

"And it was a shitty, selfish thing to do." Cooper's heart melted. "You're right. You're so right. I'm really sorry, T." She held out her arms. Tina moved in for a quick hug before letting go and eyeballing the floor. "Can I make it up to you? It's your birthday tomorrow, how about we start the celebrations early? Invite Josh over. We'll get a takeaway, anything you want."

Tina considered the offer. "Bowling. Me, you and Josh. And a burger afterwards?"

"Absolutely." Cooper laid a coaster over her wine glass. It would keep for later. "The babysitter will have to come too. Call Josh and tell him we'll pick him up in twenty, and if he keeps us waiting, I'll get Northcutt to start the siren."

COOPER HADN'T BEEN TO a bowling alley in years, but it turned out she wasn't too rusty. She bowled three strikes and a handful of spares, but it wasn't enough to beat the teenagers. Josh opened the game with a turkey, and once Tina started applying her knowledge of trigonometry and physics to the activity, no one stood a chance. It was now half eight, and Tina and Josh were in Tina's room watching Netflix, or at least she hoped that's what they were doing; she'd told them to leave the door open but hadn't been upstairs to check. Cooper finally had her glass of wine back in hand and was sat at the kitchen table with her laptop open. She wasn't supposed to do any official work, but she could use Google as much as she liked.

Starting with a simple search relating to Feisty's club, she noted down every skirmish, complaint or newsworthy event she could find. Next, she dove deeper into Nicolas Petite with a little help from Google Translate. Nicolas Petite had been awarded a substantial grant for outstanding academic success. He had hit the local headlines for blowing it all in one hedonistic night of partying that involved buying all his graduating class Champagne and hiring a bunch of strippers - male and female - for his friends' entertainment. The local press had dubbed him irresponsible, ungrateful and a bad role model. Two years ago, he'd been part of a group that climbed Kilimanjaro, raising over twelve thousand Euros in sponsorship, which they used to buy supplies for village schools in the Machame area. Nico's social media was flooded with images of him with smiling, bright-eyed Tanzanian children. Then a headline caught Cooper's eye. *Baker's Son Arrested on Drugs Charges.* Nico had been accused of distributing poppers out of his parents' bakery. According to sources, his classmates would come to the bakery on Saturday mornings when they knew he was working, order a pastry, hand over extra money and Nico would pop the pill into the paper bag along with a mille-feuille or an éclair. The charges were dropped due to lack of evidence.

"Hmm." Cooper had such distaste for Nico Petite she had to take care not to blind her own judgement. Being a drug-dealing drink-spiker did not necessarily mean he was capable of rape, kidnapping, murder or whatever cruel fate had been bestowed upon Macey. He had done a runner to his homeland, the flight manifest confirming he was on the eleven forty AirFrance flight to Paris on the Monday after Macey's disappearance and had so far not reported to his local police station or returned any of Northumbria Police's calls. Cooper cast her mind back through the various statements and pieces of evidence that had been collected so far, the van was playing on her mind. It had been in the camera footage taken from the accountancy firm and the cat café. The sliding door of a van had been near enough to Macey to be captured on the voicemail she left Walker. She braced herself and called Imogen West.

"Yah?"

"Imogen? This is DCI Erica Cooper." Loud music was thumping in the background. Cooper raised her voice. "I need to ask you a couple of questions."

"Now?"

"Yes, now." Cooper could imagine Imogen and Alison seated in a swanky bar waiting for someone to buy them drinks. "Has Nicolas Petite been in contact?"

"No."

"Are you sure? I don't need to remind you of how serious this case is. If you protect him, charges will be made against you."

"I'm sure. I haven't heard a thing. I sent him a few texts but he never replied." Her voice became muffled but Cooper picked up, "No, a double, please. Vodka."

"One last question, Imogen. Does Nico drive? Or have access to a van?"

Cooper thought she heard a snort.

"Nico thinks there are two sorts of people in this world... Thank you, darling. It's Diet Coke, right?... Those who are meant to drive and those who are meant to be driven. You can guess which category he falls into."

Cooper hung up without thanking Imogen. The news Nico didn't drive was disappointing. She'd still check if he was the registered keeper of a van, but her chances weren't good. She dialled another number.

"Erica, it's Saturday night. It's the Easter weekend. This had better be good." Fuller was not amused.

"I'm bored. Humour me."

"Make it quick," he grumbled.

"The bouncer. Tiny, I think his name was. Did you talk to him?"

"Oh, Jesus. Come on, Erica, let it go. After what you've been through—"

"Please, Neil." She sipped her wine and listened to him let out a very long sigh. "Did he mention anyone hanging around the club, or any suspicious vehicles?"

He kept her waiting, sighing again. "Nothing suspicious. Just the usual mix of taxis, Ubers and the Tyne Pastors."

"You mean the Street Pastors?"

"No. It was the Tyne Pastors. Same idea, different uniforms."

"You spoke to them?"

"Yeah. Called them. They had nothing. Can I go now, Erica? There's a bottle of Brown Ale with my name on it."

When Fuller rang off, Cooper topped up her wine and did some more digging. Try as she might, she could find no online presence for any organisation matching the Tyne Pastors. There were the Street Pastors and the City Pastors, but no Tyne Pastors. They didn't exist on Google, Facebook, Twitter, anywhere. She wondered if she'd misheard and he'd said Town Pastors, or perhaps he just told her what he thought she'd want to hear. Anything to get her off the phone. She'd probably do the same if the roles were reversed. She opened a new tab on her browser and tried one last time, searching for *Feisty's, Newcastle, Pastors* and *Van.* She scanned three pages of nothing until Reddit gave Cooper her first nugget of information.

r/NewcastleUni. Posted by Giggles768. 11 months ago

Ladies, be careful. I was worse for wear coming out of Feisty's last night and two men tried to get me to go in their van. Said they were the Tyne Pastors. Seemed a bit suspect. They didn't have any ID and their van was creepy as owt. No logo or anything.

The back of Cooper's neck tingled with horripilation. Nico had been relegated to number two; the van was now her number one suspect. Macey had walked off with a woman with dark curls. Had they both been bundled into the van? She made a note to check in with Mispers for anyone matching the woman's description and remembered that the woman was wearing some sort of work vest. She may have been a good citizen helping out the lost and disorientated of Tyneside, or the fake pastors Giggles768 spoke of could have upped their game.

Cooper continued scrolling down the thread. Most of the messages expressed concern. Some complained that the city wasn't as safe as it used to be, others suggested buying a rape alarm and a can of pepper spray. Then a reply made Cooper's heart stop for a second.

r/NewcastleUni. Posted by PopTartBoy4. 11 months ago

Something similar happened to my girlfriend. She was coming out of the club next door when she was approached by a man who claimed to be police. He said she was arrested for dealing drugs (utter bullshit) and he told her to get in his van. She ran off and the van followed her all the way down to the Quay Side. Luckily, she lost him down a side street and made it back to my place. Be on the lookout.

Cooper downed her full glass of wine and got to her feet. It was time for Josh to go home and for her to go to bed. She had things to mull over.

- Chapter 26 -

"Do I look okay?"

Cooper was flabbergasted. Her daughter looked more than okay. She looked more grown-up than ever. How could her baby girl be fifteen already? Fifteen years flew through her mind's eye. Baby-grows, bottles, dummies, hand me downs from other mums on the force, first proper shoes, first school uniform, first netball kit. "You look amazing, T."

Cooper couldn't remember the last time Tina had worn a dress. She used to wear a regulation knee-length pleated skirt to school, but ever since Lucy Parker in the year above was up-skirted and the photo circulated to every teenage boy in the borough, Tina had opted for trousers. Tina looked at herself in her mother's mirror and examined the fabric of her t-shirt dress. She was knock-kneed and adjusting her weight awkwardly as she tried to get used to a pair of heels. She'd even straightened her hair, which was a big deal for Tina. She hated brushing her hair, and the most Cooper could usually hope for was that it was secured into some semblance of a ponytail.

Cooper joined her daughter at her side and put an arm over her shoulder. "How'd you grow up so fast?"

Tina shrugged. "Listen, Mum. I wanted to ask you something. Technically, I don't need your permission, but..."

That didn't sound good. Cooper patted the bed, and they sat on the edge of the mattress. "What is it, T?"

"I want to go on the pill."

The wind was knocked clean out of Cooper. "Oh. Jeez, Tina." She suddenly felt very protective and wasn't sure how she viewed Josh anymore. Sweet, polite Josh, who was currently waiting downstairs.

"Don't panic, Mum. Josh and I aren't... You know. I just want to regulate my periods. If I go on the pill, I'll know exactly when I'm due, and I won't have any accidents."

The relief must have been etched on Cooper's face because Tina added, "You look weird."

"I'm just..."

"Glad I'm still a virgin?"

Cooper laughed. "Something like that. Listen, I never regretted having you in my life, not for one second, but I was so young, and I don't want—"

"Me to be a teenage mother? Surely, that's another reason I should go on the pill. So that when I am ready for... You know... I won't get pregnant."

"I can't argue with your logic," Cooper said, taking her daughter's hand in hers. "How about we don't mention this to your dad, though?"

Fear flashed in Tina's eyes. "God. Imagine? Yeah, best we don't say anything."

"Anyway." Cooper pulled Tina to her feet. "Your guests are waiting, birthday girl."

Tina gave a toothy grin, and she made her way downstairs, the heels causing her to teeter like Bambi on ice. A duet of *Happy Birthday*, sung by Kenny and Josh, filled the house.

Downstairs, Kenny had filled the living room with a hundred balloons, and silver confetti shaped like the number fifteen had been sprinkled over every table, mantlepiece and countertop. Josh greeted Tina with a kiss on the lips and a nervous glance in Kenny's direction before handing her a card and a small box that could only be jewellery.

Cooper joined Kenny on the sofa. "Thanks for all this," she said, motioning at the decorations.

He shrugged as if it was no effort. "She's worth it," he said with a slight blush. "You both are. I'm sorry I wasn't there for all of her birthdays. I was a selfish idiot."

Thinking back to all she'd been through as a single mother, Cooper bobbed her head from side to side and replied, half-jokingly, "Yeah. You were. But you're here now, and I'm glad you and Tina have the makings of a real relationship."

Tina shrieked as Josh secured a silver necklace around her neck. "Look, Mum! It's the molecule for serotonin." She held the pendant in her fingertips. "The happy hormone."

Josh turned purple and whispered a little too loudly, "All I want to do is make you happy."

Kenny rolled his eyes at Cooper. "Bloody millennials and their sentiments. No one talked to each other like that when we were their age."

"When we were their age, the standard chat up line was, *giz a snog.*" Cooper shuddered. She'd always hated the word snog and thought it was the most unappealing word for kissing ever invented. "Besides. They're not millennials. The millennials were born between seventy-seven and ninety-five. So I hate to break it to you - given your love of millennial bashing - but you, dear Kenny, are a millennial."

Kenny's mouth opened, closed and opened again. "No, that can't be right. The millennials are the young'uns who eat too much avocado, need twenty pronouns and are scared of handling raw chicken."

"You're a millennial, Kenny. Deal with it."

"So what are those two?" he asked, raising a can of lager in Tina and Josh's direction.

"Gen Z. Also known as iGen or the digital natives. They've never known a time without the internet."

Kenny relaxed back on the sofa. "A time without the internet? Man, I remember those days. Woah! That makes me feel old."

"Tell me about it," said Cooper, wondering how she could possibly be old enough to have a daughter who wanted to go on the pill.

Kenny looked down to the carpet. "No texting, no mobiles, no Spotify or Netflix."

"No cyberbullying, no sexting, no Twitter mobs, or online shaming."

The doorbell rang, signalling the arrival of Atkinson and the Sutherlands, closely followed by two of Tina's netball team and four friends who attended the same study group as Tina and Josh. The teenagers immediately set up camp in the kitchen as that, apparently, was where the cool people hung out. At least that was something that hadn't changed since Cooper's day. Cooper struggled to pick Caroline out of the sea of youngsters at first. She'd shot up in recent months and was now a young woman with her mother's dark blonde bob and her father's shiny grey eyes. She was immediately welcomed in by the group and Cooper caught the look of joyfulness on Sam's face.

Tinny pop music began to play out of someone's phone, and Tina embraced Atkinson in a rare hug. He added a present to the growing pile of gifts for Tina and enquired about Steven before the grown-ups retired to the living room to give the teens some privacy.

"So, Steven's moved to a bigger box?" he said as Cooper gave him a welcoming kiss and made room for him on the sofa.

"The fluffball's growing by the day. It's ridiculous."

"Steven?" asked Sutherland.

Cooper laughed as she poured Sue a glass of white and handed Sutherland a lager. "Long story."

Atkinson pulled a bottle of Carmenère from a plastic bag and poured himself a glass. He offered some to Cooper who raised her lager and said, "Thanks, I'll have some when I've finished this."

Atkinson cast his eyes around the room at the balloons, confetti, flowers and cards. "Did you find out who sent you the roses? My money's on that chief superintendent's secretary."

"Oh, they weren't from work. They were from Kenny."

Kenny shifted himself around on the sofa and gave an embarrassed nod. "Guilty as charged."

"Hmm."

Kenny's brows lowered. "What do you mean, *hmm*?"

"Forget it. It's nothing."

"It's not nothing. If you have something to say, say it, Science Man."

"Okay, okay." Cooper got to her feet, sensing a very quick change in the atmosphere. This sort of thing was bad enough when it was just the three of them, but she wasn't the only witness this time. She had a work colleague and his wife here too. "Kenny, why don't you check on the digital natives in the kitchen? See if they're hungry yet?"

Kenny lifted his bulk from the seat but didn't remove his eyes from Atkinson until he was at the kitchen door.

"For goodness sake." Cooper turned to Atkinson. "It's Tina's birthday. The last thing she needs is you two bickering and causing a scene."

"Sorry, Erica, but can't you see what's happening here?"

"He bought the mother of his child flowers after she was held prisoner by a murderer. I don't think that's anything to—"

"He's stalking you, Erica."

Cooper stared down at Atkinson, who was still seated, glass of wine in hand. "What?" she exclaimed. "That's... That's just not true. What a load of... Sorry Sam, Sue. Can I get you another drink?"

The Sutherlands looked embarrassed and held up their very full glasses.

"How many times has he texted you this week?" Atkinson pressed.

It was at least fifty, but they'd been discussing Tina's birthday and whatnot. "I don't know," she lied. "Not many, and that's really none of anyone's—"

"And how many gifts has he bought you recently? The framed picture, the flowers? Popping over to police HQ with lunch? What else?"

Cooper's blood pressure was rising. She couldn't believe that Atkinson was acting like this. They had company, and he was behaving like a jealous child. Was it so unreasonable that she and Kenny were, God forbid, getting along? Was he really so petty?

"Well?" Atkinson pressed. "What else?"

Cooper pinched her nose as she often did when stressed or frustrated with someone's attitude and hissed her answer, "A fruit basket and some chocolates. He knows I don't eat properly when I'm stressed and..."

"He wants you back, Erica. He's always sniffing around, and it makes me uncomfortable."

"Don't be daft. He's just being nice."

Atkinson slammed his glass on a side table. Red wine slipped over the lip and ran down the stem onto untreated oak. It would stain. Sue jumped and disappeared, returning a second later with a tea towel to mop at the spilt wine while avoiding eye contact with Cooper and Atkinson.

"I'm not daft." Atkinson got to his feet, towering over Cooper. "And he's not being *nice*. He's being a creep."

Cooper checked that the kitchen door was closed before hissing, "And you're being bitter and insecure. If he's making you so uncomfortable, maybe you should just leave."

Hurt painted Atkinson's face. He ran a hand over his jaw and shook his head in disbelief. He waited for a second, and when Cooper didn't retract her statement, he uttered, "Fine," and stormed from the house.

- Chapter 27 -

By Tuesday morning, the Easter holidays had ended and Tina was heading back to school. Cooper had had all the rest she could stomach and was ready to return to normality, regardless of what Nixon would say. Taking a bite of toast and fishing a fiver from her purse so Tina could buy herself some lunch, she answered the door to Kenny, who'd volunteered for today's school run.

"How're things?" he asked.

Cooper shrugged. She hadn't heard from Atkinson since their argument and she was too stubborn to text him. She wasn't even sure who was in the wrong. One of them had overreacted, and she was fairly certain it wasn't her. Atkinson was older than Cooper, and she didn't want him acting overly protective of her or treating her like a child. That wasn't healthy, and neither was a relationship where a man told his woman who she should and shouldn't spend her time with.

"Are the nightmares getting any easier?"

The corners of Cooper's mouth turned down and she flashed back to the night terror she'd suffered on Sunday night; the slave collar had tightened, and tightened, and tightened until she'd awoken in a cold sweat.

"Who said I was having nightmares?"

"Tina said something. Besides, who wouldn't have nightmares after something like that? We're still reeling from last year and with Hutchins all over the news...It must be hard."

Cooper took another bite of toast and wrinkled her nose. "I've only had a couple of nightmares. They're not bad and I'm sure they'll stop with time. If not, we have a therapist on staff. I can speak to her if need be."

He reached over and touched her shoulder. "If you need help, go and get it. There's no shame in it."

"Who are you, and what have you done with Kenny? I thought you said therapy was for fragile little snowflakes?"

Kenny put on his best look of innocence. "Yeah, but I also didn't know what a millennial was, so best not listen to me."

Cooper smiled for the first time since Sunday. Tina came rushing into the room, said "Morning" to her dad and was halfway out the door when Cooper called after her.

"Necklace!"

"Aww, Mum."

"You know the rules. No jewellery in school. You'll be put in isolation." It was hardly a threat against Tina, who would much prefer to study alone, but she held out her palm and waited for Tina to undo the catch on her necklace and hand it to her. The silver chain curled up on Cooper's hand like a Lilliputian snake as the noise of huffs and whispered insults filled the room. Tina shuffled out of the door and headed for Kenny's truck. Kenny shared a look with Cooper and followed.

Before heading to work, Cooper made two quick phone calls: one to her GP to make an appointment for Tina, and one to the Northern Centre for Cancer Care. She was kept on hold for a worrying amount of time, which did her blood pressure no good at all. Eventually, a nurse came on the line and told her that everything had come back clear and that she didn't have to visit the centre again for another three months, but if she was at all concerned about anything, to give them a call.

Cooper sunk onto a seat at the kitchen table, covered her face with her hands and waited until her vital signs returned to normal. It was a huge weight off her shoulders and the relief threatened to spill over into tears. Now all she had to worry about was her relationship with Atkinson, a murderer and kidnapper on the loose, and Macey Gallagher's disappearance remaining unsolved.

None of those problems would solve themselves, so she shelved the personal problem, jumped in the Mazda and headed to Wallsend, ready to work on the other two. But first, coffee.

At Starbucks, Cooper texted Keaton to ask what she wanted and to find out if Tennessee was back at work. She was told Hayley had the tag team help of both of Alfie's grandmas, so Tennessee was back, and he wanted a mocha-choca-something-or-other.

Later, when she arrived in the incident room with two venti cappuccinos and a grande caffè mocha, Cooper found Keaton and Tennessee drowning in a tidal wave of paperwork. They gratefully took their frothy coffees, removed the lids, inhaled deeply and sighed simultaneously.

"Reports, reports, reports," Keaton groaned. "As if we didn't have enough to be getting on with. I need to check in with Omar and give him a photographic lineup. See if he picks Bryce Morton's photo. Speaking of which, we need to go over your statement, boss. Then we've got interviews with Morton's known associates to try and work out where the fucker's most likely to be."

Tennessee got to his feet and approached a map of the northeast of England that was pinned to the wall. Tiny red, orange and yellow stickers dotted the chart. "The press room released Morton's image, warning the public not to approach but to call in with any sightings. There's been at least fifty possible sightings since Friday and we have units following up with the most likely ones."

Cooper scrutinised the map, looking for clusters and patterns. "Looks to be a lot of sightings around the edge of the national park," she said, indicating a large swath of green.

"We think he might be hiding out in that area, but the park's over four hundred square miles. It's going to take us a while to flush him out. But we will, Coop."

"I don't doubt it for a second," Cooper said truthfully. She knew they wouldn't quit, especially after Morton had gone after one of their own. "What else do we have?"

"Look North want one of us to speak on the lunchtime news," Keaton answered, "and as your neck's currently bruised to fuck, and Tennessee has bags under his eyes you could fit a weekly shop into, I guess I'll do it."

Cooper laughed and blew on her drink to cool it down. "Thanks, Paula. Just try not to swear on live television. Are we covering Morton's mother?"

"We have a unit keeping tabs on their homes."

"Good. And a case file has been opened for the murder of Derrick Morton? His father. His death wasn't accidental."

"Done," said Tennessee, "and we contacted the fire investigators so they can reopen their file."

Cooper sipped her drink. "Excellent. Looks like you two have it covered. How about I do the reports? I'm not supposed to do any fieldwork, and Nixon'll have a heart attack if I leave the building, so I may as well make myself useful."

Keaton shifted her weight back in her chair and swung her legs to plant her feet on the desk before thinking better of it. "Brilliant. You don't mind?"

"I'd rather be hunting Morton but that's not going to happen, so I'll crack on clearing this mountain of paper."

"Sweet. Thanks."

Keaton and Tennessee picked up their coffees and coats and headed for the door while Cooper made herself comfortable and typed her password into a computer. She spent the next three hours typing up Keaton and Tennessee's notes before sweet-talking Oliver Martin into grabbing her a bag of chips from the burger van on the corner. As per her instructions, he'd smothered them in ketchup and brought her a wooden fork. Chips just weren't the same with proper cutlery.

After refuelling, she sat back at her desk, ready to continue her typing, but three hours was all she could take. She wasn't a typist; she was a detective, and she wanted to investigate. There was an itch in desperate need of a scratch. She opened the database and began searching for the cases that were reported on Reddit. Nothing. That didn't mean the stories were made up, and they never happened. It just meant they were never reported to the police. It made Cooper sad to think of how many crimes went unreported because people either didn't trust the police, didn't think the police would believe them or didn't think they'd be able to help. Next, she looked for any cases with similar themes. Young women, the city centre, a van, men claiming to be the police.

"Bingo." Cooper grabbed a notepad and pen and began scribbling down the details. When the door opened and Fuller walked in with Sutherland and Nixon, Cooper switched the browser back to her reports, nodded her thanks to their greetings, and poo-pooed their concerns.

Sutherland waited for Nixon and Fuller to start talking football before taking a seat next to her and asking, "Were you okay after we left on Sunday?"

Cooper flushed with embarrassment. "I'm good, Sam. Sorry you had to witness that."

"Hey, if it's any consolation, I think the kids had a great time. Caroline keeps asking if Tina can come for a sleepover at half term."

"Well, that's something at least." She was glad some people had a good time at the party. She'd spent the remainder of the evening faking enthusiasm whenever Tina or one of her friends spoke to her. Inside, she'd been sullen and saturnine.

"Have you spoken to Atkinson?"

She ground her teeth together. "No."

Sutherland gave her a look he might give Caroline, then put his arm around her shoulders. It was a move only he could get away with. "Listen, people these days, they're all about saving face, not making the first move, not being the one to crack. When I was young... I know, when woolly mammoths still roamed, it was a good thing to make the first move. The one who apologised first was the bigger man, or woman in this case. Life's too short to be angry with the one you love."

Cooper nuzzled into his shoulder. "Right as always," she said with a smile.

"So you'll call him? Or text?"

She nodded. "Once I've calmed down. I'll say something I regret otherwise."

Sutherland gave her a squeeze and released her, getting to his feet with a groan. "You're kidding, right?" he said in Fuller's direction. "United won't stand a chance if we sell Barboza. I have ten quid on him scoring a hat trick this weekend."

Sutherland and Fuller ambled into a meeting room set aside for them, and Cooper waited until Nixon left the department in the direction of his office before she reopened the case she had found on the police database.

Two years ago, Inga Jānis, born in Riga, Latvia, accepted a lift from two men in a van outside of The River Palace. Cooper did a quick Google search and found The River Palace used to be on the same road as Feisty's. It closed nine months ago and reopened as O'Neills. When Inga realised the van was headed out of town, she opened the door and jumped from the moving vehicle. The men gave chase and she made it to the motorway only to be run over by a taxi. Cooper winced as she read the list of Inga's injuries. Cooper switched back to Google, searched for Inga Jānis, and found someone with the same name on Facebook. A pretty blonde with small features and long lashes smiled from her profile picture. Cooper flicked through a couple more photos. A recent shot taken with the Tyne Bridge in the background suggested she still lived in the area, and another shot, taken from further away, showed she used a wheelchair.

In a second case, Cooper read about Sandra Hagen. An Australian in Newcastle on a student visa. After a night out, she reported being directed towards a van by a man claiming to be a police officer. He accused her of soliciting, which she denied. Sandra kicked up a fuss and ran away, running into two real police officers who found her in a panicked state. When the police tried to trace the van, the only CCTV footage they unearthed showed the number plate was obscured with mud.

Pushing a USB stick into the computer, Cooper brought up the footage she'd taken from the accountancy firm. She paused when the van drove by and tried to make out the front number plate. The footage wasn't the best. She zoomed in, but it was too much of a blur, and she suspected it had been smeared with mud. It might be an N-reg. That was all she could tell. The footage from the cat café was largely the same. She could see the rear numberplate in this footage but it was coated in mud or dirt. The left side of the first digit was a long vertical line. That fitted with an N, but could also be a B, D or any number of letters.

Cooper got to her feet and began to pace the room, letting her brain process the patterns and parallels that were becoming apparent. She returned to her computer, bent over the desk and looked up Giggles768. Next, she found PopTartBoy4 and scrolled through his posts until she found something useful. When a photograph of him with his new wheels came up she entered the number plate into a separate database to find his name. She put that name into Facebook and again scrolled through until she found out who his girlfriend was. Clicking control and P, Cooper waited for the printer to vomit up images of all the girls involved: Macey Gallagher, Dublin; Inga Jānis, Riga; Sandra Hagen, Melbourne; Klaudija Moreno, Bucharest; and Angela Wilson, the Isle of Wight.

Cooper collated the photographs before spreading them over her desk. All blonde, all dainty, all with child-like features, and all from out of town.

"Whatever's going on," Cooper whispered to herself, "someone doesn't like to shit where they eat."

- Chapter 28 -

Cooper approached Nixon's secretary to see if she knew where the superintendent was. She'd already crept past his office and knew he wasn't in there.

"He's meeting with the commissioner, Ma'am. It's scheduled until four. I can get a message to him if it's urgent."

"No, nothing important. Thank you, Vivian."

Satisfied that Nixon wouldn't notice if she wandered off, Cooper decided to visit Inga Jānis once she'd checked in with her team. Just as she was about to dial, her phone lit up. Keaton's name appeared on the screen.

"Paula, I was just about to call you. There's been another sighting, this time on the outskirts of Otterburn. Someone matching Morton's description was seen walking along the river."

"Boss. Jack and I just finished speaking with some of Morton's colleagues." Her voice was harried.

"Go on."

"Morton's hobbies include shooting. He's a member of Roker Rifle Club in Sunderland and Elite Gun Club in Rothbury."

Cooper glanced at the map on the wall. "Rothbury's not far from some of the sightings. He must know the area. Hang on." Cooper logged into another database. "Shit. He has an SGC," she said, referring to a shotgun certificate. "Certificate states he owns a .410 gauge bolt-action. A Webley and Scott. Last inspection was eight months ago. All in order. Stored in a locked box in the loft."

"Christ."

"Right, Paula. You call the unit that's stationed at the mother's house. Have them check Morton's loft. I'll contact the units in Northumberland National Park and tell them to hold back until we know more."

"Roger."

Cooper hung up and immediately got hold of dispatch. "Tell all units in the vicinity of Northumberland National Park that suspect Bryce Morton is potentially armed. Use extreme caution."

Her mobile rang again within two minutes. "Go ahead, Paula."

"The gun case is empty, boss. We're headed to Otterburn. Armed response have been called."

"Oh, bloody hell." Cooper's heart rate doubled and her hand went to her bruised neck. Her mouth was dry and though she was certain she'd been ready to return to duty, she was scared. Undeniably scared. "Don't go to Otternburn until the armed response units arrive. Meet me in Bellingham. It's the nearest police station to our search area. We'll set up an incident room and coordinate the search from there. I'll bring vests."

"ARE WE SURE HE'S here in Otterburn?" Tennessee asked. His head low against an April shower, water dripping from the ends of his curls onto a bulletproof vest.

"Pretty darn sure." Cooper slid her hands into the back pockets of her trousers to keep them warm. "Three calls in the last two hours linked him to this place. Plus, one call mentioned a navy Barbour jacket. We didn't mention that in our media pack, but it's what he wore when he took me."

Tennessee nodded. They were stood next to a patrol car on the outskirts of Otterburn. The small village in the Cheviot Hills derived its name from the Otter Burn that branched away from the River Rede. Ahead, they watched as a tactical team inched closer to a fishing hut on the banks of the Rede. The hut was sheltered from the view of the village by a copse of trees.

"Morton was spotted walking north from where the sixty-eight meets the Birky Gill," Cooper continued. "We placed a unit there to creep north and another unit in Elishaw to creep south."

Keaton squeezed rainwater from her short ponytail. "I arranged road stops on the sixty-eight and the six nine six. He's not getting out of here by car."

"He's not getting out of here full stop," Cooper said with a grunt. "Thermal imaging suggests someone's in that hut. Besides, look around." She wafted her arms about and took in the endless green fields that contained nothing but grass and sheep. "Where else is there to hide?"

At the sound of camera shutters, all three detectives turned their heads and were greeted by flashes of light as local press revelled in the hottest news story of the week.

Tennessee scowled. "Permission to move the cordon back another hundred feet?"

"Permission granted." Cooper gave him a wry smile and turned back to the hut. If Morton weren't armed, they wouldn't have hesitated in storming the hut. As it was, Cooper didn't want to take the risk. Slowly, slowly.

Time passed, rain fell and Cooper's body temperature continued to drop. As darkness approached, she sent a text to Kenny to ask him to take care of Tina until she could get home. His reply came within seconds. *Of course. It's my pleasure. Be careful, Erica. Let me know when it's all over.*

The message warmed her, but not for long, she felt icy all over as soon as Bryce Morton emerged from the shadowy doorway of the fishing hut.

"LOWER YOUR WEAPON!" The leader of the tactical team boomed his command over and over but his words washed over Morton, whose eyes were fixed solely on Cooper.

"LOWER YOUR WEAPON!"

"I want him alive." Cooper's voice was quiet but firm as she spoke into the handheld. "Repeat. We take him alive."

"Copy."

Morton took a step forward. The thin, downy hairs on the back of Cooper's neck stood on end. She could taste the tension in the air.

"LOWER YOUR WEAPON!"

"I will only speak with DCI Cooper."

Cooper's hands shook as she picked up a megaphone and moved behind one of the cars for shelter. "I'm here, Bryce. You can speak to me."

"No." He shook his head side to side, causing his weapon to shift left and right. "Not like this. We can't talk like this. You have to come here."

Swallowing hard, Cooper brought the megaphone back to her lips. She had to handle Morton carefully. She didn't want to spook him or anger him.

"I'm sorry, Bryce, but we can't speak facc to face until you put the gun down. Can you put the gun down for me?"

Morton started to pace. Two paces left, two paces right, his gun still raised.

"What would you like to talk about, Bryce?" When he didn't answer, Cooper tried, "We can talk about Benji if you like?"

His eyes sparked and he raised his head. "Benji was a good boy."

"Yes, he was. And you miss him, don't you?"

Morton nodded and then his face crumpled. He began to cry angry sobs, the gun trembling in his arms as he realised his options were few.

"I know what it's like to lose someone you love. We can help you, but you have to help us first."

He wiped his nose on his shoulder. "It's too late for me. I'm going to prison because you know too much."

He was going to prison because of all he had done. Morton was a deeply damaged individual who needed help, but he was also a dangerous criminal and needed to be detained to pay for his crimes and for the protection of the public. With Omar and Cooper, he had made mistakes, and those mistakes had led him to this situation. There were only two ways out: Either he lowered his weapon or armed response would be forced to shoot. It was his choice.

Cooper tried one last time. "Bryce, would you like to meet one of our police dogs?" To Cooper's relief, the idea worked and he stopped pacing to look at the dogs. "Put them at ease," she hissed to the nearest handler. The Belgian shepherds sat on command and panted. Clouds of condensation billowed from long, pink tongues. "What's her name?" Cooper asked quietly.

"Nancy."

"Bryce. This is Nancy. She's lovely, isn't she?"

Morton smiled. The rain was coming down heavier now and it was causing Morton to glance back towards the shelter. Cooper wanted to keep him where she could see him.

"Nancy's very friendly. You can come and meet her if you like. But she doesn't like guns. If you want to give her a stroke, you'll have to put the gun down."

He smiled again and a dreamy look passed over him. He lowered the shotgun so the barrel pointed to the ground and took a step forward. Nancy's hackles raised, but she wouldn't move unless her handler told her to.

"Put the gun on the ground, Bryce," Cooper repeated.

Morton squatted and lowered the gun towards a muddy puddle. He paused, looking deep in thought, before standing and pointing the gun at Cooper.

- Chapter 29 -

Cooper stared straight down the barrel of the bolt-action shotgun. She was frozen, paralysed with fear. It took Tennessee's full might to haul Cooper to the ground and shield her behind the body of the patrol car. A single shot rang out and Cooper gasped for air beneath Tennessee's weight as the sound of angry dogs filled the village of Otterburn. "No," she pleaded. "I want him alive." She pushed herself to her feet and assessed the scene.

Morton was on his back. Two dogs were biting his arms, pinning him down as the tactical team raced towards him. The shotgun was kicked from his reach, and MP5s pointed at the man's chest. Watery, red blood seeped from his shoulder into the mud and grass around him. "Clear," someone called out, and a medic ambled towards Morton, pulling dressings from a shoulder bag.

"Shoulder," said Tennessee. "He's alive. It was a good shot."

Relief overpowered Cooper. She wiped her face with her hands, coating her cheeks with muddy fingerprints. If the shot had been fatal, she may never find out who Morton's other victims were. A waiting ambulance backed up towards the hut. Its back doors opened.

"Come on," said Tennessee. "You get the honours."

They squelched through the wet ground as Morton was rolled onto a stretcher. Medics worked to stop the bleeding from both the bullet wound and the dog bites. Cooper wondered if he'd continue his infatuation with dogs now he'd been chewed up by two of them.

"Bryce Morton, I am arresting you for the murder of Derrick Morton, the attempted murder of Omar Ali, the abduction and assault of a police officer," Cooper hovered over him and made sure to look him in the eyes. "Carrying a firearm to resist arrest, possessing a firearm with the intent to endanger life, and arson. Did I miss anything?"

He smirked. The painkillers he'd been injected with were starting to kick in. "You've missed so, so much, dear. There's a lot you don't know. Lots of pets you don't know about."

She'd find out. She'd get justice for every single one of Morton's victims. Taking a pair of handcuffs from her pocket, Cooper played with them as Morton watched. She couldn't restrain him while the medics did their work, but she looked forward to seeing him in chains.

"It's a shame these won't fit your neck," Cooper said just before the ambulance doors closed and its engine started.

"They're taking him to the Royal Victoria," said Keaton. "I'll head on over and let Omar know we got his attacker."

"Thanks, Paula. Don't tell him they're in the same hospital. We don't want to give Omar any extra stress or worry."

Keaton nodded. "Sure thing, boss." She clapped Cooper on the arm. "Well done. That can't have been easy."

It hadn't been. Facing Bryce Morton had been more terrifying than she had anticipated. She wasn't impervious to fear; she was human, and she'd have to face him again soon. She'd question him day and night, twenty-four-seven until she found out exactly who he'd hurt and where their bodies lay.

BELLINGHAM POLICE STATION WAS dying down for the night. Armed response conducted their debrief and waited while forensics finished up at the site. Cooper removed her bulletproof vest and washed the mud from her face in the sink of the women's toilets. She stuck her head under the tap and let the warm water run over her scalp and the back of her neck. It took some contorting, but she angled herself under the hand dryer and stayed there until her skin was dry and she'd thoroughly warmed through. While her shirt and trousers dried on an old cast-iron radiator, Cooper called Kenny to assure him and Tina that everything was all right.

"Glad to hear it," he said. "There's a couple of beers waiting in the fridge for you. Thought you'd need them. Don't worry about Tina. She's busy teaching Josh how to memorise the periodic table."

"That's my girl," Cooper laughed. "I'll still be a while. Can you hold the fort?"

"Absolutely. Do what you need to do, Erica."

Cooper hung up and read her text messages. Tina had sent her a heart emoji, and Atkinson had messaged to ask if she was okay. She didn't have the energy. Not now. Atkinson could wait.

Once the last patch of dampness faded on her trousers, she dressed and met Tennessee in her car.

"Have you called Hayley?"

He nodded. "Everything's fine. She's had a good day, and I get the feeling the mother-in-law wouldn't let her watch the news."

"Probably for the best."

Tennessee's face spread into a genuine smile. "That could have ended so much worse. Makes you feel grateful to be alive, doesn't it?"

It did, but Cooper was just about holding herself together so she responded by giving him a soft punch on the arm and calling him a big softy.

"Back to HQ?" he asked. "Write all of this up? Or we could head to the RVI, but I doubt the docs will let us start interrogating Morton."

"Actually, I want to take a detour." Cooper typed an address into Google Maps and started the engine.

INGA JĀNIS LIVED IN an impressive house on the outskirts of Darras Hall, an area famed for housing footballers and the more successful reality TV stars.

"Why do we want to talk to this woman?" Tennessee asked after Cooper rang the doorbell. "Shouldn't we hand over your findings to Fuller?"

"We should. But we're not going to. Not yet." Cooper could hear noises beyond the door, and the door opened.

"Yes?" Inga had the impossible beauty of Eastern Europe. She was blessed with a great complexion, slender build and golden locks.

"Inga. I'm DCI Cooper. This is my colleague DS Daniel. Sorry to disturb you, but I was hoping to ask you some questions about what happened two years ago."

Inga's forehead wrinkled. "Did you catch them?"

"No. I'm afraid not. But a few cases fit a similar pattern to what you went through. I'm hoping you can help me."

Inga wheeled herself backwards and turned herself in the opposite direction. "Follow me."

Inga led the pair through an expansive lobby and into a modern living room decorated entirely in white.

"Amazing place you have here," said Tennessee.

"Thank you. But it's not mine. Not really. I tutor art and design to the local school children. It's well paid but not *this* well paid." She gestured around. "Tiago pays the bills."

Cogs whirled in Tennessee's head, then a light-bulb illuminated in his mind and his eyes widened. "Not Tiago Barboza?"

Inga looked coy. "Yes. My boyfriend."

"Wow." Tennessee looked around in all directions, hoping the star Newcastle United striker was home.

Cooper moved closer to her DS and hissed, "Don't go all fanboy."

"I play wheelchair basketball," Inga continued. "Tiago and some other players had visited our practice session as part of some community work. They were in chairs and giving it a go, but they were useless, which was hilarious because I got the feeling these guys weren't used to being outplayed by little women like me. Anyway, we hit it off." She shrugged as if to say *the rest is history*. She extended an arm towards a plush white sofa. "Please."

"We're a little muddy. I don't want to stain your sofa. Is it okay if we sit at your breakfast table?"

"Of course."

Once seated, Cooper began her line of questioning. "So, Inga, two men tried to abduct you when you left the River Palace?"

"That's right."

"And that was on July seventeenth?"

"Yes, the year before last. Around half two in the morning. I wasn't sure of the exact time."

"Can you tell me what you remember about that night?"

She took a deep breath and pulled her sleeves down, so they covered her hands and began fidgeting with the fabric.

"I'd got into an argument with my then-boyfriend and he walked off. I decided to stay in the club to finish my drink but the venue was emptying out fairly quickly. When I left, the street was almost deserted. A man was talking to someone in a black van, and he asked me if I wanted to share a taxi."

"A black van?" Cooper consulted her notes. "In your original statement, it says a blue van."

"No, that can't be right. It was definitely black. That must be a mistake. Anyway, I said it didn't look like a taxi, but he said it was freelance, like an Uber or something. We were both headed to South Gosforth, so I thought *why not?* I was so, so stupid."

"You were trusting. That doesn't make you stupid."

Inga gave Cooper a thankful look. "Thank you, but on this occasion, yes, I think I was stupid. Straight away, I knew something wasn't right. It drove off towards the Tyne Bridge. I went to open the car door, but the man next to me grabbed hold of my arm. I hit him in the face with my elbow and jumped out. You know the rest." She cast her eyes downward.

"Did the men address each other by name?"

"No. I don't think so. I think the man in the back just called him Driver."

Cooper sifted her papers around and pulled out some sketches. "These are the artist's impressions of the two men that were drawn up at the time." She handed them to Inga, who examined them with a sad expression.

"Would you say they are accurate?"

"They're not bad," said Inga. "But I would make some changes." She moved to a sideboard and retrieved a pencil. "May I?"

The image was a photocopy of the original. Cooper had no problem letting Inga sketch over it, and who would be better qualified than an art tutor? "Go ahead."

"The man who lured me in and sat in the back, he was a little gaunter than this." She shaded in the hollows of his cheeks and adjusted the shape of his jaw. "His brows were thicker too." She continued sketching and moved on to the driver. "He was older than he looks in the picture." Inga's pencil moved in arcs, reforming the shape of the man's cheeks and hairline before thinning his lips. "There," she said, "That is as good as I can do."

Reaching across the table, Cooper dragged the pictures and rotated them so they faced herself and Tennessee. She examined the pictures of the lure and the driver, turned her head to her DS, and they exchanged a long, hard look.

- CHAPTER 30 -

COOPER, TENNESSEE AND KEATON huddled around an ancient computer monitor in CID. Keaton had made a FaceTime call to Tennessee and placed her phone in the corner of the hallway so it was partially hidden behind a bin. As long as they kept one eye on Tennessee's screen, they'd have at least a forty-second head start if anyone was going to disturb them.

"What am I looking for?" asked Keaton as she opened an internal search engine.

"Unmarked cars, registered here at HQ, North Shields or Whitley Bay."

"Okay. Got them."

"Narrow the search to vans, then sort by colour," Cooper instructed.

"Done."

"How many are black?"

"Four."

"How many are N-reg?"

"Two. Right, give me a second. I'll see where they were on the night Macey went missing. Here we go. One was getting into position for a dawn raid in Benton. Checked out at eight p.m. and returned the next day at seven thirty a.m. Peterson and Myers had the other one in Seaton Sluice. They were staking out a carwash on modern slavery allegations. Looks like all the Is are dotted and the Ts are crossed. Checked out at twelve noon. Back by six p.m."

Cooper folded her arms. "Good. That's one less thing to worry about."

"Can you imagine the press?" Keaton asked.

"That wouldn't bear thinking about."

Tennessee picked up his phone. "Nixon's coming."

Within seconds, the computer was switched off, Tennessee pretended to do paperwork, Keaton watched the news on the antique television, and Cooper examined the map of Northumbria that was still pinned to the wall.

"What now?" whispered Tennessee.

"For now, we do our jobs," said Cooper. "Later, we meet back up and take a little drive."

SNUGGLED BETWEEN TYNEMOUTH AND Whitley Bay, Cullercoats was a perfect crescent of golden sand, contained at each side by matching piers. The beach was favoured by the local kayaking community who, during good conditions, would kayak beyond the piers and head three kilometres south to King Edwards Bay for a hearty kipper breakfast at Riley's Fish Shack before paddling back to their starting point.

Tennessee gave a long, low whistle as he watched two kayakers drag a tandem back up the sands, their bare feet sinking deeper into the sand the further from the shoreline they walked. "A sea view? Very nice."

Behind him, Cooper and Keaton took in a double-fronted, terraced home with three storeys of bay windows. It was indeed very nice, idyllic even. "Come on," she said, checking her watch. "Let's take a look around the back."

Keaton cast furtive glances over her shoulder as they walked to the end of the terrace and took an alleyway to the rear of the expensive properties.

"Any sign?" asked Cooper.

"No. We're clear," she answered. "Doesn't mean no one's at home. Let's keep our heads down and our mouths shut."

Cooper stopped walking when she reached a double garage extension to the home they'd been watching, and her eyes immediately flicked to the windows. The windows were lined with newspaper, ensuring the owner privacy. Privacy was for hermits, people who didn't want to advertise their wealth, and people who were up to no good. She switched on a torch and raised herself onto her tiptoes, trying to angle a vantage point where some Sellotape had lost its adhesion and the paper had fallen away. "I can't see," Cooper grumbled.

"Allow me." Being much taller, Tennessee didn't have to stand on his tiptoes. He angled the torch around for a few seconds, stepped back, and wiped a hand over his brow. "Fucking hell."

"What is it?" asked Cooper.

"A black van. Tinted windows."

Cooper's mouth hung open as her worst fears were confirmed. She rested her back against the garage door, needing the support to stop her legs from wobbling. "I don't believe it."

"Me neither, boss." Keaton shook her head, disbelief written all over her face.

The three detectives stood in silence, trying to process the information, when a beeping sound preceded the garage door starting to roll upwards. They jumped, turning to face the garage and watching as the owner of the van rifled in a lockbox for a set of keys. He swung the keyring on his index finger before pressing the fob to unlock the van. It was then that he clocked his colleagues. Cooper's eyes met those of Sam Sutherland.

- CHAPTER 31 -

FOR A SECOND THAT seemed to last forever, everyone remained motionless. Sutherland's gaze moved from Cooper to Tennessee, to Keaton. All of their faces were frozen, hard and serious. Sutherland dropped the keys and charged at Cooper, knocking her into Tennessee. He ran south along the back alley and Keaton gave chase.

Cooper was quickly back on her feet and she and Tennessee followed Keaton. Their legs pumped as fast as they could and although she and Tennessee were both quick off the mark, neither of them were any match for the star athlete of the department. Sutherland didn't stand a chance. Five seconds later, he was prostrate on the black tarmac of Grand Parade with Keaton sat astride him, wrestling his arms behind his back.

Cooper caught up and read Sutherland his rights. Tears formed in her eyes as she told the man she considered a father figure that he was arrested for the kidnap of Inga Jānis and Macey Gallagher. Angrily rubbing the wetness around her eyes on the back of her hand, she instructed Tennessee to secure him in the car and call for backup to transport him to the cells to await questioning.

"You're the driver." It wasn't a question, and she noted how Sutherland couldn't meet her eyes. "The house? The new BMW? Sue didn't get you that Rolex for your anniversary, did she? What was your price, Sam? What were those girls worth?"

"I think I'd like a lawyer."

"Damn right, you'd like a lawyer. You're going to need one. You're the reason I was pulled off this case. Aren't you?"

He lowered his head, his jaw resting on his heaving chest.

"Answer me!" Cooper was beyond furious at his betrayal. She'd trusted him, confided in him.

Sutherland just shook his head and repeated his request. "Lawyer."

"Who are you working for? What did you do with Macey?" No answer. "Goddammit, Sam! Get him out of my sight. Keaton, call for forensics. We need the SOCOs to check the van for Macey's DNA and any other evidence they can find. We'll start searching the property. See what we can uncover."

Keaton pulled her phone out of her jacket pocket. "On it, boss." She gave Sutherland a scathing look, shook her head and turned away.

Tennessee led Sutherland towards where they had parked and shoved him, heavy-handedly, into the back seat of Cooper's Mazda. Meanwhile, Cooper squatted to the floor and did everything she could to stop herself from screaming. Not Sam. Not Sam Sutherland whom she'd known for over ten years and had been there with her on every step of her journey to DCI.

A UNIT OF UNIFORMS arrived to help with the search. Cooper and Keaton started upstairs and began the painstaking process of rifling through every drawer and cupboard, under every bed and behind every dresser. Opening a drawer and discovering a second Rolex caused Cooper to fume with disgust. She slammed her hand on the wooden top, an attached mirror shook in its frame.

"Let's wrap up this room, boss. There's nothing to lead us to Macey. Just flash trinkets we can use as evidence of payment. I know he's a rung up the ladder on me, but there's no way I could afford all this crap on my salary. I imagine the same would go for him."

Cooper gave the room one last look over. Expensive sheets on the bed, designer clothes in the wardrobes. Even Sue's makeup bag was stocked with the top brands. Had she been in on it? Did she question her husband's income, or just innocently revel in all the lavish gifts? "Let's move on to Caroline's room."

"You don't think he'd hide anything in there, do you?"

Cooper shrugged. "Wouldn't be the first one. Remember that dealer in Blyth? He stored all that coke in baggies and stitched them into his daughter's teddy bears?"

Keaton held the door to Caroline's room open for Cooper to go in ahead of her. "Oh, shit, yeah, I remember that one."

Caroline's room was typical of a girl in her early teens. Magazines, school textbooks and young adult novels littered the floor by her bed. Clean, pressed school uniforms of pink and navy hung in her closet and makeup brushes endorsed by the hottest influencers filled a stand on her dressing table. Tina had been invited to a sleepover. Cooper could imagine the girls painting their nails as they listened to music and talked boys. That wouldn't happen now. Cooper didn't think her daughter would be welcome in the Sutherland home now Cooper had arrested its patriarch.

"You notice how much security this place has?" Keaton asked, pointing to sensors on the bedroom window.

"I saw the cameras downstairs and the keypad by the door."

"There were sound sensors in the kitchen too. I guess Sam has a lot of pricey shit to protect."

"That he does." Cooper searched through the room but concluded that Keaton had been right. There wasn't anything tying Sutherland to the abductions in the bedrooms. She bobbed her head sideways. "Come on. What's next?"

Keaton opened the next door that led from the hallway. "It's an office."

"Now we're talking." Cooper entered the room and went straight to the desk. She tried the top drawer and found it to be locked. She found the same thing with the two drawers below it. In the corner of the room, an old black safe with a brass handle served as a plant stand for a dying yucca. Scanning about, Cooper looked for a key. When she didn't spot one, she sent Keaton to go to the garage and see if the box of keys could give them any joy.

Keaton saluted, "Gotcha," and left the room.

The desktop was cluttered with the usual household paperwork: bills, mortgage statements and insurance renewals waiting to be filed away. Cooper arranged them into a neat pile for the forensic accountants to review later.

"Here we are." Keaton dropped the metal box on the desk and it gave a loud clattering noise as its contents jumbled against each other. "Forensics have arrived. They're taking samples from the van. Atkinson asked if you have two minutes for a chat."

Cooper paused, caught off guard. "Erm. No. He'll have to wait." She wasn't being childish; she wanted to find as much evidence as she could. She needed to be in the drawers and, more importantly, the safe. But that required a combination. Besides, she was still too irate and hurt about Sutherland to have any reasonable conversation with Atkinson.

One by one, Keaton and Cooper tried the keys against the various locks.

"Most of these look like house keys and car keys, boss." Keaton held up an old fob for a Vauxhall. "And these ones are labelled *Joyce and Gary*. These ones say *number fourteen*. I'm guessing they're the neighbours."

"Urgh." Cooper ground her teeth in frustration. "Think like Sam. Where would he keep the key?"

"It wasn't in his pockets. Tennessee searched him before taking him away. But he's old school. If there's anything worth hiding in the drawers, the key'll be in the safe."

She was probably right. Sitting cross-legged in front of the safe, Cooper drummed her fingers on her thighs and then spun the dial, searching for the numbers of Sam Sutherland's birthday. When it didn't work, she turned her face up to Keaton, who was searching a bookcase. "Call Sue, his wife. She's probably been informed by now. Ask for the combination. If she doesn't know it, find out the date of their anniversary and her and Caroline's birthdays."

Keaton pulled out her phone.

"And call a locksmith," Cooper added, "in case the dates don't work."

Next to the safe, a small wastepaper basket was full of crumpled junk mail and sheets of lined paper. Cooper turned it upside down, emptying its contents over the floor. Given that she'd already had Oliver Martin sent to the dump and Tennessee elbow-deep in a bus stop's rubbish bin, she could hardly complain about searching through scrunched-up flyers for the local Chinese takeaway. It wasn't exactly attracting flies. She smoothed out each piece of paper in turn; they were mainly adverts for tradesmen and restaurants. One torn-out page from a notepad was covered in sums. Cooper was surprised anyone did sums by hand these days, not when everyone old enough to have a phone had a calculator in their pocket, but Sutherland was a traditionalist. It might well be quicker for him to do long division with pen and paper.

Keaton hung up and joined Cooper on the floor. "Try thirteen, four, ninety-three. That's the day Sam and Sue got married."

Cooper spun the dial, anticipating a satisfying click as the safe unlocked, but none came. "Damn it. Sue's birthday?"

"Three, twelve, sixty-five."

"Nope. What about Caroline's birthday?"

"Sixteenth of August, 2006."

"Let's give it a try." She turned the dial. "Sixteen, eight, six. Shit. No, that didn't work either. Let's keep thinking. In the meantime, can you read this?" Cooper handed her a piece of paper from the bin. "His handwriting's worse than my doctor's."

Keaton squinted and held the paper at arm's length. "It's an address. Unit sixty-three, Jarrow IE."

The synapses in Cooper's brain sparked into life, illuminated with urgency and excitement. She was getting somewhere. "Jack," she shouted into her phone. "Is he speaking?... Huh? ...But a lawyer's on the way? Okay. Listen. Get a unit over to Bede Industrial Estate in Jarrow. Unit sixty-three. No, sixty-three. We found an address in Sam's office. He was referred to as the driver, and the last place Macey's phone pinged was the road next to Bede Industrial Estate. That might be where he delivered her to. Great. Keep in touch."

"What did Tennessee say?" Keaton unfolded her legs and stretched them out in front of her.

"That Sam's not saying much, but he's protesting his innocence. Saying it wasn't his fault, he didn't have a choice and so on."

Keaton shrugged. "We'll find out soon enough, I guess." She rotated her ankles from side to side, her boots chiming against the side of the safe.

Sam Sutherland wasn't a complicated man. Cooper didn't mean that as an insult. He was down to earth, basic, and liked to keep things simple. "Sam wouldn't pick a random number for this bad boy. It would have to be something he could easily remember. We've tried birthdays, his anniversary..."

Keaton's arm extended and her index finger pointed to the top shelf of the bookcase. "It might be staring us in the bloody face. Look. The first three books. Catch 22, Seven Years in Tibet, Orwell's 1984." She leant forward and turned the dial to twenty-two, back to seven, then to eighty-four."

Click.

"You beauty." Cooper slapped Keaton on the back but stopped short of hugging her. "Right. What we got here?"

Three rolls of fifty-pound notes rolled off a manila folder and stopped at Cooper's feet. She bagged them as evidence. If Sutherland's accomplices had handled the money, Atkinson could get prints from them. The folder contained sheets of un-ruled paper with handwritten notes. They all appeared to be abbreviations and codes that neither Cooper nor Keaton could make heads or tails of.

"There's a mobile here. Looks like it's from the dark ages." Keaton handed Cooper a Nokia 3210.

"Christ. I had one of these when I was in school." She pressed the power button and found it still had two bars of battery. She wasn't surprised. She seemed to remember playing Snake all day, every day, and the little brick could go a week without a charge. Opening the phone's call history, she tilted the screen towards Keaton. "Only one number... Only one number in the contacts too."

"Keeper," Keaton read. "So, so far we have a driver, a lure and a keeper."

Cooper got to her feet and walked to the window.

"What is it?" Keaton asked.

"Do we take the phone to tech, have them trace the keeper's number, and try to triangulate the most recent location? Or..."

"Or we call the number? Might tip them off. But, saying that, they might know already. Sam was about to head somewhere with that van. If he hasn't shown, they might suspect something's off."

Cooper made a decision. She'd hand the phone over to tech after she'd called the number. Under her latex gloves, her hands were sweating and beginning to shake. She sat back down in front of the safe, took a deep, calming breath and pressed the call button.

"Sam! About bloody time." The keeper's voice was angry, gravelly, and his accent was distinctly northern. "Where the hell have you been? I had to hire a fucking van. The girls are loaded up and departure's at six fifty-four."

Cooper said nothing but locked eyes with Keaton. *Girls*. Plural. Loaded where? She looked at her watch; it was six thirty-three. Twenty-one minutes.

"I'm guessing you couldn't find a replacement for the Swedish bird? They're gonna be pissed we didn't fulfil the order. They wanted four. I told you, Sam, don't mess about with these guys. Their threats aren't empty. They'll do it... Sam?" His tone changed from angry to worried. "Sam?... Sam?"

The line went dead. Cooper and Keaton jumped back to their feet and raced through the house to get back to the street.

"Has to be the docks," Keaton said.

"Call the airports just in case. Newcastle, Tees, see if there are any smaller airfields too." She called Nixon. "Sir. It's Cooper... I know, unbelievable, sir, but we don't have much time. I think Sam was the driver in some sort of people-trafficking ring. Transporting young women to a unit in Jarrow and then taking them to the docks to go who knows where. Macey Gallagher wasn't the only girl taken. I think the DB at Marsden was part of the same operation. She may have been Swedish. Macey and two others are about to be shipped off. I need canine units at both the north and south banks. I want the ports closed. All available units from North and South Shields to make their way over, and I need the coast guard. Departure's at six fifty-four. We can not let that boat leave the Tyne."

Cooper had nineteen minutes until departure. The port was twenty minutes away.

- Chapter 32 -

"You," Keaton shouted to a young officer standing next to a panda car. "Port of Tyne. South side. Let's go." She jumped in the back of the car, leaving the passenger seat for Cooper. The officer looked dumbfounded as his car was commandeered. "You deaf?" Keaton yelled. "Now. Lights on. Sirens on."

Doing as he was bid, the car sped into action. It was a twenty-minute drive to the river and through the tunnel to the south side of the Tyne. Cooper hoped they could blast their way through in under fifteen if the good people of Tyneside shifted their cars out of the way. She radioed the Tyne Tunnel and gave them a heads-up. The roads were still busy, and once in the tunnel, they wouldn't be able to overtake or weave their way through. "Hold the barriers until we're clear," she requested.

"There's going to be some pissed-off commuters," the officer at the wheel murmured as cars switched lanes ahead, making way for their approach.

"Well, they'll have a pissed-off me if they don't do as I ask."

Cooper called Tennessee, told him to secure the unit at Jarrow and to meet her at the docks pronto.

The world around them darkened like a solar eclipse as they sped into the tunnel. Panels that lined the walls whizzed past in pulses until a circle of light appeared in the distance, and they emerged onto a clear motorway. Collectively their eyes narrowed to slits as they blinked away the bright sunlight.

"Time?" she asked.

Keaton glanced at her watch. "We have seven minutes."

"We should be there in under three." The officer lowered his visor and leant forward as he drove.

"Make it two." Cooper didn't want to take any chances.

Her radio crackled. "Cooper, Cooper, this is Daniel, over."

"Go ahead."

"I'm onsite. The ship's still docked. It's the Libra. Must have at least five hundred containers on it. I can see units arriving from South Shields. Awaiting instructions."

"Can you see the Coastguard?"

"The RIB's approaching, the boat's not far behind."

"Wait for the units, then board the ship. Detain all crew members. One of them will know something. Make sure to get the cargo manifest."

"Roger."

Cooper and Keaton held their breath. Even though Tennessee had told her the ship was still in port and the Coastguard were moving up the Tyne, she still had an awful feeling she would pull up to an empty port and be too late. The squad car ripped around the last bend, its tyres screeching against the road, and coming to a rest next to cars from South Shields police station. The ship was there. Looming against a Newcastle backdrop, the Libra, with a dark red hull, laden with multicoloured shipping containers stacked four high. They reminded Cooper of a giant Jenga set or Lego pieces for the gods. A van pulled up next to them and a man led three excitable spaniels from the rear. Sniffer dogs, tails wagging and mouths panting, keen to do their job and please their master.

"Let's go." Cooper jumped from the car and directed the dog handler to search for humans. Alive humans, hopefully. She picked up pace and ran towards the Libra, all the time scanning her surroundings and taking in the scene. Towards the mouth of the river, an orange boat labelled Port of Tyne Authority was descending on the Libra. Two smaller RIBs, most likely Coastguard, had positioned themselves to the stern. Arching her neck upwards, Cooper spotted Tennessee on deck. He escorted two men towards the gangway where they were met by uniformed officers. He raised his hand to Cooper and beckoned her on board.

The gangway was steep. Cooper held the rail and half ran, half pulled herself up.

"Ma'am," he paused, "Coop. We've already rounded up most of the crew. Half of them don't speak English, or claim they don't speak English. The rest are saying they don't know anything about any women or girls being transported."

"That might be true." Not everyone on the Libra needed to know what it was being used for, but it was someone's job to check the manifest against the actual cargo, and that person was the captain. "Where's the skipper?"

"On the bridge, having a tantrum."

Cooper looked upstream towards the famous bridges of the Tyne.

"He means where the helm and all that is," explained Keaton. "Like in Star Trek."

"Of course. What an idiot." She shook her head at herself. "What's he saying?"

"That he has a schedule to keep. I told him he's not going anywhere until the ship is searched, and if we find anything untoward, he'll be coming to the station for a chat."

"And the manifest?"

"Sealed in an evidence bag."

The spaniels dragged their handler up the gangway, their leads tight, choking themselves and barking from the thrill of it. The handler unclasped their leads and watched as the dogs lowered their noses to the ground and sprinted away in three different directions.

"I'll follow the one with the blue collar," Keaton said.

"Good luck with that," said the handler. The dogs were already out of sight. He held out his hand for each of them to shake. "Jared VanZant," he said. "We're best waiting here. They'll bark if and when they find anything."

Cooper didn't know if she could stand waiting around. She'd rather be part of the search but she conceded that the ship was vast and her sense of smell was far inferior to those of the dogs. It would take her a week to open up every container.

"Where was shc heading?" she asked Tennessee.

"Who?"

"The boat." At least she wasn't the only one caught out by nautical terminology.

"Ah. Cyprus."

She opened a map on her phone and zoomed in on Cyprus. "I wonder why Cyprus?"

"It's pretty central," Keaton mused. "Transfer them to a smaller boat, and then it's just a short hop to north Africa, Syria, Turkey."

"Syria?" Tennessee tapped his handheld against his leg nervously. "ISIS brides?"

"God knows. Poor girls," Cooper said. She raised and lowered her shoulders, looking around for further evidence. "We won't know until Sam starts talking."

A crew member shuffled by, speaking in broken English to an officer who escorted him off the ship and in the direction of a waiting panda car.

"Did you hear that?" Tennessee cocked his head. "A bark?"

Like members of the pack, Cooper and Keaton cocked their heads in the same direction.

"I hear it," Cooper said. Her heart thumped. She turned to VanZant. "Which way?"

"Follow me."

The three detectives took off after VanZant. Keaton radioed for assistance. They'd need bolt cutters, medics, and a few extra bodies in case the girls had a minder. Her heart thumped harder the further they ran. The Libra was a monumental labyrinth whose scale couldn't be appreciated from the shore.

"This way." VanZant spotted one of his dogs heading in the direction of the barking and they rounded a corner and came to a halt, almost falling over the other two dogs, which were sat perfectly to attention and barking at the doors to a rusty red shipping container.

"Where are those bolt cutters?" Cooper grumbled. She grabbed the heavy lock and felt the weight of the chain, dropping it again as a memory from the previous week returned to her. She froze in horror.

"Boss?" Keaton eyed her. "You don't have to be here. Tennessee and I—"

"I'm okay. Thanks, Paula, you too, Jack, but I'm all right. I just had a bit of a flashback."

"You look like you've seen a ghost. Oh, here we go. Did someone order bolt cutters?" Keaton took the cutters and played with them for a moment, snapping them shut a few times.

"You need quite a lot of strength," the officer who had fetched the cutters said. "It's not easy. Would you like me to—"

Cooper placed a hand on his arm and shook her head as a way of quieting him. He'd clearly never met Paula Keaton.

"Three, two, one..." Keaton squeezed, her bulky arms flexing against the fabric of her jumper. She scrunched up her face and grunted like a weightlifter.

Click.

The dogs were rounded up and clipped back onto their leads as two officers pulled at the doors. The doors creaked on their hinges; an eardrum-piercing squeak made Cooper shudder. Three torches illuminated dozens of cardboard boxes that were stacked neatly to the roof of the container. Cooper's hope began to slip away. Were the dogs wrong? She hoped the girls weren't already at sea on another boat.

Tennessee stepped forward and started to shift box after box. Keaton and the uniforms joined in, creating a new pile just outside the doors in the natural light.

"Hello?" Cooper called. "Is anyone there?"

No answer.

Tennessee could now see over the wall of boxes. "There is something there. At the back. I can't make it out."

Everyone picked up the pace. Moving boxes in a conveyor belt fashion, passing them back along a line of people. The boxes were heavy, easily five or six kilograms a pop. Finally, a doorway emerged and Cooper squeezed through and into the darkness. The gap in the boxes had allowed some light to enter, but her body caused a shadow and she still needed the torch to make out her surroundings. Crates of bottled water were stacked in one corner with what looked like boxes of canned goods. Two buckets the size of dust bins were fastened to a wall with a shower curtain set up around them. There was a stench of vomit mixed with something sweet, and in the opposite corner, Cooper saw a mound of blankets. She approached, Tennessee close behind her, and pulled at the corner of a raggedy blanket. It slipped away, uncovering three girls, all pale in the torchlight, lying on their sides and not moving a muscle.

- Chapter 33 -

"Hello? Can you hear me? Can you open your eyes?"

The first aid training Cooper was forced to take every three years kicked in and she knelt next to one of the girls. "Hello?" she tried again. "Can you open your eyes? Shit." She lowered her head to the girl's mouth, waiting for the sensation of breath on her cheek or the sight of her chest rising and falling. "Come on, come on, come on," she pleaded. The thought of coming this far only for the girls not to have made it was almost too much for Cooper. Acting on the instincts of her training, she gently rolled the girl onto her back, ready to start chest compressions when she saw the slightest exhalation. The girl's eyes flickered before snapping open.

Cooper felt a formidable sense of relief. "She's alive. Heavily sedated, I think, but alive." The girl blinked at her. "It's okay, we're here to help. Paula, she looks terrified, poor thing."

"This one too." Keaton pulled a second girl to her feet. She was petrified, resisting Keaton's help and backing herself further into the container.

"It's all right. My name's Paula." She spoke in soft tones. "I'm with Northumbria Police. You're safe now."

The girl didn't seem to understand.

"Police?" she tried again. Letting go of the girl's hands and giving her some space. "We'll need translators," she called back to the awaiting officers. The first girl stood up from where she was crouched and hugged her fellow captive. They were shivering and unsteady on their feet.

Tennessee moved forward to help. They flinched, their eyes somehow widening further, pupils magnified with whatever cocktail their smugglers had given them. "I'll wait outside," he said to Cooper. "I'll move the male officers away too. We don't want to overwhelm them."

She nodded to him and turned back to the girls. "Macey?" she asked gently.

One girl shook her head and placed a hand on her chest. "Nina." Her gaze dipped to the third girl, still curled in the blankets. "She is Macey."

"Macey?" Cooper crouched down and gave her shoulder a gentle shake. She was cold to the touch and looked to be sleeping, perfectly still, eyelids closed, not even flickering. She was thinner than in the photos she'd seen, her cheekbones protruding through dry skin. "Macey? Come on, sweetheart. Wake up. You're safe now. It's over." Cooper shook her harder, fear building inside her. *No*. She was too late. There was no change. Macey wouldn't wake. Cooper realised the sweet scent was coming from Macey's mouth.

"Medic!" Keaton called. "Medic. Now!" She turned to Cooper, "Have we lost her?"

COOPER HELD A SHITTY cup of vending machine coffee between her palms on Thursday afternoon. The erupting steam warmed her face and condensed on her chin. She sat in a plastic chair and watched through one-way glass as two detectives from West Yorkshire Police interviewed Sam Sutherland. She had wanted the task - but rightly - Nixon had told her to sit this one out. She was too close to Sutherland, and though she didn't want to say it out loud, she was still shaken up by her abduction. It was only right that impartial detectives be brought in from a different force. So far, they had achieved nothing much other than *no comments* and time was running out.

The three young women they'd rescued from the Libra were transferred to South Tyneside District Hospital. Nina, an Estonian, was being treated for dehydration and malnutrition. The other girl, although physically well, was in a state of shock and the doctors did not want to let her leave without a family member or close friend. Unfortunately, she was too shaken to speak to the doctors or the translators, so they were yet to establish her name or nationality. Macey Gallagher was in a diabetic coma due to advanced levels of ketoacidosis. The Gallagher family were at the hospital in time for her arrival and had fallen apart at the sight of their daughter being so ill and unresponsive. The hospital chaplain comforted the family overnight. He stayed up to pray with Iris Gallagher throughout the evening and into the early hours. The doctors were confident that Macey would emerge from her coma, but as they didn't know how long she'd been in that condition, they feared she was at risk of severe brain damage.

"Says here you have a daughter. Caroline? Right?"

Sutherland nodded at DI Eloise Wan. She had thick eyebrows and blue-black hair pulled into a long braid. Next to her, DS Darren Thompson was silver-haired and round-bellied. He could have been Sutherland's twin.

"Thirteen-years-old. That's a difficult age." Wan sat back in her chair and folded her slender arms over her chest. "When I was Caroline's age, I discovered my father was a criminal." She paused as Sutherland raised his head to look at her. "He was an assistant manager in a care home. It wasn't glamorous, but it was good, honest work. He and his team looked after the elderly, kept them safe, fed and warm. He wasn't a doctor or an engineer, something my grandmother would be impressed by, but I was proud of him. Then he disappeared one day. Prison. I was too young to be told why, but I overheard my brother talking to my mother when they thought I was sleeping. He had three of the carers stealing money from the residents. Quite a small fortune they acquired over the years." She sighed, just short of dramatically. "Anyway, I never forgave him. Never once visited him in prison. Do you think Caroline will forgive you?"

Sutherland wiped a hand over his face and gasped for air. She'd got him. *Well played,* thought Cooper. He shuffled his chair backwards and couldn't figure out what to do with his hands.

"Do you think Caroline will visit you behind bars?"

"You don't understand," he sobbed. "I did it *for* Caroline."

Cooper moved closer to the glass. Finally, he was talking.

"So you could pay for private school? Buy her pretty things so she'd love you?"

"No!" he snapped.

If his outburst had shocked Wan, she didn't show it. She didn't so much as blink.

"You don't understand." Sutherland rose to his feet and walked around in a small circle.

"Sit down," ordered Thompson, but he was quickly overridden by Wan, who didn't want her interviewee to stop talking now he had started.

"It's okay, Sam. If you'd rather stand, that's fine by me. What don't I understand?"

"It was Caroline or those girls. If I didn't help take them, they'd take Caroline." He looked to the ceiling, noticed he was staring straight into the bubble-covered CCTV camera, and looked away again. "When they approached me, they had photos of Caroline taken through her bedroom window. Photos of her walking to school, at the beach, at her fucking swimming club."

Wan poured a glass of water and slid it over the table to Sutherland. He took it and downed it in one.

"Then they showed me the auction." He gagged and asked for more water.

"What auction?"

"She was for sale. Online."

Tears formed in his eyes. One by one they burst from his lash line and snaked down his face. Beyond the glass, Cooper's eyes had done the same.

"Some Saudi bastard had bid three hundred grand for her. I was furious. Blind with rage. I grabbed that little Russian shithead, head-butted him and punched him in the gob. But I was outnumbered. They had weapons. I... I..."

Wan didn't push. She gave him time to gather himself.

"They knew everything about Caroline. Sue too. I became desperate. I bargained. I begged. I said I'd do whatever they wanted so long as they didn't touch them. He - the leader - said, *Good. We need a driver. Work for us for three years and Caroline will be considered off-limits.*"

"Who's they?"

He shook his head furiously. "I don't know. Russians? Romanians? I... I don't know."

"You could have gone to your colleagues."

"I was scared."

"I saw the security system you had installed. Your fear bought a lot of nice things. You weren't too scared to take their money."

Sutherland rested his weight against the wall and supported his head in his hands.

Cooper jumped as Keaton and Tennessee entered the observation room. She put a finger to her lips and motioned for them to sit with her.

"CPS are going to love you," Thompson said, his tone was dry and oozing irony. "Cop turned human-trafficker? Juries are famously nice to bent coppers. I bet you get off scot-free."

"You need to give us something," Wan added. "You know you're facing jail time. The best you can do now is be as cooperative as possible. Give us the ring leaders and we might be able to broker a deal."

"I don't know their names. I don't know anything about them."

Tennessee filled his cheeks with air and exhaled slowly. "Some detective," he glowered. Cooper agreed.

"I only met them once. After that, I got my instructions from the keeper."

Wan picked up her pen. "And who's the keeper?"

"I don't know. He's local though. Borough accent."

"And the lure?"

"I don't know. Fucking hell. I don't know anything. They knew my name. Insurance, I guess. I didn't get to know theirs. She was a thin girl with curly hair, big eyes and some scars on her arm. An ex-cutter, I'd say. She got the girls to trust her, then led them to the van. She replaced a bloke they had. I don't know what happened to him."

"You really don't know much, do you?" Thompson said scathingly.

Sutherland's chest fell in defeat. He had nothing to offer them. Nothing to save his skin.

"How long have you worked for these mysterious Eastern Europeans? You said they told you they'd leave you alone after three years."

"Two years and nine months."

"Ooh." Thompson pouted, mocking Sutherland. "So close. You nearly made it. Bet you thought you were home and dry."

Sutherland returned to his seat as if he didn't even have the energy to stand anymore.

"Who else is involved in this little operation? There's you - the driver - the keeper, the lure, the unnamed bosses."

"There's a guy who works at the docks. He's the keeper's contact. He makes sure the containers are loaded up, and if any crew ask too many questions, they get a backhander to keep quiet."

Wan pulled her braid over her shoulder and ran her hand down the length of it. "Do the boats always go to Cyprus?"

Sutherland shook his head. "Depends who won the auctions. Sometimes it's Cyprus and on to the Middle East and Persia. Sometimes it's Morocco and into northern Africa."

"How many?" Thompson leant forward, propping his elbows on the table.

"How many what?"

"Bent coppers does it take to screw in a lightbulb. Girls. How many girls did you ship off as sex slaves or wives to order, or whatever you want to call it?"

Shrinking back, Sutherland lowered his gaze. Cooper wondered if he was counting them up in his head. Wondered if he was seeing each of their faces in his mind's eye.

"Since I started... Maybe twenty."

"Fuck me." Wan wrapped her braid around her fist as if it were a silky knuckle duster. "You coward. You could have asked for help, but instead you did as you were told like a good little soldier."

"It might have started as cowardice," said Thompson, "but it finished as greed. Twenty young women's lives ruined so you could cash your cheques." He got to his feet. "Sam Sutherland, you will be taken downstairs and charged. You will either be remanded or released on bail."

Thompson continued to explain to Sutherland the procedures he was already familiar with, but his words faded in Cooper's head. She watched Sutherland rise to his feet and be escorted from the room and from her life.

Twenty young women. She wiped her eyes and drew her shoulders back. She had phone calls to make. The National Crime Agency would no doubt want a word. Interpol too. Then there was the press; she had to do some damage control. This was going to be a long afternoon.

- CHAPTER 34 -

THE WATER WAS WARM and comforting. Cooper slid down the bathtub until she was fully submerged. A bath bomb turned the water a purply pink, and the room smelled of passionfruit. Beneath the water, she held her breath as the events of the last few days played in her mind like a video stuck on a loop. She saw Pearl Baxter's worry and Omar Ali's bruised face. She saw Sutherland flashing his new Rolex and Elin Karlsson - the Swedish girl's - swollen body. She saw Bryce Morton's maniacal demeanour and the pair of scissors twirling between his fingers. She saw the man slamming his brakes as Cooper fled from Morton's bunker. The look on Tennessee's face when Inga altered the sketches. The look on Morton's face as he was rag-dolled by the Belgian shepherds. Sutherland's face when he realised she knew his secrets and the poor girls' faces, stained with confusion when she helped escort them out of the dark and into the sunlight.

She exhaled one bubble at a time until her lungs were empty. Her body twitched and fought against her mind, willing her to sit up. She held on. Heat filled her chest, and orange spots flashed in front of her closed eyelids. Only when she couldn't hold on a second longer did she erupt from the water and gasp for air.

She was alive. Cancer hadn't got her, and nor had Morton. She was alive and thankful for it. It didn't mean she was happy.

Cooper pulled herself from the bath. Her skin was red with heat but the cool air from the open window caused goosebumps to form over her entire body and the tiny hairs on her head prickled as they stood on end. She checked the time on her phone. Kenny and Tina would arrive any second and her solitude would be over. She wrapped a towel around herself and shuffled to her bedroom, where she examined her scars in front of the mirror again. Fuck Justin Atkinson. She didn't know where they stood with each other, but she knew that if she wanted tattoos, she should get them. She imagined a floral design she'd seen, applied body lotion and got dressed. She'd just about buttoned up her jeans when the noise of Tina, Josh and Kenny floated up the stairs. Kenny had taken the digital natives to play mini-golf after school and had promised to pick up some fish and chips on the way home. Judging by the smell of vinegar, he'd made good on his promise.

"Mum! I got a hole in one! Didn't I, Dad?"

Kenny grinned while dishing up his quarry. "She sure did. I'd say it was a fluke, but knowing Tina, she probably applied some advanced trigonometry and factored in the wind speed and direction, and accounted for the camber of the grass, and—"

"It was a fluke, Dad." Tina winked at her mother to show that it most certainly wasn't a fluke before squirting a huge dollop of ketchup over her chips.

"Loads of mushy peas and extra vinegar," Kenny said. "Just the way you like it."

She was impressed. She took her plate and sat down at the kitchen table.

"Beer?"

"Hell, yes."

"Can I have one?" asked Tina.

"Yeah, can I have one?" Josh added. He was growing in confidence. Once upon a time, he'd barely look at Cooper, let alone Kenny.

"On a school night? Nice try." Cooper clinked her bottle against Kenny's and felt her body relax as the three others recalled the game, telling her who flunked on the ninth and who aced the third. It was nice to focus on something outside of CID. Once the food was finished and the dishes loaded into the dishwasher, Tina and Josh went upstairs to watch some show everyone at their school had apparently been talking about. Kenny got her another beer.

"Just us millennials," he said with a sheepish grin.

"So you finally accept it?"

He looked awkward. Usually, his big frame made him look formidable. Awkward looked plain weird on him. "Are you okay?" he asked.

"Yeah. I'm good."

"Erica. I've known you for a long time. I know I was away for a huge chunk of it... but anyway, it's been a long time. I know when you're not quite right. Is it work?"

She picked at the label on her bottle. "I had to arrest a colleague. It hit me like a truck."

"Shit. Sorry, Erica. That's got to suck. Want to talk about it?"

Cooper shook her head. She did want to talk, sort of, but there were too many thoughts in her head right now to make sense of it all.

"Well, when you're ready, you know where I am." He reached over and placed his hand on hers. The pads of his palms were calloused from his manual job. They rubbed against the moisturised skin of her knuckles. It wasn't a bad thing. It was nice, protective even. Her eyes met his, igniting an invisible spark, one that she'd thought she'd buried many moons ago. "I mean it. You know you can talk to me, right?"

"I know."

He hesitated, then leant in to kiss her cheek, but Cooper turned her head and their lips touched. Muscle memory controlled her. She wet her lips and went back for more. It was the briefest of kisses. Soft, with trembling lips and over fifteen years of build-up. She bit her lip and pulled back.

"Sorry," he said.

"Don't be. You didn't do anything wrong."

They sat there, quite still, for a good minute, just holding hands and contemplating in the silence where they should go from there.

Kenny spoke first. “I know it’s not the most romantic thing to say, but I need the loo.”

Cooper laughed. “Not romantic at all. But better than wetting yourself.”

He squeezed her hand before letting go of it and heading for the stairs. A few seconds after he’d left, a phone began to vibrate somewhere in the kitchen. Cooper scavenged the room and found Kenny’s phone just as the caller rang off. She unlocked the phone; his code hadn’t changed since they were teenagers.

What she saw made her heart stop.

She blinked, unsure if what she was seeing was really real. It was a colour feed of her bedroom. It was definitely her bedroom. Her bed, her books, her towel on the floor from the bath she’d just taken. Her breathing came quicker, in shallow bursts of disbelief. Kenny was in her room. He looked directly into the camera before pulling four circular batteries from his pocket. The screen went black for a moment and then burst back to life. The angle was facing the dresser and Cooper’s bed. It could only be coming from the mantlepiece and the framed Metallica poster. One of the buttons on the frame had to be a camera lens.

Nausea swept over her. She raced to the sink, vomiting her fish supper into the stainless steel. She gagged again before more came up. She knew she hadn’t mentioned the nightmares to anyone. He’d watched her. Watched her sleep. She ran the tap, but her sick clogged the plug, and the water began backing up. Chunks of fish and potato swam in the cloudy water. She turned the tap off, wiped her hand over her mouth and turned her eyes back to the camera, though her brain willed her not to. Kenny opened a drawer in Cooper's dresser, removed a pair of French Connection briefs and slid them into his pocket.

As she raced back to the sink to finish emptying her stomach, all she could think was that he was right. *Justin was right.*

- Chapter 35 -

Friday morning at eleven a.m. on the dot, Cooper, bleary-eyed and sulky-mouthed, walked to the Gibraltar Rock, a pub overlooking King Edward's Bay, and dragged herself to the upstairs bar. Superintendent Nixon had ordered she take a mental health day. Actually, he'd ordered she take a mental health week, but she didn't know if she could handle that. Last night, a squad car had been sent to find Kenny after she'd thrown half the contents of her kitchen at him and chased him out of her house. He'd been arrested on stalking charges, and Cooper was beside herself with mortification and isolation. His phone and the photo frame had been seized as evidence, and officers would be, at this moment, looking at footage of her in various stages of undress, crying after returning from her abduction, drunk dancing to Hush In Hell, and making love to Atkinson. Her cheeks burned. The files would be handled with sensitivity and stored securely, but the fact remained that her colleagues would see her in her worst moments of vulnerability.

There was a table in the bay window that overlooked the North Sea. A couple enjoyed a morning stroll on the sand. A Yorkshire terrier fruitlessly chased a whippet. A surfer briefly caught a wave before falling into the numbing sea. She ordered a double vodka. Straight. No ice. She wanted desensitising. She wanted to forget. She craved a day of complete numbness.

Her finger circled the rim of the glass. It emitted a low hum that groaned through her bones as she dwelled on her situation. Cutting Kenny from her life meant cutting him from Tina's life. Her daughter deserved a father, but she deserved better than Kenneth Roberts. She'd alienated Atkinson and left herself exposed at work. She was alone, and the person she'd usually turn to for wisdom was locked up on human-trafficking charges. She watched the surfer paddle out beyond the break, turn and pop to his feet. She willed him to fall again. An elderly man on the adjacent table rose and finished his pint, leaving a copy of the Evening Chronicle. Cooper reached across and took the paper. The headline caught her eye: *Tarot Card Killer's Legs Broken. Brian Hutchins brutally attacked in own cell.*

A glass collector looked over her shoulder. "Couldn't have happened to a nicer bloke."

Cooper snorted and sipped her vodka.

"My little sister was in one of his classes. Hope his arms are next."

Cooper didn't reply. She downed the rest of the drink. She'd wanted to be alone with her thoughts. To stew in peace. Not make small talk with an adolescent.

"They reckon it was that gangster, Blackburn, who did it. But my cousin's ex-boyfriend's mate is in Frankland, and he said Blackburn doesn't get his hands dirty. He just gives the orders."

Cooper had to get out of there. She felt as if the walls were closing in on her. She stood. "Blackburn didn't give the order," she said, handing him her glass and turning away.

"Oh yeah? How'd you know?"

Because I did, she thought. When it came down to it, was she any better than Sutherland? She hadn't kidnapped anyone and sent them overseas to live a life of torture and slavery. She wasn't the reason Elin Karlsson was dead or the reason Macey Gallagher was showing signs of brain damage. But she had broken the rules. She was crooked.

She descended the stairs and emerged onto the street. She turned her face to a cloudless blue sky and let the sun warm her skin. She checked her watch; the tattoo parlour would be open.

DCI ERICA COOPER WILL return in Roll The Dice.

- Message from the Author -

I hope you enjoyed reading Rock, Paper, Scissors and would wholeheartedly appreciate it if you could take the time to nip over to Amazon and leave a review.

While writing Cut The Deck and Rock, Paper, Scissors, I felt a little guilty for using Newcastle and North Tyneside as the setting for some awful crimes, but I'm a crime writer, and that's what we do! In real life, Newcastle upon Tyne is a fantastic city, filled with warm, caring, friendly people. Geordies have long claimed Newcastle to be the best place in the world and we were proved right last year when Newcastle topped Rough Guides' list of must-see places for 2018.

I am always seeking inspiration from the world around me, and although Rock, Paper, Scissors is a work of fiction, I'd like to point out two events that gave rise to sections of the book. Firstly, Cooper being annoyed at having to take the stairs from the rooftop car park at the Freeman Hospital is a nod to my mother who faced the same thing when undergoing radiotherapy. Second, Steven Seagull was a hatchling who fell off our roof and landed on our neighbour's extension along with his brother who we named Terrance. The entire seagull family relocated to the roof of the extension and we were enthralled by their daily coming and goings. We even set up seagull cam! Sadly, there was a terrible storm one night, and Steven didn't make it. Terrance went on to fledge in early August. I still kind of miss him.

I'd like to give a special mention to those people who have offered feedback and provided encouragement. Rob, Mum, Shaun, Ian, Julie and Christie, thank you for the support, and suggestions and for spotting many, many typos. You've all been wonderful.

- About the Author -

Betsy was born and raised in Newcastle upon Tyne, living first in Gosforth, then Jesmond. In 2013, she moved to North Shields and enjoys walking her Welsh terrier along nearby beaches and learning about local history.

At school, Betsy struggled with spelling and grammar. However, she doesn't believe in giving up on something because it's difficult. She finds writing novels can be compared to martial arts. They are both thrilling, exhausting, and rewarding.

It's no secret Betsy considers herself part ninja. She also works as a taekwon-do coach and is a self-confessed UFC geek. Her ideal Saturday begins with an intense workout, followed by a long bath, a spot of writing, steak and red wine, and then retiring to the sofa to watch the latest title fight. She came up with the idea for her debut novel, The Only Weapon In The Room, the morning after Rousey vs. Holm.

Betsy's writing process involves drinking ridiculous quantities of tea and hot chocolate, bouncing ideas off her friends and family and getting distracted by Twitter and TikTok.

- Be Sociable -

Facebook: B Baskerville - Author

Twitter: B__Baskerville

TikTok: B_Baskerville

Instagram: B_Baskerville_Author

Newsletter: You can subscribe to the B Baskerville newsletter using the form on BetsyBaskerville.co m. You'll mainly hear from B when she has something to share, such as a pre-order going live, a new book release or sale etc.

- Also By B Baskerville -

The DCI Cooper Series:
Cut The Deck
Rock, Paper, Scissors
Roll The Dice
Northern Roulette
Hide & Seek
Finders Keepers

Stand Alones:
The Only Weapon In The Room
Dead In The Water

Printed in Great Britain
by Amazon

37406137R00179